LUMBERJACKS OF TIMBER RUN

A DEEPWOOD MOUNTAIN COMPLETE SERIES

LEXI HAYES

Published by No Regerts Press, LLC

NO REGERTS
PRESS, LLC

Cover Designed by R Agung Nugraha

ISBN 978-1-957933-47-4 (print)

Join my mailing list here:
www.lexihayes.com

CONTENTS

AXE ME BABY ONE MORE TIME

DON'T GO SAWING MY HEART

CLIMB ME MAYBE

LOG IT LIKE IT'S HOT

AXE ME BABY ONE MORE TIME

CHAPTER 1
SKY

I adjust my phone on its tripod, framing the rustic wooden sign that reads *Timber Run Eco-Historical Lumberjack Camp.*

The camp sprawls before me, a collection of cabins built from reclaimed timber, boardwalks in strategic places protecting the delicate forest floor, and demonstration areas where various lumberjack skills are brought to life.

In the distance, I can see an axe-throwing range with painted targets on massive log rounds.

"Hey adventure fam!" I beam at the camera, sliding my sunglasses atop my head. "Sky here at the newest sustainable tourism hotspot in Deepwood Mountain. This place is like lumberjack heaven meets eco-warrior paradise!"

I back up, gesturing expansively at the camp entrance. "Today we're going behind the scenes at—"

My back suddenly collides with something solid—like hitting a brick wall—then a strong hand grabs my arm. But instead of finding my balance, I stumble forward, a deep "oomph" reverberating near me as we both go down, tools clattering around us.

"Christ on a cross," growls a voice rumbling below me.

I push myself up, my hands pressing against a slab of granite covered in flannel. Looking down, I find I'm straddling a very thick, very warm body.

Dark hair with gray streaks at the temples frames a ruggedly handsome face. Silver threads glint in his short beard, while his brow furrows over espresso-dark eyes blazing with irritation.

The man is built like a redwood—broad shoulders, powerful chest, and strong hands that clasp my waist.

"Hi," I manage, suddenly very aware of our compromising position. My thighs are practically hugging his hips, and I can feel the heat of him through my hiking pants.

"You always wander around backward with your face glued to a screen?" Each word is clipped, precise, and rumbles through his chest directly into me.

I scramble to my feet, nearly tripping over what looks like an axe handle.

"I'm sorry! I didn't see you there. I was just filming my intro and—"

"Filming." He snorts, pushing himself up more slowly, a fleeting grimace crossing his face as he straightens his right leg. He quickly masks it, but I catch the careful way he distributes his weight once standing. "*Of course* you were."

His disgust is impossible to miss. He bends to retrieve his scattered tools, muscles flexing beneath his rolled-up sleeves. I stare at the veins running along his forearms, the way his hands grip each tool with practiced ease.

A flame of heat pools low in my belly.

Too low.

"Let me help," I offer, reaching for a strange metal contraption.

"Don't touch that." He snatches it away, his calloused

fingers brushing mine. An electric zing skitters up my arm at the contact.

Oh no, no no. I am *not* attracted to this walking thundercloud.

Even if his big hands make mine look like a child's. Even if the way he hoists that equipment shows off arms corded with muscle. Even if that damn scowl somehow makes him more appealing.

"I really am sorry," I try again, putting on my brightest smile—the one that usually softens even the grumpiest people. "I'm Sky, by the way. Sky James."

"Don't care." He adjusts his load and glares at my phone, still recording on its tripod.

The casual dismissal stings more than it should. I'm used to winning people over quickly (it's my job), but this mountain of a man seems immune to charm. For a split second, uncertainty flickers through me before I push it down.

He grunts. "You plan on standing in the entrance all day, or can people who actually work here get through?"

His eyes briefly drop to my lips as I form a retort, then lower still, sweeping over my body. He immediately scowls harder, as if angry at himself for looking.

Before I can respond, a cheerful voice calls out, "Graham! I see you've met our special guest!"

A woman with auburn hair tied back in a thick braid hurries over, followed by another burly mountain man with striking blue eyes. I recognize them from the website as the camp's founders.

"Is *'met'* what we're calling it when someone bowls you over while talking to their phone?" the grump mutters.

Teagan offers me her hand. "You must be Sky. I'm Teagan Leigh, and this is my husband Connor. We spoke by email?"

"Yes! Thank you so much for having me." I shake her hand

enthusiastically. "Your camp is even more gorgeous than your website shows. The way you've integrated the structures with the natural environment is exactly what my followers are looking for. Sustainable, authentic experiences that balance both nature and tradition."

"Wonderful!" Teagan smiles brightly, and gestures to the grump. "This here's Graham D'Amico."

Connor claps the big bear on his massive shoulder. "He's our master wood cutting and axe-throwing expert."

Graham grunts an acknowledgment, eyes still narrowed at my camera setup.

"*Another influencer?*" he asks Connor, the word 'influencer' dripping with the same disdain someone might use for radioactive waste.

"Sky specializes in eco-tourism," Teagan explains. "Her audience is exactly the demographic we're hoping to attract."

"I've visited sustainability projects all over the country," I add. "But nothing like this. The way you're combining traditional skills with environmental education is revolutionary. My audience has already been buzzing about this visit for weeks. My preview posts about Timber Run generated *three times* my usual engagement."

Graham's jaw ticks as if my words offend him. But his gaze drops to my mouth again, then snaps back to my eyes with renewed irritation.

"I've built a following of over half a million people who are genuinely interested in this stuff. They're not just here for pretty sunset pics—they want the real deal."

Connor nods approvingly. "That's exactly why we invited Sky here. Her platform aligns with our mission to preserve traditional logging practices while promoting responsible environmental stewardship."

"The camp represents such beautiful harmony," I say,

turning to Graham. "Honoring tradition while protecting the environment. I'd love to highlight how those two values can coexist. Show my followers how much skill goes into what you do."

Graham's expression softens slightly—*very slightly*.

"Speaking of which," Connor says, "Graham, Sky will be with us for the week documenting the camp. We thought you could...give her lessons for her channel. Show her audience some of what we teach here."

Graham's face darkens like storm clouds rolling in.

"No." He adjusts his grip on the tools he's gathered. "I don't perform tricks for internet points."

"It's not tricks," I protest, stepping closer. My pulse quickens as his worn leather and freshly split pine scent washes over me. "My followers want to learn."

"Your followers," he interrupts, "wouldn't know an adze from a froe if it hit them in the head, which it might if they learn from watching two-minute videos."

"Graham," Connor says quietly, "we talked about this. Expanding our reach is part of the mission."

Graham looks from Connor to my camera setup, then back to me.

There's something primitive and compelling about this man that scrambles my insides, even as he's being a stubborn ass.

"The whole point of this camp," Teagan adds, "is to preserve traditional skills by teaching them to new generations. Sky's platform helps us reach people who might never find us otherwise."

Graham's nostrils flare.

"Not going to happen," he finally growls.

And without another word, he turns and stalks off toward

a wooden building his brawny frame radiating tension with every step.

I watch him go, oddly captivated by the confident way he moves, the power evident in each stride.

Despite his rejection, my pulse races.

Wonderful.

CHAPTER 2
GRAHAM

Connor's boots crunch behind me before I even reach the workshop. "We need to talk about this, Graham."

I walk in the door and slam the tools onto my workbench harder than necessary. "Nothing to talk about. She's here to turn us into circus acts. I won't do it."

"She's here to *help*," Connor says, leaning against the door-frame. "Teagan vetted her. Sky's content is super heavy on education."

"Education? You can't be serious." I bark a laugh, whirling to face him. "You think her followers give a damn about grain patterns or proper splitting technique? They want flashy clips of axes spinning through the air and six pack abs. Not the *work*."

Connor crosses his arms, unflinching. "You sound like my father when I first proposed solar panels."

"Your father was right about *some* things."

"And wrong about so many others." He steps closer, voice lowering. "This camp will survive by adapting, Graham. Sky's platform reaches thousands. Imagine if even a fraction of them care enough to visit, take classes, and support what we're building here."

I grind my molars. The old injury in my knee throbs. Of all the ways to dishonor my father's legacy—playing entertainer for strangers who'll forget this place by next week.

"The camp needs exposure," he says. "If we don't get more guests soon, we won't make it."

"Connor, she creates content for people with the attention span of squirrels," I growl, organizing my workbench. "You can't teach proper axe handling in a fifteen-second video with pop music in the background."

My hands work automatically, a welcome distraction from the memory of the woman who'd knocked me flat, literally *and* figuratively.

Sky James. Even her name sounds made up.

Like something a marketing team would create to sell over-priced hiking boots to people who've never set foot on an actual trail.

"You've seen her channel?" Connor raises an eyebrow.

"Don't need to." I pick up a splitting maul that needs sharpening. "I've seen enough 'influencers' to know the type."

The way she'd felt sprawled on top of me flashes unbidden through my mind. Honey blonde hair escaping from a carefully styled ponytail, bright blue eyes wide with surprise, the warm press of her thighs against mine. Petite but solid. Not the fragile doll I'd expected.

Connor huffs. "Look, I'm not asking you to perform tricks. Just teach her the same way you'd teach anyone who comes to the camp."

I run a thumb along the maul's edge, finding it duller than I'd like.

Much like this conversation.

"Just a few sessions," he presses. "Wood splitting, and some axe throwing. Then she'll be the rest of the crew's problem for a while."

I lick my lips.

"For the camp," he mutters.

That's always the clincher with Connor. He knows I believe in what we're building here. Traditions my father passed down to me...that are disappearing faster than old-growth forests.

"Fine," I concede, pointing the maul at him. "But I'm not dumbing it down for views or likes or whatever the hell she's after."

Connor grins. "Wouldn't expect anything less."

"And I'm *not* smiling for the camera."

She's waiting at the woodpile when I arrive after lunch, phone set up on a tripod nearby.

Her hair's twisted into two silky braids that I have the inappropriate urge to pull. Even dressed more practically now in hiking shorts and a simple T-shirt rather than the Instagram-ready outfit from earlier, she's still too...sexy.

And she looks young, too young for me to be thinking such dirty thoughts about her.

"Safety glasses." I shove a pair at her, laying a splitting maul near her. "And if you drop anything on your foot, I'm not carrying you to the medic."

She slides the glasses on, transforming her heart-shaped face into something absurdly adorable. "Wouldn't dream of inconveniencing you."

I demonstrate the stance—feet shoulder-width apart, grip low on the handle—then nod at the log. "Show me."

She grabs the axe and finds her grip. Her first swing goes

wide, the blade flying into the dirt. The second glances off the log's edge.

"You're choking the handle," I snap. "Loosen your grip."

"I'm trying—"

"Try harder."

She glares, but resets. Third swing. The maul bites deep, wedging in the wood.

"Stuck," she huffs, yanking uselessly.

I push her aside and free the axe, then hand it back to her.

When I step behind her, I tell myself this is purely instructional.

My chest nearly brushes her back.

Focus on the lesson, Graham. Not the woman.

"Hips forward," I grunt, adjusting her stance with a nudge of my boot. My hand wraps around hers on the handle. "Follow through *with* the blade, not against it."

She leans into the motion, the curve of her ass pressing against my inner thigh.

Heat floods my veins and my cock stirs.

I grit my teeth.

This is just biology. Nothing more.

"Like this?" she breathes.

I jerk back like she's branded me. "You got it." I move away from her. "Now, again."

She takes another swing.

"You're still dropping your shoulder. Remember, it's about control, not force," I offer. "You need to guide the axe through its arc, not muscle it."

She nods, concentration furrowing her brow. There's a determination in her stance that surprises me. She's listening, not just going through the motions for her *audience*.

"Keep your core tight, and let the weight of the axe head do the work."

She swings, her form still awkward, but improving. The blade connects with the log, sinking in halfway.

"Not bad." The words slip out before I can stop them.

A smile lights up her face, transforming her features from merely pretty to something that burns my insides. "Really?"

"For a beginner," I clarify, crossing my arms. "Again."

For two hours, I push her hard, expecting her to quit.

Instead, she absorbs every correction, asking smart questions about grain direction and swing mechanics.

Maybe she's not the vapid social media princess I'd expected.

"Why does this one keep cracking sideways?" She gestures at the splintered mess.

I crouch, tracing the growth rings. "You're hitting the knots. Grain's twisted here." I point, then stand wiping the sweat from my neck. "Aim *here.*"

She does and gets a nice split.

"There you go. Strength without strategy's useless." I look her over. "You've got the basics. For today."

She's sweating—her braids disheveled, dirt streaking her arms. But there's satisfaction gleaming in her eyes.

I take the axe from her. Our fingers brush, and I ignore the heated jolt that races up my arm. "Let's try some axe throwing."

Her smile brightens as we walk over to the range.

I line up the throwing axes. "Grip the handle like you're shaking hands. And step into the throw."

I demonstrate, my axe hitting dead center.

"Easy," she mutters, mimicking my stance. Her first throw sails over the target, burying in a tree.

"Easy," I mimic her.

She sticks out her tongue.

I shouldn't find that charming. "You're releasing too late."

"Show me again?"

"Throwing is about consistency. Same stance, same grip, same release point, every time."

I let the axe fly. It rotates once, the blade once again embedding itself in the center of the target with a satisfying thunk.

"That was amazing," Sky breathes, her eyes wide. "How many rotations should it make?"

"Depends on the distance and the axe. For beginners, we aim for a single rotation."

She positions herself again, and I find myself noticing the lean muscles of her legs. I've lost count of how many times my eyes have slid over them.

Her stance is wrong. Before I can think better of it, I'm back behind her.

"Feet wider," I murmur, my voice rougher than intended. "And your grip is still too tight."

I reach around, and cover her hands with mine. Heat spreads wherever our skin connects.

"Feel the balance point." I instruct.

She's warm, sweat-slicked, and *still* smells like sunshine and wildflowers.

Damn her.

I'm suddenly aware of how easily my arms wrap around her smaller frame, and how nicely she fits against me.

"Now, focus on the target," I manage, my mouth too close to her ear. "Draw back, keeping your elbow at this height, and release when your arm is fully extended."

I step back, putting a welcome distance between us. She exhales shakily, then follows through with the motion I showed her. The axe spins, hitting the target handle-first and bouncing off.

"Keep trying."

She retrieves the axe, determination written across her

features. Three more failed attempts follow, each one met with increasing frustration.

"I can't get the timing right," she admits, blowing a strand of hair from her face.

"Everyone struggles at first," I find myself reassuring her. "It's muscle memory. You can't think your way through it."

"How do I not think about it?"

I consider her question seriously. "Focus on the feeling, not the mechanics. When it's right, you'll know."

She nods, taking a deep breath. This time when she throws, her movement is fluid, natural. The axe rotates cleanly and sticks into the outer ring of the target.

"I did it!" She spins, eyes alight with genuine joy, and launches herself at me in an impulsive hug.

I freeze, her arms around my neck, her body pressed against mine.

For one dangerous moment, I'm tempted to return the embrace, to feel more of her beautiful body. Instead, I gently disentangle myself, stepping back.

"Good job," I say stiffly.

She blushes, seeming to realize what she's done. "Sorry, I got excited."

Me too, honey. Me too.

"It's fine."

But it's not fine. Nothing about her effect on me is fine.

"I'll help you clean up," she says.

I shake my head. "You should go get changed. Dinner's soon."

"You sure?"

I nod, and start picking up the site, eyes averted.

"Okay, then. Tomorrow?" she asks.

I nod again, not trusting my voice. She gathers her camera equipment, packing it away in a case.

I watch her out of the corner of my eye with a sinking feeling.

This woman is trouble—she's everything I can't stand, all flash and filters and fleeting attention.

But she didn't complain once about the work today.

And that smile when she finally hit the target...*that's* going to stay with me well into the night.

CHAPTER 3
SKY

I stare at my phone in disbelief as I finish lacing up my boots.

635,472 notifications.

"Holy crap!" I whisper to my empty cabin.

I scroll through the tsunami pouring over my screen. My hands are still sore from yesterday's wood-splitting lesson, but the ache fades as I process what I'm seeing.

Half a million views overnight of the first couple of videos I posted last night. The main start snippets of my lesson with Graham set to a remix of "Timber" by Pitbull.

Comments are pouring in by the second.

Shares *skyrocketing*.

I'd kept the editing simple—just Graham demonstrating perfect form, followed by my pathetic first attempts, and then that first moment when he stood behind me, those massive hands engulfing mine on the axe handle.

I hadn't even realized how intimate it looked until I reviewed the footage. I mean, it *felt*…intimate. I had wanted him to drop the stupid axe and slide his big hands into my shorts…into my panties—

A ping for a new notification startles me back to the present.

The comments are savage:

> OMG WHO IS THIS LUMBERSNACK DADDY?? 😭😭😭

> That man could split me in half any day 🪓

> I've watched him grip that wood more than 27 times already 👀

> Booking my stay at Timber Run NOW. Does the hot grumpy instructor come with the... package?? 😏🖤

And those are the tamer ones.

My inbox is flooded with questions about Graham. Where to find him. Whether he's single. If *all* the instructors at Timber Run look like that.

With such an explosion in followers, I'd normally be ecstatic. This is exactly what I'd hoped for—engagement, visibility, interest in the camp—but I hadn't anticipated how raunchy it would get. I guess that was a little naive.

Still, I'd focused on the educational aspects in my caption, explaining sustainable forestry and traditional skills. Yet the comments are 90% thirst and 10% everything else.

The hashtag #LumbersnackDaddy is trending.

My phone pings with a text from Teagan.

> Have you seen our numbers? Connor's ecstatic. This is exactly what we needed.

> Right?! I'm thrilled 😄 ...Is Graham aware?

The three dots appear, disappear.

Not yet. He doesn't do social media. But the
rest of the crew have seen it. Brace yourself.

Oh god. Just what I need before today's lesson, more fuel
for Graham's anti-influencer fire. I can already imagine his
scowl when he discovers he's become an internet thirst trap
overnight.

I grab my gear and head to breakfast, wondering how I'm
going to navigate this new complication. I need more content
with Graham, but I don't want to alienate him further.

The dining cabin buzzes with energy when I arrive.

Ewan, the sawyer, spots me immediately and breaks into
raucous applause.

"There she is! The lass who's made our Graham an internet
sensation!" He raises his coffee mug in salute. "He's got dozens
of marriage proposals before breakfast, and one of them
from me!"

Rourke, the log-roller, slides his phone across the table.
"Look at these comments! This woman wants to—" he
squints at the screen, "—climb him like a redwood and—*fuck
me*, I can't say that out loud." He cackles. "Still...quite
poetic!"

"Please stop," I groan, sinking onto a bench. "Where is he?"

"Stormed out about ten minutes ago," Brady says, the tree-
climber's quiet voice somehow cutting through the chaos.
"After Rourke read him some of the spicier comments."

My stomach drops. "How bad was it?"

"On a scale of one to volcanic eruption?" Ewan considers,
stroking his beard. "I'd say Mount St. Helens, 1980."

Oh no.

After a quick breakfast, I head to the wood-splitting area, a
cleared section between Graham's workshop and the equip-

ment shed, marked by stumps of varying heights and a growing pile of kindling.

I'm unsure if Graham will even show up. The woodpile stands empty, no intimidating figure waiting to critique my form.

I set up my tripod anyway and do a quick intro while I wait, explaining the basics of what I learned yesterday.

But my heart isn't in it.

I keep glancing over my shoulder, hoping to see him trudging toward me with that signature scowl.

After twenty minutes, I give up and pack my equipment. Graham isn't coming. I've pushed too far, too fast.

I should've accounted for this kind of response, and tried to mitigate it.

What was I thinking?

I wander over to the axe-throwing range and find him hurling axes with laser focus, each one landing with a solid thunk in the center of the target. He retrieves them with swift, practiced movements, his shoulders rigid.

"I gather you saw the video," I say, approaching cautiously.

He doesn't turn. "You made me look like some kind of...performing bear for bored, thirsty women to ogle." Another axe flies, splitting the air. "I told you I'm not entertainment."

"That wasn't my intention," I reply, setting my camera bag down. "I focused on the technique, the history—"

"Don't bullshit me." He finally turns, and the outrage in his eyes makes me step back. "I saw the comments. 'Daddy this, lumbersnack that.' 'Climb him like a fucking tree.' That's what you wanted."

Heat rises to my cheeks. "I'm sorry. I can't control what people fixate on."

"But you can control what you post." He gestures dismissively at my equipment. "And you chose to post...*that*."

"I posted an educational video about axe-throwing technique," I counter, frustration building. "You do realize I could film you reading the phone book and you'd probably get the same response. It's not *my* fault you happen to be..." I gesture vaguely at him, "...you."

His eyebrow quirks slightly. "What's that supposed to mean?"

"Do you ever look in the mirror, Graham? You're a smoke show! Hot, sexy, built like a goddamn boulder. Good with your hands. You smell incredible—" I stop myself, and swallow hard. "Sorry, nevermind. Look, people are interested. They're asking about the camp, about booking experiences. Isn't that the point?"

"They're not interested in *the camp*," he says, frowning.

"That's not *completely* true."

He glares.

"Fine. You're right," I say, hands on my hips. "I'm being disrespectful to you and your wishes. I could create something more professionally conservative when you're involved. And I could keep filming of you to a minimum." I take a deep breath.

He studies me, suspicious.

"I'll re-edit the first video accordingly. And if the rest of the crew doesn't mind it, I'll focus on them for the more hardcore lumbersnack daddy enthusiasts."

His lips twitch. "Really?"

I nod. "Why would I want to make you do something you don't want to do? Especially on social media."

Something shifts in his expression, so subtle I almost miss it.

"So how about my lesson?" I ask.

"You going to film it?"

I shake my head.

"Then why, if you're not getting content out of it?"

"Because I actually *want* to learn," I admit. "Yesterday, when I split that log correctly? That felt amazing. Better than a thousand likes."

He considers me for a long moment. "Okay then."

We head back to the wood splitting area and work in silence for the next hour, my muscles burning as I practice proper stance and swing. The repetitive motion is strangely meditative.

Just as we're finding a rhythm, dark clouds roll in from the mountains and the wind picks up.

"Spring squall," Graham says, glancing at the sky. "They hit fast up here."

With the oncoming drizzle, Graham gestures toward the camp. "Follow me to my workshop."

We grab the axes and head for the building, as distant thunder booms, my hair whipping into my eyes.

Inside, the workshop is meticulously organized, thick with the scent of wood shavings and oil, a sturdy workbench scarred from years of use in the center.

It's intimate in a way I hadn't expected, like glimpsing a private piece of the man himself.

He moves around the space with easy familiarity, past the wall of hanging axes to the corner where more woodworking tools rest in careful order.

He lights an old kerosene lamp as the storm darkens the windows. The warm glow softens his features, illuminating flecks of gold in his dark eyes I hadn't noticed before.

"While we're cooped up here," I venture, perching on a stool. "Why don't you tell me about how you got started with logging?"

He eyes me warily. "Why you want to know?"

"Just curious about your story."

He hesitates, then sighs. "Third-generation logger. Grandad started after the war, taught my father, who taught me."

"What was that like? Learning from your dad?"

Graham shrugs. "Hard. Demanding. But he knew his craft. Taught me to respect the forest, not just take from it." He runs a hand over a piece of wood on his bench. "Said a good logger is like a good doctor—knows what to remove, what to leave, how to help the forest grow stronger. Told me men who understood trees understood themselves."

"That's really wise," I say, genuinely touched. "Could I...would you consider letting me record you talking about that? Just audio. It would be so valuable for people to hear."

To my surprise, he doesn't immediately shut me down.

The lantern flickers, and he studies me like I'm a knotty piece of timber. "Maybe. If you make it about the tradition, not about me. And no silly music."

"I promise. Raw footage. Tasteful, educational, focused on the craft. Just your voice."

He nods slowly and I grab my phone, pressing record. He cradles a piece of wood, thumbs testing resilience. His low voice fills the humid air, recounting midnight felling trips, the hymn of saws in frozen dawns. When he mentions his father's death, crushed by equipment during a winter storm, his fingers curl into a fist.

My chest aches. "Is that why you left logging?"

"No. Knee injury." He rotates his right leg with a wince. "Rain's got it acting up."

"I can help." The offer escapes me before I think it through. "My sister blew out her ACL skiing. I learned some PT moves."

He looks genuinely startled. "That's not—."

"Just for the pain," I clarify quickly.

After a long hesitation, he moves his chair to sit awkwardly beside me. I guide his long, muscled leg across another stool and stand up.

His muscle jumps under my hands as I begin working my thumbs gently through the nylon and polyester of his hiking pants.

"Christ," he grits out.

"Too much?"

"No. It's—keep going."

I focus on the task, trying to ignore how intimate this feels. My fingers trace circles around his kneecap, and down the sides out into the muscles that attach to his thick thighs.

"How's this feeling?" I ask, not quite meeting his eyes.

His voice comes out rougher than usual. "It's...good. Real good."

Rain crescendos overhead. His eyes drift shut, lips parting slightly. I press deeper, tracing the corded muscle up to his quad. His heat seeps through the fabric as my body responds to his ragged breathing.

Maybe this *wasn't* a good idea.

It's taking all my willpower not to massage further up his thigh...

Oh god, his bulge is definitely growing.

Is he turned on, too?

It's probably a purely physical reaction to massaging so close to his—

Don't look, Sky.

And stop drooling!

My phone chimes loudly, snapping me out of my haze. I get up and check the notification.

"Oh wow," I breathe, eyes widening as I read the email.

"What?" Graham asks, the warmth from moments ago already fading from his voice.

"Alpine Horizon—they're one of the biggest sustainable outdoor apparel brands—they want to discuss a potential sponsorship deal!" I can't keep the excitement from my voice. "They specifically mentioned the Timber Run videos. They love the authentic wilderness skills angle!"

"Congratulations," Graham says, and I think he means it, but his posture has already changed, shoulders going stiff, jaw tightening. He stands, putting distance between us. "Sounds like a big deal."

"It could be huge," I agree. "They have partnerships with National Parks, conservation efforts...exactly the kind of alignment I've been hoping for."

Graham nods, his expression now unreadable as he tidies tools that don't need tidying. "You should probably get on that, then."

"I...yeah, I should respond," I say, feeling oddly deflated despite the good news. "And do some editing on today's footage."

The intimacy of minutes ago has vanished, replaced by an awkward tension that feels almost worse than his initial hostility.

"I should go," I say, standing. "Thanks for everything today."

He reaches for something on a shelf. "Take this," he says, handing me a worn, forest-green poncho. "Rain's not letting up."

Our fingers brush as I accept it, but he pulls away quickly.

"Thanks," I say again, wrapping the poncho around my shoulders.

It smells like him.

I pause at the door, hoping he'll say something more, but he's already turned back to his workbench, shoulders a rigid line of dismissal.

CHAPTER 4
GRAHAM

The storm's long gone, but my head's still thundering inside.

I slouch on my bed, my phone opened to YouTube. Thankfully, Sky posts there, because I don't have any social media accounts.

The screen glows with her latest video, the one she re-edited and promised would focus more on the camp values than me.

My finger hovers over the play button, half-expecting to see myself once again turned into some kind of sex-fueled spectacle.

I tap and the video loads.

Sky's voice narrates clearly over footage of me demonstrating proper stance (from my chest down) and discussing the history behind each technique.

There's no flashy music, no quick cuts designed for goldfish attention spans, just the crisp *thunk* of steel biting wood.

"The splitting maul isn't just about brute force," her voice-over explains while the camera zooms in on my grip. "As Graham showed me, it's about understanding the wood, reading its unique structure, and working with its natural tendencies rather than against them."

She then included everything I told her earlier; the knowledge my father passed down to me. She edits in historical photos of loggers and overlays text of important facts.

And in the comments, between the thirsty remarks and fire emojis, there are actually people asking legitimate questions about sustainable forestry practices.

Dammit. Why do I hate that she got it right?

I make the mistake of clicking over to her profile.

It's research. That's all.

Videos flood my screen showing Sky at various eco-tourism sites—a sustainable farm in Oregon, a conservation project in Colorado. Then she's rappelling into a canyon and interviewing a Navajo weaver. She seems genuinely engaged in each one, asking thoughtful questions, and highlighting environmental initiatives.

And god, the way she moves...

There's a video of her demonstrating stretches for hikers. Her lithe body bends and tightens in form-fitting gear, ponytail bouncing. My mouth goes dry as she demonstrates a hamstring stretch, bending over in those ass-cheek-gripping yoga pants.

Jesus almighty.

And when she looks back over her shoulder with that damn sweet smile...*hnnfgh.*

I chuck the phone onto the bed with a huff and palm myself through my jeans.

Gritting my teeth, I groan.

I unzip roughly, fist squeezing my cock. I'm already rock-hard.

"Fuck," I mutter, disgusted with myself.

But I don't stop.

I think about how she felt pressed against me during our lessons—the heat of her firm body, the scent of her hair, the determination in her blue eyes when she finally split that log. I think about her fingers massaging my knee in the workshop, and how desperately I wanted her to move higher up my thigh.

Goddammit.

I stroke faster, thinking how she said I was hot, good with my hands, and that I smell incredible...

My cock throbs in my hand as I imagine what those soft pink lips might feel like wrapped around my aching dick. How she would sound moaning my name as I take her against my workbench...

Before I know it, I'm coming hard and fast, spilling over my fist with a strangled groan.

It's intense, leaving me panting, pulse racing.

I clean up with rough, angry movements. Forty-four years old, jerking off to some influencer half my age.

Talk about pathetic.

The next morning at breakfast, my eyes feel like sandpaper as I nurse my third cup of coffee.

Sky breezes into the dining cabin, past the stone fireplace where Rourke's tending the morning fire, weaving between the long pine tables where guests and crew mingle over breakfast.

Her hair is in a simple ponytail instead of those silky braids and her cheeks are flushed from the morning chill, smiling bright as she greets everyone.

"Morning, sunshine!" Ewan calls, pulling out the bench

beside him. "Ready for your sawing lesson? I'll have you handling my blade like a professional in no time."

The innuendo is obvious, and something hot and unfamiliar twists in my chest.

"I've been practicing my grip," Sky responds playfully, accepting a mug of coffee from Brady.

She casts a glance in my direction, her eyes meeting mine for just a second.

Heat rushes through me, pooling low in my gut. I shift in my seat, jeans suddenly too tight.

Jesus, I'm getting hard at the breakfast table like some hormonal teen.

Rourke leans across the table. "Ah, tomorrow then! After Ewan and Brady have had their way with you, I'll be teaching you the fine art of staying upright on my log."

The entire table erupts in laughter. Teagan snorts into her oatmeal, while Brady nearly chokes on his coffee. Ewan pounds the table, and even Connor cracks a grin.

"Sheesh, Rourke," Ewan wheezes, "warn a lad before you unleash that kind of double entendre."

This is typical camp banter, the same crude jokes we've always shared. But watching Sky blush and laugh along with my crew, I have an irrational urge to flip the table and toss her over my shoulder marching away from these idiots.

"Don't you all have actual work to do?" I growl, standing abruptly. "Or is harassing our guest part of the job description now?"

An awkward silence falls over the table. Connor raises an eyebrow at me. Brady's eyes flick between Sky and me with too much understanding for comfort.

"Just having a laugh," Ewan says carefully. "Sky knows we're joking. I'd never do anything to make her feel uncomfortable."

"It's fine, really," Sky assures me. "But I appreciate your concern, Graham."

"Whatever." I dump my remaining coffee in the bin and stalk out, feeling like an ass but unable to tamp down this unfamiliar wave of possessive angst.

What the hell is wrong with me?

She's a temporary visitor who'll be gone in a week, back to her digital world of likes and followers and sponsorships.

But this feeling doesn't ease up as the day unfolds.

Through my workshop window, I watch her laughing with Ewan at the two-person saw station, her small hands gripping the massive saw as he guides her through the motions.

Later, I spot her with Brady, securely harnessed as he demonstrates climbing techniques, his hands adjusting her safety gear with professional efficiency.

Each time a crew member touches her—even innocently—that achy feeling returns. I've never been the jealous type. Never had reason to be. But this feels different, almost innate.

It's stupid. And I hate it.

That night, after I choose to eat my dinner in my workshop and sulk, I venture out for a walk and find Sky alone by the dying campfire. Everyone else has turned in, but she sits wrapped in a thick flannel blanket, staring into the embers.

"They all behave themselves today?" I ask, settling onto the log beside her.

She startles slightly, then smiles. "They were perfect gentlemen. Well, mostly." She laughs. "Ewan has quite the repertoire of dirty lumberjack jokes."

"He thinks he's charming."

"He kind of is," she admits. "In an uncle sort of way."

I grunt, oddly pleased by the 'uncle' categorization. "Learn anything useful?"

"So much," she says, eyes brightening. "Brady's knowledge

of tree health indicators is amazing. And Ewan showed me these old-school cutting techniques that weren't in any of my research notes."

I nod, watching the genuine enthusiasm in her expression. It hits me that she's actually absorbing all this, not just collecting content.

"Why do you do the influencer crap?"

She stiffens. "It's not *crap*." Her fingers twist in her lap. "I started for the likes. The validation. But then..." She looks up at the stars. "I met a shaman in New Mexico who said his sacred dances would die with him since he had no one to pass them on to. And then I met a marine biologist in Hawaii who'd said tourists didn't understand the negative impact they had on sea turtles." Her voice cracks. "I realized I could... *amplify* these kinds of things. Make people care."

"I guess that's admirable," I say.

Really admirable.

The fire pops.

"Can I ask *you* something?" she says after a moment of silence.

"Depends what it is."

"Why do you do *this*? The camp, the demonstrations."

I stare into the fire, considering. "After my father died, my mother followed six months later. Heart attack, though I think it was grief." I don't know why I'm telling her this. I never talk about them.

Her eyes soften. "I'm so sorry."

I shrug, looking down at my knees. "For a while, I lost my way. Connor and the crew dragged me here, refusing to let me rot. Gave me purpose when I thought my career was over."

I look up and she's smiling at me. "Sounds like you have some amazing friends."

"I owe them a lot." I take a deep breath. "My dad died

thinking his life's work was obsolete. So when Connor had this mad idea about preserving these skills, teaching them, giving them a future. I knew I had to hear him out. Couldn't see it at first, but now..."

"You're keeping your family's memory alive," she says quietly. "Through the traditions."

"Something like that."

Her hand brushes mine—quick, electric. "Well, they're lucky to have you."

"Thanks."

She pulls away, then stands to gather her blanket. "I should probably head in. Long day tomorrow with more lessons."

As she moves to leave, the corner of her blanket catches on the log, and she stumbles forward, landing directly in my lap with a surprised yelp.

"Oh god!" she gasps, her face burning red as she tries to untangle herself from the blanket.

How can a woman so natural in front of the camera—and who now can even handle an axe, a saw, and climbing tall trees—trip over her own feet? Twice?

The absurdity hits me, and I start laughing. Deep, genuine laughter that hasn't happened in a long while.

Her embarrassment melts into giggles at my reaction, then full laughter as she joins in. "What is my problem?" she manages between breaths. "I'm such a klutz."

"Smooth as silk," I tease, still chuckling.

When our laughter finally dies down, she's still perched across my thighs, her hands resting on my chest for balance. Her blue eyes drop to my mouth, and for a moment, I consider closing that small distance. Taking what I've been thinking about since yesterday in the workshop.

Her lips part slightly, and I can feel her breath against my face.

God, I want to taste her.

And there go my jeans, getting much too tight.

"It's getting l-late," I stutter, standing abruptly, pulling her up with me. "You should probably rest up for tomorrow." I hurriedly step back away from her.

Confusion flickers across her face, quickly masked with a smile. "Right. Thanks for...catching me. Sorry about that."

I shake my head and wave her off. "No big deal. Night." I walk away quickly, cursing myself with every step.

Getting involved with her would be a bad idea. I could make a list of reasons why we shouldn't go down that road. The last one being the heartache when she inevitably leaves for her next trending destination.

Still, as I glance back at her silhouette, I can't help wonder what might happen if she decided to stick around.

CHAPTER 5
SKY

G raham's axe hits the target with lethal force, dead center —as always.

But today, when I lift my own axe, my muscles hum with newfound confidence. The handle feels like an extension of my arm now, the weight familiar. I step into the throw, release... and the axe leaves my hand in a perfect arc, spinning once before the blade sinks right into the outer ring of the target.

Not perfect, but close.

"Hell yeah!" I pump my fist in the air, grinning as I turn toward Graham. "Did you see that? Finally, I'm getting somewhere!"

The corner of his mouth twitches as he leans against a tree, arms crossed. "Beginner's luck," he says, but I catch the wink.

It caught me off guard when he broke into laughter yesterday by the campfire, even if it was at my expense. His smile is gorgeous, and I really want to see it again...along with that carefree laugh. But since he ran off right after, who knows what he's thinking today.

"Admit it. You're impressed," I tease.

"Don't let it go to your head, Slick," he teases right back.

"But yes, much better," he acknowledges. And I'll take it. Because from Graham that might as well be high praise.

I retrieve the axe and land another solid hit. The repetitive motion feels genuine now, and I'm proud of my improvement. I'm buzzing, the adrenaline of progress crackling under my skin.

And the crisp scent of sap mingles with Graham's heady musk.

I've memorized that smell now.

Hell, it follows me into my dreams.

"I think I've earned some exploration time," I announce, pulling out my phone to check the map screenshot I'd saved earlier. "There's supposed to be this incredible waterfall nearby—Timber Creek Falls. Seems perfect for some nature content."

"Planning to hike there alone?" Graham stiffens, his brow furrowing.

"That was the idea. It's only a couple miles according to the trail app."

"Trail's washed out near the ridge. Roots you could trip on. And bears."

I snort. "Bears?"

"You think that's a joke?" His scowl deepens. "You're not trekking solo."

Is he really that worried about me? "I'll be fine. Promise."

"No." The word lands like one of his axe strikes. "I'll go with you."

I blink, surprised by his sudden resolve. "You don't have to do that. I know your knee's been bothering you."

He waves off my concern. "It's fine. Trail's not well-marked anyway. Easy to get lost if you don't know these mountains."

"Are you sure? I don't want to make it worse—"

"Sky." His tone brooks no argument. "I'm going."

Something warm unfurls in my chest at his protectiveness.

He pushes off the tree, all broad shoulders and stubborn swagger. "Be ready in ten."

An hour later, we're hiking through dense forest that reminds me why I fell in love with wild places. The leaves in the canopy above rustle in the breeze, air smelling like pine and moss and growing things.

The trail is a narrow, winding beast that climbs steadily uphill. Graham moves like the forest itself—steady, surefooted, his boots barely disturbing the moss underfoot.

You'd never guess he had a bad knee.

I scramble behind him, sweating through my tank top, hyper-aware of the way his jeans cling to his thighs with every step.

"You good back there?" he calls over his shoulder.

"Peachy," I lie, swatting a mosquito.

He pauses, waiting for me to catch up. Sunlight catches the silver in his stubble. "Told you it was rough."

I grunt and he turns, chuckling...a low, rumbling sound that does dangerous things to my core.

"These woods remind me of where I grew up," he says, pausing beside a massive hemlock. "Back in Maine. Different trees, but same feeling."

His expression softens as he continues. "Dad started teaching me when I was barely tall enough to hold an axe properly. Said the forest was the best classroom in the world."

I follow him over a moss-covered boulder, accepting his steadying hand when I slip slightly. "It must have been amazing, learning all that from him."

"It was." His fingers linger on mine a moment longer than necessary before he releases them. "Course, I didn't appreciate it then. Thought I knew everything."

"Pretty standard for kids," I reply.

He chuckles. "I sure was a handful."

I think about Graham as a rebellious boy and a pleasant ache fills my chest.

We continue to hike in silence for a while, the air thick with the scent of damp earth and wild mint. Birdsong trills overhead.

"What draws you to the nature stuff?" Graham asks suddenly.

I glance at him, then side step a muddy patch. "When I'm out here…it's the only time I feel *honest*. No filters, no algorithms judging my worth. Just…*this*." I sweep a hand at the towering pines. "I want people to feel that too. That they're lucky to be part of all of it."

He studies me, his gaze weighted.

The sound of rushing water grows louder as we climb, and suddenly the trees open up. Sunlight fractures through the mist, painting rainbows over the plunging cascade. The clear pool below churns, framed by ferns and ancient, gnarled trees.

"Oh my," I breathe. "Graham, this is absolutely gorgeous."

For a long moment, we stand there in the mist, the roar of water filling the silence. Then Graham crouches, plucks a smooth stone from the bank, and skips it across the pool. It dances four times before sinking.

I'm already framing shots when I notice he's watching me, his dark eyes intense.

"What?" I ask, lowering my camera.

"Just…watching you work." He clears his throat, looking almost embarrassed. "You get this look when you see something beautiful. Like you're a child seeing the world for the first time."

Heat creeps up my neck. "With places like this…I do feel like a child. Such beauty never gets old."

"No," he agrees quietly. "It doesn't."

"Graham," I say softly.

37

He nods, wary.

"Do you…like me?" I take a breath. Shit, Sky. Did you just ask a grown ass man if he *liked* you? What are you…back in high school?

His face flushes red above his beard. "Sky—"

I'm probably completely out of line here. Would he really want anything to do with a woman half his age? Especially one that asks childish questions. Ugh. "Nevermind," I hedge. "You don't have to answer that. I'm being silly."

He rubs the back of his neck. "You're not being *silly.*"

I groan. "*I am* though. It's just I've been thinking about you a lot and—"

Shut up, Sky! You're rambling and digging yourself into an even deeper hole!

His eyes widen.

"But I know you probably think I'm too young and that I'm not your type. Plus, those thirsty comments make you uncomfortable."

He blinks, then swallows hard. "Sure, you're young…and I may have thought you weren't my type, but you've surprised me at every turn."

I smile, a giddy feeling in my belly.

"Coming from you, those comments…wouldn't be so bad." He scrubs a hand down his face.

I chuckle and move closer, reaching up to trace the line of his jaw. The coarse hair of his beard grazes my palm. "Can I tell you what I think about?"

His nod is subtle.

"I think about your big hands and how they feel when you adjust my grip on the axe. How gentle they are despite all that strength."

His breathing quickens.

"I think about what it would feel like to have them all over me," I continue, my voice dropping. "Touching me everywhere."

"Sky..." His voice is rough, strained.

"I think about how you smell—like cedar and leather. And how you most definitely would taste even better." I look up at him through my lashes. "I think about you taking me apart with those skilled hands, making me scream your name."

He groans, his control visibly cracking. "Fuck. You can't say things like that."

"Why not?"

"Because *you* could have any man you wanted. Why would you want some broken-down logger who's twice your age and would rather be hiding in his workshop than out making content for strangers?"

My heart clenches. "Hey." I cup his face, forcing him to meet my eyes. "You want to know what I see when I look at you?"

He doesn't answer, but he doesn't pull away.

"I see strength. Not just physical, though god knows you've got that in spades." I stroke my thumbs across his cheekbones. "I see integrity. Passion for what you do. Loyalty to your friends. Patience with a woman who didn't know a maul from a hatchet."

His eyes search mine, vulnerable in a way I've never seen.

"I see a man who honors his father's memory by preserving something beautiful. Who protects what matters to him." I press closer, feeling the heat from his body. "I see a man I can't stop thinking about, despite every rational reason I should."

That breaks the last of his resistance.

He pulls me to him. "Christ," he breathes against my lips. "I may not fully understand it. But I want you so fucking bad."

Then he's kissing me, and it's nothing like the gentle first kiss I might have expected. It's desperate, consuming, like he's been holding back for much too long.

I melt into him, my hands fisting in his flannel as his tongue sweeps into my mouth. He tastes like black coffee and maple bacon, exactly like I'd expect a mountain man to taste.

"Wanted this since you fell on top of me that first day," he growls against my throat, backing me toward a massive pine. "Even when I was telling myself you were trouble."

"Me, trouble? You're the one with the brooding lumberjack act—"

He silences me with another kiss. He lifts me easily, pressing me back against the tree trunk as my legs wrap around his waist. The bark bites into my shoulders, but I don't care—not when Graham is looking at me like I'm something precious and irresistible. Nor when he's grinding against me, his erection pressing insistently into my hip.

"Tell me you want this," he demands, palming my breast through my sports bra. "Tell me you're sure."

"I want this." I roll my hips against him, feeling his hard length through his jeans. "I want you."

He makes a sound low in his throat, part growl, part groan. "Jesus, the things I want to do to you."

"Yes, tell me," I breathe, working at the buttons of his flannel.

"Want to put my mouth everywhere," he confesses, his voice rough with need. "Want to taste every inch of you."

"Graham..." I shiver at his words, my shirt falling away under his hands.

"Want to be inside you so deep you'll feel me for days," he continues, his mouth moving down my throat. "Want to fuck you until all you can think about is me, and how good I make you feel."

I never expected to hear him talk like this—so raw, possessive, and desperate.

"Yes," I gasp. "Yes to all of it."

He makes quick work of my bra, and then his hot mouth is tasting each of my breasts. I arch into him with a cry that echoes off the rocks.

"The noises you make," he murmurs against my skin, his beard scratching deliciously. "Gonna make me lose my damn mind."

His hands are everywhere—spanning my waist, groping my ass, sliding between my thighs.

He undoes my shorts, shoving his fingers inside them to rub my pussy through my panties. "Teasing me with these shorts. Those *legs*," he grumbles, and I nearly come just from his touch alone I'm so on edge.

"Need to touch you," I pant, trying to unbutton his shirt.

I manage to spread it wide enough to take in his mesmerizing chest…all bulging pecs, tan skin, and sexy as hell tattoos. *Damn boy.* I lower my head as best I can and drag my tongue over him, grazing his nipple.

"Fuck, yes," he breathes, and I move my hands down, fumbling with his belt.

He helps free his huge cock from his jeans.

He's really big, and so thick and hard in my hand. When I stroke him, he drops his forehead to my shoulder with a shuddering moan.

"Goddammit, Sky. Your hands…"

I work him slowly, marveling at the weight of him, the way he pulses in my grip. When I twist my wrist on the upstroke, he bites my shoulder with a gasp.

"Want to taste you," I whisper in his ear.

He pulls back to look at me, eyes wild. "Little menace."

I give him a wicked grin as I slide down his body until I'm on my knees before him.

His cock is beautiful—flushed and veined, already weeping at the tip.

I take him in my mouth, reveling in his sharp intake of his breath, and how he grips my ponytail with his fist. He tastes like salt and musk.

"Fuck," he groans, his hips bucking. "Your mouth is...just heaven."

I work him deeper, using my tongue in ways that make him curse creatively. When I message his balls, rolling them gently, he tugs on my hair with such a frantic sound.

"Enough," he pants, pulling me up quickly. He claims my mouth with a possessive kiss. "Need to be inside you, now, or I'm done for."

He makes swift work of my shorts and panties, his fingers finding me slick and ready.

"So wet," he marvels, stroking through my folds. "Soaked like a good little girl."

Oh god. I whimper.

"I'm on the pill, and it's been a while since..."

"Same," he says roughly, sliding his cock along my pussy, positioning himself at my entrance. "Can't even remember the last time. Been so long."

Then he's pushing inside me, slow and careful despite his obvious need.

The stretch is delicious, overwhelming.

"Okay?" he asks, his jaw clenched with the effort of holding still.

I gasp, rolling my hips experimentally. "Yes. So much, yes. Please move, Graham."

He doesn't need to be told twice. His hips snap forward, finding a rhythm that has me crying out with each thrust. The waterfall's roar creates a wall of sound around us, our own private world.

"That's it, baby girl. Squeeze me just like that," he growls against my throat, his movements becoming even more erratic.

"Love hearing you say that," I say, dragging my nails down his back.

"Good," he grunts, and shifts his angle slightly, spiraling me toward the edge almost embarrassingly quickly.

"Graham..." I say, voice shaky. "That's...I'm so close."

"Do it. Come for me," he commands, his voice rough with need. "Let me feel that sweet pussy shiver."

He drives into me deeply—I swear even the tree is shaking—then suddenly I'm shattering around him.

My cries mingle with the sound of rushing water, my body clenching and trembling as pleasure lights me up.

Graham follows seconds later, his release pulsing as he buries his face in my neck.

We stay like that for a long moment, breathing hard, hearts racing.

Slowly, he lowers me to my feet, both of us wincing at the separation.

"You..." I begin, then trail off.

He reaches for his clothes, smiling. "No, you..."

We laugh and dress in companionable silence, the awkwardness from before replaced by something deeper, more complex.

"We should head back," Graham says, checking the position of the sun through the canopy. "Don't want to be caught on the trail after dark."

The hike back is quieter, but not uncomfortable. When Graham offers his hand to help me over obstacles, he doesn't let go afterward, and I nearly swoon.

As Timber Run comes into view through the trees, I squeeze his fingers.

"Thank you," I say softly. "For joining me."

He stops walking and turns to face me, his dark eyes serious. "Anytime."

The words hang between us, loaded with meaning that goes far beyond waterfalls and forest trails. Whatever's developing here is bigger than I expected.

And I have no idea what comes next.

CHAPTER 6
GRAHAM

The taste of Sky still lingers on my lips as we walk back into camp, her hand warm in mine.

My body hums with satisfaction, but there's something else settling in my chest; something that scares the shit out of me.

It's dangerous, this feeling. Like standing on a rotten log— one wrong step, and I'm falling.

I keep replaying the way she looked at me by the waterfall, like I was a goddamn hero. And the way she felt in my arms, against that tree, crying out my name.

Christ, I'm getting hard again just thinking about it.

"You okay?" Sky asks, squeezing my fingers. "You've gone quiet."

"Just thinking," I mutter, forcing myself back to the present.

She grins up at me, cheeks still flushed. "Good thinking or bad thinking?"

"Good," I admit, and her smile brightens.

Fuck, that smile. It does things to me I'm not prepared for.

Later at dinner, I can't keep my eyes off her. Her laughter seems to seep into my very bones. The way she giggles at Ewan's ridiculous stories, how she listens intently when Brady explains tree biology, the crinkle around her eyes when she catches me staring—even the pines seem to lean closer, just to be near her.

Everything about her seems amplified now, like someone turned up the shine on the world.

"Graham's looking mighty pleased with himself tonight," Rourke observes, waggling his eyebrows. "Must've been a… satisfying hike."

Sky nearly chokes on her water, and I feel heat creep up my neck.

"Waterfall's beautiful this time of year," I say gruffly, focusing on my plate.

"Aye, I bet it was," Ewan chuckles, not fooled for a second. "Nothing like nature's beauty to put a spring in a man's step."

Sky gently kicks me under the table, her eyes dancing with mischief.

For once, I don't mind the crew's teasing. Let them think what they want. What happened between Sky and me feels too good to spoil with embarrassment.

When she reaches for the salt, her fingers brush mine, and that simple contact sends electricity up my arm. I catch her eye, and the heat there promises more of what we shared by the falls.

She heads over to help Rourke and Connor with dessert.

"You gonna keep mooning, or grab a beer?" Brady says beside me, handing me a bottle.

I crack it open, the hiss drowned by Ewan's booming laugh. "Just enjoying the view."

Brady follows my gaze to Sky. "She's good for you. Lets you pretend you're not a walking fossil."

"Fuck off." I shove him, with a small grin.

But he's right. She's scraped off layers of rust I didn't know I had.

Now, she catches me staring and winks, her tongue darting out to lick marshmallow off her finger. Jesus, even that's obscene.

"Graham!" Teagan calls from the kitchen. "Sky says you two found bear tracks near the falls. Show me the photos?"

Sky holds up her phone, grinning. "I got a great shot of his track identification face."

The crew whoops as I shake my head, but I'm already moving toward her. Her eyes darken when I get behind her, my chest brushing her back as I reach for the phone. "Which one?" I murmur, inhaling her citrus shampoo.

"The one where you're scowling at dirt like it insulted you." She swipes to a photo of me squinting at paw prints, my beard flecked with pine needles.

"Delete it."

"Never." She tilts her head. "It's my favorite."

The crew's laughter fades as I wrap my arms around her. I kiss her cheek. Let them see us.

After we finish eating, most of the crew disperses to their cabins or the fire pit.

I'm helping clear plates when I hear Teagan call Sky over to the corner of the dining hall.

"Got a minute? I wanted to talk to you about that email you mentioned."

My hands still on the stack of dishes.

The sponsorship thing. I'd forgotten about that in the haze of everything that happened today.

That's the problem with happiness. It lowers your guard.

"Oh, right!" Sky follows Teagan to a quieter spot. "Alpine Horizon got back to me with more details."

I shouldn't eavesdrop.

Should mind my own damn business and finish cleaning

up. But my feet seem rooted to the spot, ears straining to catch their conversation over the clatter of dishes.

"They're offering a year-long partnership," Sky says, excitedly. "Twelve different locations across the country, featuring sustainable outdoor experiences. The exposure would be incredible for my channel."

My chest feels like someone's tightening a logging chain around it.

"That sounds amazing," Teagan responds. "What kind of timeline are they looking at?"

"They want to start next month. I'd be traveling constantly, a new location every three to four weeks. Colorado, Utah, Oregon, Alaska..." Sky's voice carries that breathless quality it gets when she's passionate about something. "It's everything I've been working toward."

The plate in my hands suddenly feels too heavy. I set it down carefully, my father's voice echoing in my memory:

People leave, son. Job opportunities, better offers, greener pastures. Don't get attached to things that ain't built to last.

I'd watched it happen my whole life—friends who moved away for work, relationships that couldn't survive competing ambitions. Even my mother chose to follow my father to the grave rather than stick around.

And now Sky's getting exactly the kind of opportunity that takes people away from places like this.

Away from me.

"And the compensation?" Teagan asks.

"More than I made all last year. Plus gear, travel expenses, the works. They specifically mentioned how much they loved the Timber Run content—apparently it's exactly the vibe they're going for."

Of course it is. We're just content to her, *including me*. A stepping stone to bigger and better things.

I force myself to keep moving, stacking plates while their voices fade into background noise.

But the damage is done.

What the hell did I *think* was going to happen?

That she'd give up her career to stay here with me? That someone like her would choose a grumpy, aging logger over bigger and better opportunities?

By the time I finish cleaning up, Sky and Teagan have wrapped up their conversation. Sky bounces over to me, practically glowing.

"Hey, sexy" she says, slipping her arms around my waist. "Want to come to my cabin? We could...talk about our hike some more."

The suggestive tone in her voice makes my cock twitch, but the joy in her eyes—the same joy she had talking about leaving —kills any arousal before it can fully form.

"I'm beat," I say, gently removing myself from her embrace. "Long day."

Confusion flickers across her face. "We don't have to do anything. I just thought maybe we could cuddle, talk..."

"About what? Your big opportunity?" The words come out sharper than I intended.

She blinks, taken aback. "I...well, yes. I wanted to share it with you. I thought you'd be happy for me."

Happy. Right. Happy that the woman I just fucked against a tree, who's embedded herself in my heart like the head of sharpened maul, is planning her exit strategy.

"Congratulations," I manage. "Sounds like exactly what you wanted."

"Graham, what's wrong?" She reaches for me again, but I step back. "Did I do something?"

"No," I say, and it's the truth. She didn't do anything except be exactly who she's always been—a woman with ambition, talent, and a life that extends far beyond this mountain. "You didn't do anything."

"Then why do you look like someone just ruined your favorite flannel?"

Because I'm an idiot who thought this afternoon meant something more than it did. Because I let myself forget, for a few hours, that we're two completely different people.

"I'm just tired, Sky. It's been a long day."

She studies my face, those sharp blue eyes seeing too much. "Is this about the sponsorship?"

I shrug, aiming for casual and probably missing by miles. "Your career's got nothing to do with me."

"Doesn't it?" Her voice softens. "After today, I thought...I mean, what happened between us..."

"Was good," I finish. "Really good. But it doesn't change anything."

The hurt that flashes across her face nearly breaks my resolve. But I force myself to remember what I overheard—the excitement, the plans, the future that doesn't include me.

"I should go," I say, backing toward the door. "Early day tomorrow."

"Graham, please! We should talk about this."

I move close to her, towering over her. "You want to talk? Fine. You're using this place. Using *me*. Another checkmark for your influencer bingo card."

She reels back. "You know that's not true!"

"You'll film your little videos, fuck the local lumberjack, then jet off to your next *authentic experience*." The words taste like ash. "Just don't pretend it's more than that."

Her eyes glisten. "You're wrong."

Am I? I saw her profile, her videos...the globe-trotting, sponsorships, a life as rootless as dandelion fluff.

She'll forget me soon enough.

I turn and walk off, blood pounding in my head.

I hated the wounded sound in her voice. Hate myself for putting it there. But it's better this way. Better to end it now before I get in any deeper.

Before it destroys me when she leaves.

My cabin feels smaller than usual, the walls pressing in as I strip off my clothes and collapse onto the bed. I can still smell her on my skin—sunshine and wildflowers and the heady scent of sex.

This is why I don't do relationships. People leave. It's what they do.

Sky's got the whole world waiting for her. Why would she stick around here?

I roll over, punching my pillow harder than necessary. Whatever we were, whatever we could have been, it's over now.

Has to be.

CHAPTER 7
SKY

The hurt sits like a stone in my chest.

I barely slept last night, replaying Graham's cruel words over and over.

After everything we shared...the conversations at the range, the vulnerability in the forest, that mind-blowing sex by the waterfall...he *still* thinks of me as nothing more than a shallow social media princess.

Well, *screw that*. And *screw him*.

The morning air is crisp as I head to our usual lesson spot. Graham's already there, setting up the wood splitting station. I see the tension in his shoulders.

"Morning," I say, keeping my voice carefully neutral.

He grunts an acknowledgment without looking at me.

We work in strained silence for the first few minutes.

"Wasting good wood with that weak follow-through," he finally says, voice slicing through me like a blade. Gone is any warmth from yesterday, any hint of the man who whispered filthy promises in my ear.

I grit my teeth, yanking the axe free from where it embedded crookedly in the grain. My palms sting.

"Your stance is wrong," he snaps when I swing again. "Feet wider."

I adjust, and try again.

"Christ, Sky. Your form's gone to shit." His voice carries an edge of disgust. "Swing like you actually want to split the wood, not like you're worried about breaking a nail."

Heat flares in my chest. "Excuse me?"

"You heard me." He crosses his arms, towering over me with that intimidating scowl. "Yesterday you were making progress. Today you're swinging like a delicate little flower who's afraid of actual work."

The unfairness of it steals my breath. "That's not—"

"What? Not true?" He steps closer, his voice dropping low and mean. "Face it, sweetheart. You got your viral moment, your big sponsorship offer. Now you're just going through the motions until you can move on to the next trending destination."

The accusation burns. I stare at him, my vision blurring with angry tears. But his stony expression is as unyielding as the Montana granite.

I square up for another swing. "Maybe I'd listen better if you weren't being such a dick."

The log splits cleanly. "Amazing. You managed not to maim yourself."

I glance up and his eyes have gone cold.

He's a glacier now, determined to freeze me out.

"Would you grow up?!" My voice cracks. "Did yesterday mean nothing to you?"

"Yesterday was fun," he says with a casual shrug that destroys me. "But let's not pretend it was more than that."

That's it. I throw the axe down, not caring that it clatters against the wood pile.

"*Fuck you*, Graham."

I storm off toward the dining cabin, my chest heaving with rage and pain. Behind me, I hear the solid thunk of his axe hitting wood with violent accuracy.

Teagan looks up from her laptop in her office, when I burst through the door, my face undoubtedly streaked with tears.

"Sky? What happened?"

"Your instructor is being a complete asshole," I manage, sinking onto a bench. "And I'm done being his emotional punching bag."

Connor and Brady exchange glances from across the room. Brady quietly sets down his coffee and approaches.

"Take a breath." His calm voice is soothing after Graham's verbal assault.

"He's being cruel," I whisper. "Deliberately cruel. I don't understand."

Teagan closes her laptop, her expression concerned. "Did something happen between you two?"

I laugh bitterly. "Yesterday we...uh...connected. *Really connected.*" I shake my head. "And now he's acting like I'm some kind of predator who's using him for content."

"That doesn't sound like Graham," Connor says, frowning.

"It doesn't?" I snap. "Well, he's back to thinking I'm the enemy again."

Brady sits across from me, his dark eyes thoughtful. "Sometimes people lash out when they're scared."

I snort. "That grizzly bear of a man, scared? Of what?"

"Getting hurt," he says simply. "Graham's lost a lot of people he cared about. Maybe he's protecting himself the only way he knows how. By pushing you away first."

Teagan nods. "He *was* pretty upset after he heard us talking about the sponsorship last night. Maybe he jumped to conclusions."

My anger crystallizes into fierce determination. "Then I need to set him straight." I stand, wiping my eyes.

Connor grimaces. "Sky, maybe give him some time to—"

"No." I shake my head. "I'm not letting him do this. He needs to hear me out before it festers any further."

The workshop door is closed when I reach it, but I don't knock. I push it open hard, and find Graham hunched over his workbench, attacking a piece of wood with a hand plane like it personally offended him.

"Here to film the 'grumpy lumberjack'? Get your fucking quota?"

I cross my arms and narrow my eyes. "Here to talk. Like an adult."

He doesn't look up. "Nothing to talk about."

"Like hell." I step further into his space. "I don't believe you think what happened between us yesterday meant nothing."

"It was just sex, Sky." His voice is flat, emotionless. "Good sex, but that's all."

The casual dismissal feels like a slap. "You're lying."

"Am I?" He finally looks at me, his dark eyes cold. "You got what you wanted—content that went viral, a big sponsorship offer. Mission accomplished."

"You think this is about my career?" My voice rises.

"I know you're using me." He turns back to his work. "It's what you do. What influencers do. Find something authentic, package it for consumption, then move on."

Rage boils over. "You stubborn, pigheaded jerk!"

"So you're good at your job," he says with devastating calm. "You almost had me convinced that..." He trails off.

"That it's real?" I slam my hand on his workbench, making his tools jump.

"You're scared," I press. "Terrified I'll walk away, so you're pushing first. Classic wounded bear crap."

"Damn right I'm scared!" The roar startles us both. He scrubs his face, voice fraying. "You think I don't see how you light up places? The way people flock to you like you're magnetic? You're a fucking supernova, Sky. And I'm…" He kicks at the sawdust at his feet. "A relic. Why would you ever want to stick around here? With me."

My anger dissolves.

"You idiot." I close the distance between us. "You think I'd throw away what we have for a *sponsorship*? I've been negotiating with Alpine for weeks to make Timber Run their flagship! Quarterly features here, touring other sites in between. They *adore* this whole 'grumpy lumberjack' aesthetic."

His brow furrows and he straightens slowly. "So you're not leaving?"

The question hangs in the air between us. I blink, as understanding floods through me.

"You were practically glowing with excitement about traveling constantly, seeing the country, building your brand." His eyes look like a puppy dog's. "It sounded like exactly what you wanted."

"It would have been," I say, quietly. "A month ago, that offer would've have been everything I dreamed of."

He goes very still.

"I asked them to structure it so I'd spend most of my time here, with shorter trips to other locations throughout the year. Because this place and everything you're all building here matters." I step closer, my heart pounding like mad. "And what's happening between *us* matters more than anything else, sponsorships included."

His eyes search my face.

"I want my career *and* you," I admit, my voice raw. "I've been fighting for a way to make that work because you and I… we're worth it."

His body seems to relax. "Sky..."

"I'm not going anywhere, Graham. Not unless you want me to." I reach for him, relief flooding through me when he doesn't pull away.

I watch his throat work as he swallows, then run my palms over the coarse hair of his beard. "I'm stubborn as hell, and when I find something (or someone) I care about, I don't give up easily."

"Shit, I'm a moron," he says.

"And I'm falling in love with you, regardless, you gigantic ass."

My confession makes his eyes widen and his hands slide up my waist.

"Say that again," he rasps.

"I'm falling in love with you, Graham."

He groans, crushing me against him, mouth claiming mine with hunger.

I claw at his flannel, relishing the feel of his lips and the swipe of his hot tongue.

"I'm falling in love with you too," he whispers, as we break apart. "Christ, Sky, I'm so sorry. I said horrible things I didn't mean—"

"You were protecting yourself," I interrupt. "It's no excuse, but I get it. But please don't do that again."

"Never," he promises.

"I'm here, and I'm staying."

"Even if it means changing your whole life?"

I smile, tracing the line of his jaw. "My life was missing something before I came here. Missing someone. Now it's not."

He kisses me again, slower this time, full of hope and relief. When his hands frame my face, I can feel them trembling slightly.

"I want you," he murmurs against my lips. "Not just now,

but...permanently. Want to wake up next to you every damn morning. Want to teach you everything I know about these woods. Want...to watch you turn Timber Run into something bigger than any of us imagined." He sighs. "Even if it means being a lumbersnack daddy."

I chuckle. "You're only *my* lumbersnack daddy."

His hands slide down to my waist, pulling me closer. "The crew's going to be insufferable about this."

"They already are. Ewan's been making innuendos about how I handle your wood since breakfast."

His eyes crinkle with the first genuine smile I've seen from him all morning. "So, about this sponsorship negotiation of yours..."

"Alpine Horizon is actually excited about the anchor location concept. They think it'll show deeper authenticity than the usual nomadic influencer approach." I grin up at him. "Plus, having gorgeous lumberjacks as a regular feature doesn't hurt their engagement metrics."

He groans.

"I promise to protect you from the thirstiest comments," I say.

"My hero," he says dryly, but his eyes sparkle.

I pull him down for another kiss, pouring everything I have into it. He rests his chin on top of my head when we come up for air.

"You know," he says casually, "Connor's got an empty cabin near the west ridge. Big windows. Good light for filming."

I blink. "Are you...offering me a room?"

"Offering you a home." He meets my gaze. "If you want it."

There's a lump in my throat, but I manage a quiet, "I do," as he grins back at me.

Through the workshop window, I can see the rest of the camp buzzing with life. This place, these people, this incredible man holding me close—it's everything.

And I'm never letting go.

EPILOGUE - GRAHAM
SIX MONTHS LATER

I'm pacing like a caged bear outside the main dining hall, checking my phone for the hundredth time. Sky texted from the rental car she picked up from the airport that she'd be here any minute.

The ring box in my pocket feels like it weighs fifty pounds.

"Och, you'll be wearin' a groove clear through to bedrock at this rate," Ewan observes from his perch on the porch railing.

"Shut up," I mutter, running a hand through my hair.

"Graham's nervous," Brady announces matter-of-factly as he carries supplies past us. *"It's adorable."*

I glare at him. "I'm *not* nervous."

Rourke snorts from where he's stringing up twinkle lights. "Right. And I'm not Irish. Mate, you've been jumpier than a long-tailed cat in a room full of rocking chairs."

Fine, I *am* nervous as hell.

Not about Sky saying yes, we've talked about our future enough that I'm confident she wants this too.

But proposing on camera, with everyone watching like it's dinner theater? That's terrifying for a man who's spent most of his life avoiding attention.

I'd rather wrestle a bear.

Yet Sky deserves something she can treasure forever, something that matches the way she's transformed not just my life, but this entire place.

When she first suggested the anchor location concept to Alpine Horizon, I figured we'd see a modest uptick in visitors. What I didn't expect was for Timber Run to become the most sought-after eco-tourism destination in Montana. We're booked solid through next fall, with a waiting list longer than three arms.

The "Lumbersnack Daddies" phenomenon—hell, I still cringe at that name—has taken on a life of its own. Sky's quarterly features showcasing our skills and the camp's mission have garnered millions of views.

We've been featured in *Outside Magazine*, *National Geographic's* adventure blog, and somehow ended up on a "Most Eligible Bachelors in Outdoor Recreation" list that had Connor laughing until he nearly choked on his beer.

The attention means we've had to establish some pretty specific boundaries at the camp. After an incident where someone tried to "accidentally" walk in on Brady's shower, and another where a guest slipped Rourke her cabin key, we implemented what Teagan diplomatically calls our "Professional Interaction Policy."

In plain English: look but don't touch. You can fantasize all you want, but keep the fantasies to yourself.

Most of our guests are genuinely here to learn—sustainable forestry practices, traditional logging techniques, and wilderness skills. They leave with real knowledge and a deep appreciation for what we're preserving.

But obviously I'd be lying if I said the eye candy aspect wasn't a huge part of the draw. Our "Lumbersnack Daddies" merch sells faster than Connor can restock it.

Ewan's embraced his heartthrob status with characteristic Scottish flair. During our monthly "Heritage Nights," he dons his family tartan and regales guests with stories of Highland logging traditions.

The man's shameless, using his accent like a weapon. He makes ladies (and some men) blush with his charm. Last week he nearly caused a riot when three female guests tried to peek under his kilt. Before that, a woman from Phoenix tried to propose to him during the evening campfire.

"She was a lovely lass," he'd said afterward with a grin. "But I told her my heart belongs to the forest."

Lying bastard. His heart belongs to whatever pretty lady happens to be batting her eyelashes at him that week.

But it's working. Sky's content strategy has attracted exactly the kind of visitors we want. The educational programs Teagan developed are now booked months in advance.

More importantly, the revenue has allowed us to expand our conservation efforts. We've purchased three adjoining parcels of old-growth forest.

Connor's dream of creating a lasting legacy has become reality, and Sky helped make all of that possible.

The sound of tires on gravel snaps me out of my thoughts.

A car rounds the bend, and my heart starts hammering wildly like a woodpecker on speed.

She's back.

I watch through the windshield as she spots me and breaks into that radiant smile that never fails to knock the wind out of my lungs.

Even after six months together, two of which included her traveling for various Alpine Horizon projects, she still makes me feel like a teenager with his first crush.

As soon as the car stops, she's jumping out and running toward me. I catch her in a bear hug that lifts her clean off the ground, breathing in her delicious scent. Her gasp melts into a moan as I kiss her.

"Miss me?" she asks against my ear, her arms tight around my neck.

"Maybe," I growl, setting her down but not releasing her.

She pinches my side. "Liar. Teagan said you've been moping by the fire pit every night."

"Teagan talks too much."

Her fingers thread through my beard, tugging gently. "You're cute when you're pining."

I grunt. "How was Utah? I see the Canyonlands gave you a tan." I kiss her neck.

She chuckles. "It was incredible. The slot canyon footage is going to be amazing." Her eyes sparkle with excitement. "But I'm so happy to be home."

Home. The word hits me square in the chest every time she says it.

"The crew's inside," I tell her, nodding toward the dining hall where warm light spills from the windows. "Dinner's waiting."

She grins. "Did Ewan make his famous shepherd's pie, like he promised?"

"With extra whiskey in the gravy, just how you like it."

"I do love that man." I'm tempted to spank her sweet ass for talking about another man like that while she's in my arms. But that would lead to skipping dinner entirely and taking her straight to my cabin.

And I've got plans tonight.

Plans that require an audience.

Dinner is chaos, as usual—packed with guests. Sky holds court at the head of our table, her foot hooked around my ankle beneath the table, regaling everyone with stories from her latest adventure while the crew hangs on her every word.

Watching her interact with these guys who've become family to both of us, I'm struck again by how well she fits here.

She's not just tolerated or accommodated, she's genuinely one of us now. Teagan is basically her BFF, and the rest seek her advice on everything from social media strategy to relationship problems. She mediates disputes, celebrates successes, and she and Teagan somehow manage to keep us all in line without any of us realizing it.

"So the park ranger says to me," Sky continues, gesturing with her fork, 'Ma'am, we don't typically allow influencers to rappel into the sacred petroglyphs area,' and I had to explain that I wasn't just any influencer, I was representing Timber Run. And he's like, 'In Montana?' Turns out, he's a big fan of grumpy Graham, and after he realized I was his girlfriend, he let me do whatever I wanted." She winks at me. "Though, you owe him a personalized video, babe."

I shake my head.

"Oh," Teagan says, and I catch the meaningful look she gives me. "Graham wanted to film something with you real quick before it gets too late, didn't you?"

I freeze. This is it.

"Right," I manage. "Nothing fancy. Just wanted to...record a little welcome home message. By the camp sign."

Sky tilts her head, curious. "That's sweet. Of course."

As we make our way to the entrance of the camp, I pat the ring box in my pocket. Behind us, I can hear the crew finding excuses to linger outside the dining hall, positioning themselves for the show.

The sky's bleeding indigo, the lights twinkling like trapped stars. The carved wooden sign that welcomes visitors to Timber Run looks particularly magical tonight. Connor and I built it together when we first established the camp, never imagining it would become the backdrop for marriage proposals and viral content.

Sky positions herself beside me as Teagan sets up the shot.

I clear my throat, suddenly tongue-tied. All the words I'd practiced evaporate.

You can do this, D'Amico.

I take a deep breath and look at Sky.

Really look at her. Her blonde hair effortlessly sexy as it falls around her shoulders, wavy tendrils brushing her cheeks, and her blue eyes soft with affection. She's still wearing her travel clothes, rumpled from the flight, but she's never looked more beautiful.

"Rolling," Teagan nudges, quietly.

I take Sky's hands in mine, feeling their familiar warmth.

"I missed you," I start, my voice huskier than usual. "These past two weeks felt like two months. The cabin was too quiet, the bed too empty. Even Ewan's terrible jokes weren't funny without you there to laugh at them."

"Arse!" comes an indignant shout from behind us, and Sky giggles.

"I used to think this place was complete," I continue, finding my rhythm. "The camp, the crew, our mission. But then you crashed into my life—literally like a tornado in hiking boots—and showed me what I was missing."

Her eyes start to glisten.

"You didn't just bring your camera and your followers, which I fought tooth and nail. You brought purpose, vision, and a way to share what we do with the world." I squeeze her hands. "You brought joy. Laughter. Light. And you brought a dying relic back to life."

"Graham..." she whispers.

"You brought love," I finish. "The kind I never thought I'd be lucky enough to find."

I release one of her hands to reach into my pocket, and her eyes widen as I drop to my good knee.

"Sky James," I say, opening the ring box to reveal the vintage art deco setting I'd chosen, with clean lines and classic beauty, just like her. "Will you marry me?"

She's down on me in seconds flat, knocking us both into the dirt. "Yes," she chokes out. "Yes, my stubborn, sexy grump. I'll marry you!"

The camp erupts behind us. The crew cheers and whistles as I slide the ring onto her finger with trembling hands. Our kisses are salty from both of our tears.

"Did you plan this whole thing?" she asks breathlessly.

"For a month," I admit. "Teagan coordinated everything. The crew helped me write the speech. And before you ask— yes, we're streaming this live to the main hall. Our guests are watching."

She laughs, the sound bright and beautiful. "My fiancé, the secret romantic."

Fiancé. I like that.

My phone dings, and I pull it from my pocket, turning the screen toward her.

She bursts out laughing.

The live stream of the proposal is already going viral, *#LumbersnackDaddyHusband* trending.

I groan. "You've got to be kidding me."

"Oh come on. You love being my viral fiance."

"I love *you*," I correct, pulling her in for another kiss. "The rest is just noise."

∼

DON'T GO SAWING MY HEART

CHAPTER 1
HAZEL

Y*ou've got to be kidding me.*
I stare through the windshield of my rental car as I pull into the *Timber Run Eco-Historical Lumberjack Camp*...what can only be described as a fantasy camp for lumberjacks...or at least a fantasy camp for those with a lumberjack fetish.

Pine trees tower over the clusters of platform boardwalks, demonstration spaces, and log buildings like judgmental spectators as I make my way to the main lobby for check-in.

My stomach churns with familiar anxiety.

What were you thinking, Hazel?

I was thinking about the promotion hanging in the balance, about my two years of research on recreational risk assessment, about proving that I can handle a simple conference presentation.

What I wasn't thinking about was the fact that a conference like "Risk Assessment in Outdoor Recreation" would be held at an *actual* outdoor recreation facility crawling with *actual* people—both social *and* outdoorsy.

The worst possible combination.

But I paid extra for a private cabin specifically to avoid this exact scenario.

While my colleagues are networking in the main lodge, sharing meals, and doing whatever socially competent people do at conferences, I'll be safely tucked away in Cabin 12 with my laptop, my research, and my carefully planned meal delivery schedule.

Breathe in for four, hold for seven, out for eight.

The familiar mantra does nothing to quiet the math humming in my skull—72% chance of embarrassment if I have to make small talk with staff, 89% likelihood of spilling coffee on myself during orientation.

I brace myself as I head into the lobby. The woman at the registration desk—Kaylee, according to her name tag—is blonde, perky, and exactly the kind of person I'd avoid at places like this. She hands me my cabin key with a smile that suggests she might actually be happy to be here.

"Your cabin's on the west ridge," she says, pointing toward a winding path. "Beautiful views, and nice and quiet for conference prep. The welcome mixer starts at seven in the main lodge, and—"

"I'll be working tonight," I interrupt. "Big presentation to prepare for."

Kaylee's smile doesn't waver. "Of course! Be sure to pick up your conference materials from the event center. It's the big building over there." She points across the way. "If you need a break from work, Heritage Night is out at the fire pit at 9pm. Only if you want the full lumberjack experience."

I don't.

But she continues anyway. "Ewan tells the most amazing Highland logging stories. He's very entertaining…and really nice to look at." She winks.

"Wonderful," I say, then leave before she can share more details about social events I have no intention of attending.

Cabin 12 is exactly what I'd hoped for—small, private, with a desk positioned to face the wall rather than the windows. No distracting mountain views or wandering lumberjacks to derail my focus.

I unpack my clothes into neat stacks, arranging my pencil skirts, slacks, and blouses in the closet. Then I set up my laptop, and lay my research materials and presentation notes precisely perpendicular to the desk.

Safety lives in right angles.

Within an hour, I've recreated my home office environment, complete with the statistical comfort of familiar routines.

I order dinner from the camp's meal service, and when it arrives, I barely look up from my actuarial models to accept it.

This is good. This is safe. This is exactly how I'll survive the next five days.

But as evening settles over the mountains, I panic. I forgot to grab my conference packet.

My presentation materials rely on the data in that packet—the charts, graphs, and handouts I spent months perfecting.

In my rush to escape social interaction, I didn't even think to get it before hightailing it to my cabin.

I stare at my laptop screen, running probability calculations in my head. The event center will be empty now, right? Everyone's at dinner.

That Heritage Night thing starts in twenty-six minutes, giving me a nine-minute window where foot traffic between cabins and the main buildings drops to an estimated 12% occupancy.

If I time this correctly, I can retrieve my materials without encountering a single human being.

At 8:41 PM, I venture out of my cabin. The path to the

event center is well-lit but mercifully empty. Through the trees, I can hear chatter and distant laughter coming from the main lodge area where the welcome mixer is still going on, but the conference building sits in blessed silence.

I slip inside and locate my packet on the conference registration table, next to a pile of name badges and lanyards.

Success!

I grab it and pivot to go when I hear movement off somewhere in another room. Ready to dash out the way I came, someone curses.

Are they in trouble?

The smart thing would be to leave immediately. The statistically sound choice would be to return to my cabin with my materials and avoid any further human interaction.

But if someone needs help, I can't ignore it.

I may have social anxiety, but I'm not a monster.

"Och, not again—" A man grunts.

I find myself walking toward the distraught voice. The door is slightly ajar, as I push it open and freeze.

Warm lamplight spills over a cacophony of flexing muscle, the man standing with his back to me. My brain temporarily stops processing information beyond "holy statistical outliers."

He's enormous—way over six feet with shoulders that could support actual architecture—and he's bare-chested, holding several yards of tartan fabric that pools around his hips wearing an expression of someone trying to solve advanced calculus.

His body is a masterpiece of functional anatomy. Broad shoulders that roll down to contoured hips, every muscle defined from what's obviously years of physical labor. His sun-streaked locks curl slightly at the nape of his neck, and he's muttering what sounds like Scottish curse words at the kilt in his hands.

I should absolutely, definitely turn around and pretend this never happened.

Instead, I stand there like an idiot, clutching my conference packet and trying to remember how breathing works.

"Come on, you stubborn piece of shite—" He breaks off, apparently sensing my presence, and whirls around.

"Christ, you're tall," he exclaims, as crystal blue eyes meet mine, and my statistical understanding of anything flies straight out the window.

He's even more devastating from the front—broad chest covered in tattoos and just the right amount of hair, defined abs that suggest he does more than demonstrate logging techniques for tourists, and a striking face with a thick beard that belongs in Highland romance novels.

Words evaporate. I open my mouth to apologize, to explain, to flee, but what comes out is a strangled noise that might charitably be called a squeak.

I manage to turn, ready to run.

"Please don't go." He grabs the collapsing fabric at his hips. "I can't give chase, as you'll learn the secret of what a Scotsman wears under his kilt, if I do."

His accent wraps around the words like warm honey as his mouth curves into a grin that should be registered as a lethal weapon.

I don't move, but then his voice is doing something illegal to my vertebrae.

"You wouldn't happen to know anything about Highland dress, would you, lass?"

"I—what?" I blink at him, trying to process the question while my brain is still stuck on the visual of all that exposed muscle and skin.

He holds up the tartan fabric, and I notice his hands are calloused, strong, entirely too attractive for someone who's playing dress up. "The pleats are giving me trouble. I can fell a tree in under five minutes, but apparently dressing myself like a proper Scotsman is beyond my capabilities."

"I don't know anything about kilts," I manage, then immediately feel stupid for stating the obvious.

"Aye, well, neither do I, apparently." He gestures helplessly at the fabric. "I usually have a helper, but Sky's on her honeymoon." He glances up at a clock on the wall. "And Heritage Night starts in ten minutes. The good news is I can't possibly embarrass myself more than I already have."

Something about his self-deprecating humor breaks through my paralysis. "You're not embarrassing yourself. You're just...geometrically challenged."

He raises an eyebrow. "Geometrically challenged?"

"Your pleating's inverted. The pleats follow a mathematical pattern. If you think of it as a series of calculated folds rather than random fabric manipulation..." I trail off, realizing I'm about to explain Highland dress construction using statistical principles to a half-naked Scottish lumberjack.

"Go on," he says, not mocking. "I'm listening."

I step closer, drawn by the intellectual puzzle. "See, if you start with the back panel centered on your spine, then create uniform pleats at measured intervals..."

I reach out to demonstrate the folding pattern, and my fingers brush against his forearm as I position the fabric. He goes very still, and I take a deep breath to focus.

It's nice to be able to look up slightly to meet his eyes, rather than constantly gaze downward or hunch to make myself look shorter. At 5'11, it's hard for me to fit in.

"Like this," I whisper, trying to concentrate on the fabric instead of the way his muscles shift under my touch as I arrange the pleats. "Each fold needs to be equidistant from the center point."

"You're brilliant," he murmurs, and something in his tone makes me look up. His blue eyes are warm, appreciative, focused entirely on my face like I'm the most fascinating thing he's encountered all evening. "For someone who doesn't know kilts, you sure understand them. You must be a sorceress."

"Actuary," I reply.

"Even better." He turns carefully, kilt clutched like a towel. His chest hair glints above the bunched wool.

"It's just basic geometry," I offer weakly.

"Nothing basic about it when you can't figure it out yourself." His smile is soft, easy.

I swallow. "You need a 45-degree fold every three inches to maintain pattern continuity. Here—may I try?"

His brow shifts. "As long as you're not angling for a peek, lass."

I level my gaze at him. "This is a geometric *emergency*."

Teasing crinkles bloom around his eyes. "Aye. Let's fix it then."

Cold brass buckles bite my palms as I kneel. His spruce and bergamot scent overwhelms the rational part of my brain.

Statistical anomaly: 98.7% of theoretical probabilities cannot account for this man's gravitational pull.

"You start here." My voice sounds alien, assured. "Each pleat overlaps at a ratio compensating for the uneven length."

His rough fingertips brush mine, adjusting the wool. "Like rigging sails."

"Exactly. The Fibonacci sequence in wool."

His low chuckle vibrates in my bones. "Now there's a pickup line I'll need to steal."

I'm imagining our intimate position—down on my knees in front of this Scottish rogue. My blouse brushes his scarred knees, competent hands smoothing wrinkles from his clothes. He shifts, cords of muscle sliding beneath golden skin.

Hell, don't look up at him. It's much too…accurate for something inappropriate I really shouldn't be thinking about right now.

"Tell me, Miss Actuary—"

"Hazel."

Even without looking up at him, I can feel his smile lines deepen. "Hazel." I resist the shiver at the way his accent caresses the syllables. "What's your professional opinion?" He gestures to his half-clad form. "Survival odds for a Scot in the wilds of Montana?"

"D-depends." I fumble the final clasp. "Your BMI suggests above-average cardiovascular health, but that kilt's a liability…in many ways."

"Duly noted." He pivots as I finish and stand up, the movement bringing his bare chest inches from my mouth. "Better?"

Catastrophic.

I move back and rake my eyes over him. The finished drape showcases his powerful thighs and decadent abs. My nod comes out jerky.

"Sensational." His kindness unfurls something behind my ribs. "I'm Ewan MacLeod. And I'm in your debt for your geometric expertise."

"Glad I could help," I say, my face feeling like it's radiating enough heat to power the entire camp.

"Seriously. Most women don't solve my problems within ten minutes of meeting me."

Reality slams back. *Women.* Plural. Of course.

I grab my conference packet. "I should go."

"Wait—" He catches my elbow and everything in my packet comes flying out, papers scattering all over. In my hyper focus on geometric pleats and mouth-watering Scottish anatomy, I apparently picked it up upside down.

"Oh no," I breathe, dropping to my knees to gather the materials.

Ewan immediately joins me, after he finishes tugging on a white tunic.

Our hands collide retrieving pages, his engulfing mine completely.

As he hands me a chart showing "Probability of Injury During Sawing Demonstrations," he glances at the data with what looks like actual interest.

"Fascinating," he murmurs. "According to this, I've got about a fifteen percent chance of surviving my next demonstration."

I stare at him. "That's... that's not what that means. These are baseline risk assessments for insurance purposes, not individual probability calculations, and besides, your safety protocols would significantly alter the—"

I stop, realizing I'm babbling about actuarial science to a man I just helped dress while trying to pretend I wasn't memorizing every inch of his drool-worthy torso.

His grin widens. "Ah, so you're the clever statistician who's going to tell us all how dangerous we are."

"Safety saves lives," I mutter.

"Aye. But living's more than risk mitigation." His thumb traces a whorl of ink—the Venn diagram where preparation meets luck.

"I'm not—I mean, I don't—this isn't—" I scramble to my feet, clutching my papers like armor. "I should go. You have Heritage Night to get to."

"You're not attending?" He tilts his head, studying me with an intensity that makes my stomach do things that violate several statistical models. "And here I was hoping you might stay to see how well your geometric expertise holds up under performance conditions."

The thought of sitting in a crowd watching him tell stories while remembering exactly what he looks like underneath those clothes makes my face burn even hotter. "I really have to get back to my cabin. Work to do."

"Of course," he says easily, but something in his expression suggests this conversation isn't over. "Sleep well, Hazel. And thank you—for the lesson in geometry."

The way he says my name, with that rolling Scottish brogue, makes something flutter in my chest that has nothing to do with anxiety and everything to do with a massive Scottish lumberjack who's looking at me with those heavenly blue eyes.

I flee.

Back in Cabin 12, I lean against the closed door and try to understand what just happened. I just spent fifteen minutes in close physical proximity to the most attractive man I've ever met, helped him get dressed while desperately trying not to stare at his perfect body, and had an intelligent conversation about mathematical principles.

And I didn't *completely* humiliate myself.

This is a problem.

I have five days to give the presentation of my career, prove my professional competence, and return to my carefully ordered life. I don't have time to be distracted by crystal blue eyes, Highland kilts, and the memory of his warm skin under all that fabric.

But as I organize my rescued materials and prepare for tomorrow's conference sessions, I can't stop thinking about the way Ewan said "clever" like he actually meant it, or how he'd watched me work—not a quirky nuisance, but a puzzle he wanted to solve, and how for a few important moments, I forgot to be terrified of human interaction.

Statistical anomaly, indeed.
I bury my face in a pillow.

CHAPTER 2
EWAN

The fiddle feels too light in my hands tonight, the firepit smoke stinging my eyes as I spin another tale of Highland ghosts for the crowd.

Normally, I'd savor this—the crackle of flames, the wide-eyed tourists, the way women blush when I lean in to whisper a tale's chilling climax.

But all I can see is *her*.

Hazel.

Even her name rolls off my tongue like liquid caramel.

I nearly botch the finale of "The Selkie's Curse," forgetting the third verse entirely.

After the encore, Rourke catches up to me by the snack table. "You okay? You seem distracted tonight?" He licks s'mores off his thumb, squinting.

"Aye, got someone on my mind." I swipe a spare chocolate bar from his plate, ignoring his *oh-this-again* eyeroll.

As I finally get to bed, I can still smell her.

Unfortunately, I'm awake before dawn, replaying last night's encounter again and again.

Och, the way she looked at me when she first turned

around—those intelligent eyes going wide, her face flushing pink. But it wasn't just the physical reaction that's got tied up in knots. It's what came after.

Most women who stumble across me half-naked giggle, flirt, or flee. Hazel jumped right in and solved my problem like a professional, her clever mind turning Highland dress into a geometric equation.

Those long, elegant fingers arranging pleats with scientific accuracy while I stood there like a lovesick fool, memorizing the way she bit her lower lip in concentration.

The lass had knelt before me like some dark-haired goddess, hands steadier on my kilt pleats than my own heartbeat. I used every ounce of willpower to keep my erection at bay.

Even now, my skin prickles where her fingers brushed my hips, her analytical muttering about *Fibonacci sequences* echoing in my skull.

And those legs. Christ almighty, those legs that went on for miles, bringing her nearly to my eye level. Do you know how rare that is for a man my size? Most women have to crane their necks to look up at me, but Hazel easily met my gaze, like some statuesque Amazon.

Watching her work, seeing those statistical charts scattered across the floor—she's not just any number-cruncher. She's bloody brilliant.

I drag myself out of bed and into my clothes, mind already working on a plan.

Over breakfast in the main lodge, I corner Kaylee, our newest hire. She's a whiz with recalling faces and names.

"You remember a really tall, skittish lass checking in?" I ask without preamble. "Know her story?"

Kaylee grins knowingly. "Hazel Phillips? With the risk assessment conference? Paid extra for the private cabin, number 12, and orders all her meals to be delivered. Hasn't been to a single social event as far as I can tell. She hasn't picked up her lanyard or name tag."

"Is she presenting or on any panels?"

Kaylee gives me a sideways glance.

"I'm just curious. I want *all* of our guests to enjoy their stay," I say, innocently.

Her lips twitch. "She's on the schedule for a big presentation and panel talk on Thursday." Kaylee leans closer conspiratorially. "Between you and me, she's got some serious social anxiety. I know the type. My little sister's the same way."

My protective instincts kick in immediately. The woman who confidently solved my geometric clothing crisis is hiding from people—even other actuaries, insurance industry enthusiasts, and fellow number-crunchers like herself? That gifted mind that impressed me so thoroughly is being wasted in isolation?

Not on my watch.

By noon, I've gathered intelligence from the kitchen staff about her meals and found the conference schedule posted in the main lodge. She's missed three sessions she was supposed to attend.

"I'll take this one, mate," I tell the kitchen runner, intercepting her lunch delivery. "I promise to give you any tip she leaves."

He just shrugs. "Fine with me. I've got plenty more to deliver."

The walk to Cabin 12 gives me time to think about my approach. Clearly, direct Highland charm might be a bit much for someone who's actively avoiding human contact. But maybe the woman who appreciated geometric solutions might respond to more...practical help.

I knock on her door, balancing the lunch tray.

"Food delivery!" I call out in my cheeriest voice.

The door opens a crack, revealing one gorgeous green eye peering out suspiciously. When she sees it's me, the eye widens.

"What are you doing here?" She doesn't sound upset at least.

"Bringing you lunch. May I come in?" I hold up the tray. "And I swear to keep my clothes on this time."

Her face flushes that delightful pink again.

"Turkey sandwich, Earl Grey tea, and a side of Highland kindness." I grin. "Though the last bit was my addition."

She hesitates.

I lean against the doorframe, the cold mountain air biting through my flannel. "Come on, brilliant minds need fuel."

A beat. Two. Then the door swings wider, revealing her fully—long dark hair in a frazzled bun, glasses smudged, wearing leggings and a cardigan that swallows her whole.

She's fucking glorious.

Her cabin's a nest of spreadsheets and highlighters, a half-empty coffee cup abandoned beside charts, tables, and other printed documents.

I step into her makeshift office. Her laptop is open on a desk positioned to face the wall, papers arranged in precise stacks, everything organized to a T.

"Impressive," I say, setting down the tray and gesturing to her setup. "Like mission control for statisticians."

"It's just work," she mumbles, but I catch the hint of pride in her voice.

"Just work? Lass, I glimpsed those charts last night. You're calculating risk probabilities for recreational activities. That's not 'just' anything—that's bloody amazing."

She blinks at me like I've grown a second head.

"According to your models from last night," I begin,

settling into the chair across from her desk. "Do your calculations regarding my sawing demonstrations account for my biceps and Highland stubbornness? Because that might improve my odds of survival significantly."

For the first time since I've met her, Hazel smiles—a big, sweet smile that transforms her entire face. "That's not how actuarial assessment works. These are baseline risk calculations for insurance purposes, not—"

"Individual probability models, aye. But surely proper equipment, experience, and training factors alter the baseline?" I lean forward, genuinely interested. "I've been doing sawing demonstrations for fifteen years without a serious injury. Doesn't that data point matter?"

Her eyes light up. "Actually, yes. Expertise and safety protocol adherence significantly reduce individual risk below baseline calculations. Your experience would move you into a completely different risk category."

"So I might actually survive the week?"

"You might actually survive the decade," she says, and there's warmth in her voice now, the sharp mind I glimpsed last night coming to the surface.

"Excellent. Now, how about you eat your lunch while telling me why you've been hiding in here instead of attending your conference?"

Her walls go back up immediately, as she sinks into her chair. "I'm not hiding. I'm working."

"Hazel." I use my gentlest tone, the one that works on spooked animals and guests that get nervous around my saws. "You've missed three sessions today. Sessions where they're discussing the very research you're an expert on."

"How do you know what sessions I've missed?"

Uh. "Because I looked at the conference schedule, and I asked around." I hold up my hands when she looks alarmed.

"Nothing to worry about. Just curiosity about the bright statistician who solved my kilt crisis."

She fidgets with her napkin. "I just...crowds aren't really my thing."

"Neither are kilts, apparently, but you managed that just fine." I lean back, studying her face. "What's really going on, lass?"

For a long moment, she's quiet, and I can practically see the numbers formulating odds in her head.

Finally, she sighs. "I'm supposed to give a presentation on Thursday. Two years of research on actuarial models for adventure tourism liability. It's important. For my career."

"And you're worried about presenting to a crowd of people who do exactly the kind of work you're an expert on?"

"I'm worried about *everything*. It's kind of what I do. Worry." Her voice is small. "What if I mess up? What if they ask questions I can't answer? What if—"

"What if you're a bloody star and they recognize it?" I interrupt gently. "Because that's what's going to happen, you know. You're going to get up there and show them research that could revolutionize how the industry thinks about risk assessment."

She stares at me like I've spoken in ancient Gaelic. "You can't possibly know that."

"Sure, I can. I spent fifteen minutes watching you work last night, and I've never seen anything like it. You took one look at the chaos of fabric around me and solved it in moments. You're not just smart, Hazel—you're clever in a way that most people can only dream of."

Her throat works as she swallows hard. "Ewan, I don't know how to do this. The networking, the presenting, the..." She gestures helplessly. "The *people* part."

"Lucky for you, I happen to be excellent at the people part."

I fold my hands in my lap, decision made. "Let me help you. We'll start small—maybe one conference session this afternoon. I'll sit with you, and if it gets overwhelming, we leave."

"Why...why would you do that?"

The question catches me off guard with its honesty. Why would I? Because something about this wonderful, terrified woman calls to every protective instinct I have. Because I want to see her succeed almost as much as I want to see her smile again. Because last night, I met someone who interested me for reasons that go beyond the physical...and god help me, *that's* bloody sexy.

"Because you helped me when I needed it," I say simply. "And because I think you're someone special, who just needs a little nudge."

She studies my face, those green eyes searching for something. "That's why you're really here?"

"Couldn't stop thinking about you." The truth slips out, rough and unpolished.

She drops her spoon in her tea. "Wh-what?"

"Not like that," I lie. "Well, not only that..." I shake my head. "Okay, let me start over." Why am I so flustered?

I gesture at her walls of data. "You're...fascinating. Like a spy novel, but with spreadsheets."

She snorts, surprising us both. "You're mocking me."

"Never." I move closer to her, ignoring for a moment the way her breath hitches. "Hazel, I've met CEOs less intelligent *and less intimidating* than you. Saw your presentation topic in the program. Even the title's a masterpiece."

Her lips quirk. "You understood it?"

"Not a word. But these people will." I pull her conference badge out of my pocket. "I grabbed this for you."

She watches me place it in her hand.

Then she nods slowly. "One session. But if I panic, we leave immediately."

"Deal." I stand, offering my hand. "Now eat your lunch, freshen up, and when I return we'll go show those conference attendees what real expertise looks like."

As she shakes my hand, her fingers slightly tremble in mine.

I show myself out, but as I turn to go, her voice stops me.

"Ewan?"

I turn back. She's backlit in the doorway, all long limbs and tangled hair.

My cock stirs.

"Thank you." She smiles.

I smile back. "Of course, Hazel."

I'm in deeper trouble than I thought.

CHAPTER 3
HAZEL

I stare at the conference schedule in my hands, my stomach a riot of knots.

"Risk Assessment in Extreme Weather Conditions" starts in twelve minutes, and despite every probability calculation screaming that this is a terrible idea, I'm actually going to attend.

With Ewan.

Who somehow convinced me that hiding in my cabin for five days isn't a viable career strategy.

Who the hell is this man?

I count my breaths—*in for four, hold for seven, out for eight*—but my pulse still thrums like an overclocked processor.

"You ready, lass?" His voice rumbles behind me as I hover outside the conference center like a deer calculating predator proximity.

"I'm ready to vomit into the nearest potted plant," I mutter.

"That's the spirit!" His laugh is rough and rich, as he holds the door open, ushering me into a room buzzing with conference attendees. When I freeze at the threshold, his hand finds the small of my back. "Breathe. I'll be right beside you."

He looks devastatingly handsome in a navy flannel that stretches across those firm, broad shoulders, and worn jeans that should be illegal in how well they fit him. The memories of helping him with his kilt the other night come flooding back.

All that warm flesh under my hands.

My face goes up in flames.

"I calculated the probability of humiliation at approximately 73%."

"And the probability of success?"

I bite my lip. "27%."

"Did you include me being here with you in those numbers?"

No. I shake my head.

"Regardless, those are betting odds I'd take any day." He offers his elbow. "Come on, let's go prove your models wrong."

The session room is packed with insurance professionals, safety consultants, and outdoor industry representatives—exactly the kind of networking nightmare I've spent my career avoiding. But as Ewan steers us to two empty seats in the back, knowing he's there beside me somehow makes my lungs continue to function.

"See? Strategic positioning. Less eyeballs, quick escape route."

The presenter, a woman with a sleek gray bob, begins discussing weather-related liability figures, and within five minutes, I realize she's using outdated models that significantly overestimate certain risks.

"She's wrong about the temperature coefficient," I whisper to Ewan.

"Tell her."

I stare at him. "What?"

"During Q&A. Tell her." His blue eyes are serious. "That your research accounts for variables she's missing."

"I can't just—"

"You can." His voice is gentle but certain. "Trust me."

The man is insane.

When the presenter opens for questions, I start to raise my hand, and Ewan taps under my elbow to push it up higher. The presenter nods at me, and suddenly forty pairs of eyes are focused in my direction.

Sweat trickles down my spine.

Help.

Then I feel Ewan pat my knee and whisper. "You can do this."

I lift my chin. "H-Hazel Phillips, Senior Actuary," I hear myself say, standing up despite my knees threatening mutiny. "Your temperature coefficient assumes linear risk progression, but current data suggests an exponential model would more accurately reflect—"

I stop, realizing I'm about to deliver a mini-lecture to a room full of strangers.

"Please, continue," the presenter says, genuinely interested. "I'd love to hear your thoughts."

So I do.

For three minutes, I explain the statistical models I've been perfecting, watching faces around the room shift from polite attention to actual engagement. When I finish, I see several people are taking notes.

"Fascinating approach," the presenter says. "I'd love to discuss this further sometime after the session."

"Oh, of course. Thank you." I sink back into my seat, adrenaline making my hands shake.

Ewan's grin could power the entire camp. "Told you," he murmurs.

After the session, five different attendees approach me with questions about my research.

Panic starts rising in my throat as they crowd around, but Ewan runs interference beside me like some Scottish guardian angel.

"Fantastic presentation in there," he tells the group with his charming smile. "But I promised Ms. Phillips a tour of our safety protocols. Perhaps you could all continue this conversation at tonight's mixer?"

They agree enthusiastically and we exchange business cards before they disperse.

I realize I just agreed to more social interaction. Voluntarily.

I take a deep breath as we walk outside. "Thank you, Ewan."

"For what?"

"Saving me from turning into a stammering mess."

"You didn't need saving. You were magnificent. And I'm proud of you." He leads me over to a stand selling lemonade and pays for two drinks. "But in case you hyperventilated I thought a tactical retreat was in order."

He hands me a lemonade, and I thank him, grateful for the cool hit of sugar. "I can't believe all those people wanted to talk to me."

"Of course they do," he takes a sip from his straw. "You're hot shite."

I choke. "Don't say that."

"Why not? It's true."

My face combusts. "Stop."

As we stroll along the boardwalk, I find myself studying his profile—the strong jaw, groomed beard with those silver streaks, the afternoon sun turning his hair a soft shade of copper. He's stunning, and yesterday he was practically naked

91

in my hands. Now he's helping me navigate professional situations like *he's* enjoying it.

"I'm still not sure why you're doing this?" I ask.

"Doing what?"

"Helping me. Being kind. Spending time you could be spending doing anything else. Acting like..." I gesture helplessly between us. "Like this matters."

He turns to face me fully, and something in his expression makes my chest tight. "It does matter. *You* matter."

"You don't even know me."

"I know you solved a geometric crisis that had me stumped. I know you're clever enough to revolutionize risk assessment models. I know you worry about everything, but still make brave choices every day." His voice softens. "And I know you're terrified of taking up space in the world, when you should be owning every room you walk into."

Heat prickles behind my eyes. "I'm too tall, too awkward, too socially inept, too—"

"Perfect." The word cuts through my self-deprecation like a blade. "Christ, Hazel, those legs that go on for miles, the way you don't have to crane your neck to meet my eyes, how you stand like some gorgeous Amazon who could conquer continents if she just realized her own power."

I stare at him. In my twenty-six years, exactly no one has described my height as an asset. Except maybe my four foot ten roommate who loved that I could reach everything in the house for her. Otherwise, I've spent my life hunching, slouching, trying to minimize my presence.

"You're just being nice," I whisper.

"Am I?" He reaches over and gently touches my chin. "Look at me, lass. Really look."

I do. Our eyes are nearly level. Usually, I'm looking down

at men, and it makes me feel even more awkward and loom-
ing. But with Ewan, everything feels...proportional. Natural.

"See?" His thumb traces along my jawline. "Perfect fit."

Something flutters low in my belly at his calloused fingers
softly caressing my skin.

"Ewan..." I start, but I don't know how to finish.

"Tell me," he says.

"That this is statistically improbable."

"What is?"

"You. This. Someone like you being interested in someone
like me."

His expression seems to turn to hurt. "Someone like you?"

"Self-conscious. Antisocial. Better with numbers than
humans."

"Remarkable. Beautiful. Courageous enough to stand up in
a room full of strangers and share expertise that could change
an entire industry." His voice is fierce. "Don't you ever minimize yourself, Hazel Phillips."

I take a deep breath in and stand a little taller, his words
coaxing my shoulders back.

"How tall are you in these shoes?" He asks, eyeing my flats.

"Maybe six feet?"

"Perfect."

"For what?"

"This." And he presses his mouth to mine.

Soft. Gentle. Questioning.

My brain shorts out completely.

I've never been kissed before. And I never expected it to
feel like this—sweetness and fire simultaneously.

My lemonade drops from my hand.

He pulls away and I'm breathing hard, staring at him like
he's solved the unified field theory.

"Was that..." he starts.

"Yes," I say quickly, bending down to pick up my drink. "I'm such a clutz."

His smile is tender. "You okay?"

My face burns as I nod.

"I'm sorry, I should've asked permission. Forgive me."

"It's okay. I really liked it." I pause. "It was my...first kiss."

He groans softly. "Mo chridhe." Something protective and hungry flickers in his expression.

"What does that mean?"

His thumb strokes across my lower lip and I fight a moan. "Means I get to be the first man to kiss you properly." He winks. "Because I intend to do it again soon."

Reality, and anxiety, come crashing back. "Ewan, I'm only here for five days. After Thursday's presentation, I go back to Boston and—"

"Hey," he interrupts, caressing my cheek. "We don't have to worry about that right now. Let's just enjoy this."

He's right. Enjoy this.

CHAPTER 4
EWAN

Hazel's a virgin.

I haven't been with a virgin since...back in Scotland. *Och.*

I lie awake in my cabin, staring at the ceiling, replaying every moment of that sweet kiss. When she said it, I nearly staggered. Not because it changes how I feel, but because it means every touch, every glance, every moment between us carries weight I can't afford to mishandle.

It also makes perfect sense why she froze up after our kiss, anxiety overtaking her.

I'm completely fucked.

I'm the first man to kiss those soft lips, the first to see her face flush with desire, the first to make her breath catch with want.

And it only makes me want her more.

But the responsibility of that hits me square in the chest. This isn't some casual flirtation or one night stand with a temporary guest.

This is Hazel—brilliant, anxious, inexperienced Hazel who's never had someone see her worth.

95

I need to prove I'm serious without overwhelming her. Show her I'm interested in more than just being her first every-thing, even though the thought of teaching her about pleasure makes my cock throb against my sheets.

I'm sure she'll hear things. My reputation around here isn't a secret, but I don't want her thinking she's just another fling.

After breakfast, I find Brady by the equipment shed, methodically checking his climbing gear and the saw chains with his usual quiet efficiency.

"Need a favor, mate," I say.

He glances up, dark eyes curious. "What kind of favor?"

"The conference lass—Hazel. She's got some social anxiety. Needs some low-key practice."

Brady's lips twitch. "The tall one who helped you with your kilt?"

"How did you—never mind." I wave him off. "Aye, that one. Think you could help create some non-threatening inter-action opportunities? Nothing obvious, just...casual encounters where she can build confidence."

"You mean like accidentally running into her while she's walking to the conference center?"

"Exactly. You're good at reading people. She needs to hear she's impressive from sources other than me."

Brady nods slowly. "She is impressive. Overheard her talking to some other attendees yesterday—she knows her stuff."

"That she does. Will you help?"

"Course." He returns to his work. "But Ewan? Don't fuck with this woman's feelings. She's...different."

"I know," I murmur.

An hour later, I'm delivering Hazel's breakfast when Brady appears on the path, perfectly timed.

"Hello there," he calls out, approaching Hazel's cabin just as she opens the door. "Thought I could catch you in between sessions. Had a question about your presentation topic."

I watch Hazel's posture straighten slightly. "Oh. Sure."

"Been thinking about your actuarial models since yesterday's session. How do you account for equipment maintenance variables in your risk calculations?"

For the next ten minutes, Brady draws her into a technical discussion while I listen from the porch, watching her confidence bloom as she explains complex statistical concepts to someone eager to listen.

"That's amazing," Brady says when she finishes. "You really are doing great things when it comes to safety. Especially here at Timber Run."

After he leaves, Hazel turns to me with something approaching wonder. "He actually understood what I was talking about. Isn't he one of the camp instructors?"

"He is. See? Even loggers recognize the good you're doing." I hand her the breakfast tray. "Ready for today's session?"

We had stayed at last night's mixer for a whole thirty minutes, chatting with the others who wanted to meet her, until she began to yawn. Then I walked her to her cabin and gave her a kiss on the cheek.

Anything more than that and I would've been ravaging her all night.

And she needed sleep.

The morning conference session goes even better than the first. Hazel asks three questions, offers input on two presentations, and actually stays for the networking break afterward. When other attendees approach her, she doesn't bolt—she engages.

"Did you hear what Dr. Morrison said about my research?" she asks as we walk back toward her cabin, eyes bright with excitement.

"That you're going to change the industry? Aye."

"I can't believe people are actually interested in my work."

"Hazel." I stop walking, turning to face her. "You need to stop being surprised that you're remarkable. Smart people recognize smart people. It's not charity, it's professional respect."

She studies my face. "You really mean that."

"Every word." I step closer. "Now, about that presentation practice we discussed..."

Her anxiety flickers back. "I don't know. What if I freeze up? What if I forget everything?"

"Then we'll practice until forgetting becomes impossible." I gesture toward the workshop. "Come on. Let's use my buddy Graham's workshop—it's got good acoustics and no distractions."

The workshop smells like wood shavings and oil, thick beams overhead creating an intimate atmosphere. Graham's tools hang in perfect order, and we get plenty of light from the high windows.

"Stand here," I position her at the front of the space. "Pretend I'm your audience."

"This feels silly."

"Humor me." I settle onto a workbench, crossing my arms. "Start with your opening."

She clears her throat. "Um. Good afternoon. My name is Hazel Phillips, and I'm here to discuss—"

"Stop. It's too dry." I hold up a hand. "You're reciting, not telling. This is *your* story, lass."

She frowns. "It's a statistical model, Ewan. Not a fairy tale."

"Everything's a story." I circle her.. "For instance, injury probability. Instead of rattling off numbers, make them *feel* it.

Tell them about the logger who almost lost his thumb because someone ignored your data."

"That's...not exactly professional."

"It's human." I stop behind her, hands resting on her shoulders. "You want to change minds? Make them care."

She shivers under my touch. "How?"

"It's *your* research, your insights, your moment to shine." I lean toward her. "What's the most exciting thing about your work? The thing that makes you light up inside?"

She thinks for a moment. "The patterns. When I realized traditional risk models were missing entire variables, that we could predict and prevent accidents more accurately..."

"There." I grin. "*That's* your story. Start there."

For the next hour, I coach her through the presentation using every storytelling technique I know. How to pause for emphasis, where to make eye contact, when to use her hands for gestures. Slowly, her rigid academic delivery transforms into something altogether passionate.

"The implications for adventure tourism safety are revolutionary," she says, gesturing to invisible charts with growing confidence. "We're not just calculating risk—we're *redefining* it."

"Brava!" I stand, applauding. "That was great!"

Her face glows. "Really?"

"Really." I smile, enthralled by her excitement and the way her confidence makes her stand even taller. "You're going to be spectacular."

"I couldn't have done any of this without you," she admits. "I'm grateful."

"Watching you succeed is the most beautiful thing I've ever seen," I say simply. "You're extraordinary, and I want the whole world to know it."

Her breath catches. "Ewan..."

"I know you're leaving in a few days. And I know this is

complicated. But Hazel," I reach up to stroke her face. "I'm just asking for this moment, this feeling, this chance to show you how incredible you are."

She searches my eyes, and I can see her trying to calculate the risks, weigh the probabilities.

Then she pushes forward and kisses me.

It catches me off guard, and I groan like a desperate man.

I kiss her right back, deeper than yesterday, with all the passion I've been holding back. Her mouth opens under mine, tentative at first, then bolder as I coax her with gentle strokes of my tongue.

"So sweet," I murmur against her lips.

She moans, and the sound nearly undoes me.

My hands find her waist, pulling her closer until we're notched together, our bodies fitting like missing pieces finally joined. Made just for this.

Her hands explore my chest through my flannel, curious and careful. When she reaches the buttons, she hesitates.

"Take whatever you want, mo chridhe," I encourage.

She fumbles with the first button, then the second, until my shirt falls open. Her palms flatten against my chest, and I have to bite back an eager groan at the contact.

Lowering her head, she kisses across my pecs. "You're so warm," she marvels, fingers following her mouth.

"Hazel," I warn, voice rough. "If you keep that up..."

"What?" Her eyes meet mine, innocent but curious.

Instead of answering, I lift her onto Graham's sturdy work-bench and step between her long legs. I claim her mouth while my hands slip under her top to caress the bare skin of her back.

She gasps, and I feel her skin prickle underneath my fingers. When I nip at her earlobe, her legs instinctively wrap around my hips.

We both groan—and I know she can feel exactly how much I want her, her heat blazing through our clothes.

"You're so hard," she says, breathlessly. "*And big.*" She arches her back as we continue to kiss, rocking against my raging cock.

"Hard just for you," I growl and suck on her neck, tasting the salt and sweetness of her skin, while her hands slide into my hair. Every soft sound she makes, every tremor that runs through her, only makes me more needy.

Her hips grind against me, faster, and the friction is hurtling me toward a fierce orgasm.

"I think...I think I'm about to come, Ewan," she pants.

And I grip her ass in her conference slacks, and thrust against her in my jeans. "Do it, sweetness. Come for me."

I run my mouth along her jaw, pumping hard, feeling my own orgasm building. But I don't care about me. I only want to make her see stars.

"*Oh god... oh fuck... oh...*" and she's suddenly convulsing, moaning...and I grab her face and kiss her, swallowing all of her gorgeous sounds, my hips still grinding away.

I could come, but I'm too busy making sure I wring every last drop of pleasure from her climax.

She trembles with aftershocks in my arms as I hold her against me, slowing my thrusts.

"Och, Hazel, you're stunning when you come," I whisper in her ear, then look into her pretty green eyes.

"Wow," she breathes.

"Wow is right," I reply.

She runs her hands over my chest, pupils still dilated. "I want you to come."

Oh, love. I chuckle and shake my head, despite my aching cock's protest.

"I will, eventually. But we should stop now." We're in

Graham's workshop, and she needs her rest. The right thing to do is slow the hell down.

"We should? Don't you want to come?" Her voice is dazed, lips swollen from my kisses, breathing still slightly ragged.

"Aye, more than anything," I say. "Christ, I could take you right here on Graham's workbench."

She shivers at the suggestion, and I have to close my eyes and count to ten in Gaelic to keep from acting on the fantasy.

"Soon," I promise, helping her down from the bench. "I need to keep you well-rested and conference ready. I'd rather wait until we have the time we need to make it amazing."

She nods, straightening her clothes with shaking hands. But there's a smile on her face. "You're a good man, Ewan."

As I walk her to her cabin and give her a goodnight kiss on the cheek, I realize that for the first time in my life, I'm terrified of the future.

But for her, I'll pretend to be brave.

CHAPTER 5
HAZEL

I stare at my reflection in the bathroom mirror, smoothing down my forest green blouse—the one Ewan said brings out my eyes.

Tonight's networking mixer is my chance to prove I can handle professional social situations without Ewan as my security blanket.

"You can do this," I whisper to my reflection. "You've successfully attended three conference sessions, asked intelligent questions, and only had one minor panic attack in the bathroom yesterday. That's progress."

My phone pings with a text from Ewan.

> You're sure you don't want me to come with you?

It's the third one I've gotten since I saw him at lunch.

I adjust my blazer and square my shoulders, channeling the assertive tone he'd coached me to use during presentation practice.

> I need to do this alone.

> Text if you need extraction.

> Extraction protocols already calculated. But thank you.

The dining hall thrums with conversation and clinking glasses when I arrive, an array of attendees clustered around high-top tables with wine and appetizers. I notice familiar faces from earlier sessions, and approximate about sixty people.

Totally manageable numbers.

Breathe. Four in, seven hold, eight out.

For the first thirty minutes, I'm unstoppable. Everything goes better than my most optimistic projections. I discuss my research with a safety consultant from a Colorado dude ranch, explain my statistical models to a risk manager from Seattle's tourism board, and even laugh at someone's actuarial joke.

My confidence builds with each successful interaction.

"You're Hazel Phillips, aren't you?" A curvy woman with long blonde curls approaches me. "I've been hearing about your upcoming presentation. Dr. Morrison mentioned your research approach sounds fascinating."

My chest swells with pride. "Thank you. I'm nervous about tomorrow, but it's been two years of work, so I hope it resonates."

"I'm sure it will. Your questions during the sessions have been incredibly insightful. You clearly know your material inside and out."

Is this what professional success feels like? Being recognized for expertise rather than awkwardness?

It's really nice.

"Th-thank you." My pulse stutters, but her smile steadies me.

"We'd love to consult your team on our new protocols." She hands me her card. "Can I give you a call?"

"Of course." I excuse myself to get another club soda, practically floating with accomplishment.

That's when I hear it.

"—wonder what Ewan sees in her. He spends so much time with her."

The voice slices through my focus, sharp and snide. Two women hover near the appetizer table, backs turned, oblivious.

I freeze, pretending to study the drink menu.

"That socially awkward woman?"

"Yeah, you know, the dark-haired giraffe."

"I heard he's got quite the reputation." Another voice says, amused. "Different woman every week."

"He's a hottie though. I'm sure he gets any woman he wants. Why her?"

"That lumberjack daddy's got a weakness for challenges."

My stomach drops all the way down to my sensible flats.

"Sweet of him to take her under his wing. Like a project."

Take me under his wing? Like I'm some pathetic charity case he's amusing himself with between romantic conquests.

The voices fade as they move away, but the damage is done. Every doubt I've been suppressing comes crashing back.

Of course this was too good to be true. Men like Ewan don't fall for women like me—they pity us. *Fix us.* I'm his current project, the socially inept statistician he's coaching for entertainment.

My face burns with humiliation. The hallway tilts, fluorescent lights buzzing like angry wasps as I abandon my drink. I collide with a waiter—*sorry, sorry*—pushing through the crowd toward the exit. Outside, the cool mountain air hits my overheated cheeks, but it doesn't stop the spiral of mortification.

I'm so stupid.

I practically run back to my cabin, fumbling with the key card through my blurred vision. Once inside, I slump against it, knees buckling as tears come hot and fast.

Of *course* this was just a game. A flirty lumberjack amusing himself with the anxious freak.

A knock at my door makes me jump.

"Hazel?" Ewan's voice says, concerned. "I saw you leave. Are you alright?"

"I'm fine," I lie.

"You're clearly not fine." He says through the door. "What happened?"

I scramble upright, swiping at my face, then open the door a crack.

"You happened. Was this fun for you? The ultimate challenge—recluse to ravished in five days flat?"

His brow furrows. "What the hell are you—"

"I heard them!" My voice cracks. "'Ewan always needs a project.' Am I your latest charity case? Some…" I gesture wildly, "…math-themed pity fuck?"

Something flickers across his face—hurt, then maybe anger. "And you believed them?" He goes utterly still. "You think that's what this is?"

"Why wouldn't I? Gorgeous, Highland playboy lumberjack decides to help the pathetic woman who can't function at social events. Very *noble* of you."

"Hazel—"

"I'm just entertainment. The weird tall girl who stumbled into helping you with your kilt, who begged to be *fixed* before she leaves."

"Stop." His voice is sharp enough to cut through my spiral. "Christ, woman." He pushes through the door, and kicks it shut, then strides forward, crowding me against the wall. "You think I've spent every waking moment this week coaxing you out of your shell for shites and giggles?" His voice breaks.

He braces his arms on either side of my head. "You want to know what I think when I look at you?" His accent thickens with emotion. "I think about how you're a problem-solver without even thinking about it. How your face lights up when you talk about statistical models. How you stand nearly eye-to-eye with me like some bloody goddess."

"Ewan—"

"I'm not finished." His crystal blue eyes are blazing, and I'm stunned silent. "I think about how brave you are, walking into conference sessions despite your anxiety. How your laugh makes my chest tight. How I've never met anyone who makes me want to be better just by existing."

My breath hitches.

He continues. "Eight times I checked my phone waiting for your 'extraction' text. Zero seconds spent with anyone else because all I want is *you*."

The air crackles.

His hands frame my face, thumbs brushing away fresh tears. "Hazel, you're the most beautiful woman I've ever met. I'm helping you because watching you succeed is the most incredible thing I've ever been a part of."

I search his face, but all I see is honesty and something that looks terrifyingly like love.

"I—I'm sorry…" I trail off.

But before I can think of something else to say, he kisses me. I can taste his sincerity, feel his desire in the way his hands quiver as they touch me.

"I'm falling in love with you, you clever, stubborn woman," he murmurs against my lips. "Not helping you, not fixing you —*falling* for you."

My heart jumps in my chest. "Ewan…" I want to fight it,

tamp these crazy feelings down. But it's hopeless. "I'm falling for you, too."

He lifts me easily, carrying me to the bed where he sets me down gently. His hands work slowly at the buttons of my blouse, eyes never leaving mine.

"I want you," he says. "Are you sure you want me?"

I've wanted him from the moment I saw him. I just never thought I could be so lucky. "God, yes I do."

My blouse falls away as he pushes it off my shoulders, then my bra, and his sharp intake of breath when he sees my bare breasts makes me feel powerful instead of self-conscious.

"Och, mo chridhe," he breathes, running his rough hands over my skin. "You're so beautiful."

He starts with gentle kisses along my shoulders and chest that make me arch beneath him. His beard tickles my sensitive skin as he trails lower, and when his lips close around my nipple, I gasp at the unexpected bolt of pleasure.

He lavishes attention on one breast, sucking and licking, twirling his tongue in circles and flicks around my peak, then repeats everything on the other. I'm trembling, as my hands fist in his hair.

"You like that," he states, humming as he takes his time moving lower, pressing hot kisses to my ribs, my stomach, the sensitive spot just below my navel. When he reaches the edge of my panties, I whimper.

"Still alright, sweetness?"

"Yes," I breathe, lifting my hips as he slides the fabric away.

His first touch is feather-light, just his fingertips tracing along my inner thighs. I'm shivering with anticipation when he finally grazes my folds, exploring gently, brushing his fingers along my tender flesh.

"Oh…" I groan, at the tingling, pulsing sensations.

"So wet for me," he whispers reverently, fingers teasing me, learning what makes me gasp and what makes my hips buck toward his touch.

He finds a spot that makes me tremble, and focuses there with gentle circles and pressure until I'm panting and gyrating with his hand.

"Hazel, your body is so responsive. Such a dream come true."

When he lowers his head and replaces his fingers with his mouth, it's overwhelming in the best way.

His tongue slides over me, moving in slow, deliberate strokes, tasting and exploring while I writhe beneath him. He discovers which parts make me whimper and those that make me arch off the bed...with such patient thoroughness.

"Ewan," I gasp, my hands gripping the sheets as the pressure builds to an almost unbearable peak.

All thoughts are completely forgotten in the haze of pleasure he's creating.

It's just him.

He worships my pussy with his mouth, kissing and licking, and sucking until I can't take it anymore. I cry out.

"That's it, love," he encourages as his mouth works me over with expert skill. "Let me hear you."

His tongue swirls around my clit and that's it.

"Ewan, *god!*" I come apart, my climax wracking my body.

And he doesn't stop until I'm jerking with sensitivity, my flesh tender and spent.

"Fuck, you taste good, Hazel," he says, climbing back up my body.

"Need you," I gasp as the aftershocks fade.

"Are you certain?"

"I've never been more certain of anything in my life."

He strips down to his boxers, revealing the magnificent body I first glimpsed in the Heritage Night prep room. But this time, instead of fleeing in embarrassment, I reach for him.

My hands shake slightly as I trace the broad expanse of his chest, marveling at the contrast between the coarse hair and smooth skin beneath. I follow the lines of his thick, tribal tattoos that wrap around his shoulders with my fingertips.

His breathing goes ragged, his muscles flexing under my touch.

I grow bolder, exploring the defined ridges of his abs, feeling how his breathing quickens as my hands move lower. When I reach the edge of his boxers, I hesitate.

"It's alright, love," he encourages, voice rough. "Touch me however you want."

I push the fabric down, and my breath catches. I've never seen a man naked before, never touched one, and he's... intimidating. Beautiful, but intimidating. The skin is softer than I expected, and when I wrap my fingers around him experimentally, he groans low in his throat.

"Like this?" I ask, stroking tentatively.

"Aye, just like that," he pants, his hips jerking slightly. "You can be firmer—oh, fuck, yes."

I'm fascinated by how responsive he is, how my touch makes him moan and curse in that thick accent. When I discover the sensitive spot just beneath the head, he actually shudders.

"Hazel, if you keep that up—" His words cut off in a harsh breath as I lean down to taste him, curious about everything. "Bloody hell."

"Tell me what you like," I whisper against his skin, growing drunk on the power of reducing this strong man to desperate sounds and trembling muscles.

"All of it," he gasps, his hand threading gently through my hair. "Your mouth, your hands—Christ, as long as it's you."

I experiment with my tongue, learning the taste and texture of him, noting how he responds to different suction and movements. The skin is like velvet, and I'm fascinated by how he grows even harder under my attention.

"*Jesus*. Slower, love," he instructs breathlessly when I take him deeper. "Use your tongue right there—aye, just like that. *Fuck*...you're a natural."

His praise makes heat pool low in my belly, and I become more confident in my exploration. When my tongue delves into the slit at his tip, his whole body jerks.

"Hazel," he moans, his accent so thick now I can barely understand him. "Ye're gonna ruin me."

I pull back to look at him, taking in his flushed face and the way his chest heaves. "Am I doing it right?"

"More than right," he pants, cupping my face tenderly. "But I need to be inside you. I can't wait any longer or I'll burst."

The raw need in his voice sends a thrill through me. This powerful, experienced man is completely undone by my inexperienced touch, and the knowledge fills me with a confidence I've never felt before.

"I need to feel you inside me, too," I whisper, and mean every word.

He climbs over me, then slides his cock against my entrance. Even that feels like heaven.

"Hazel..." he whispers. "Look at me." He enters me slowly, carefully, his eyes locked on mine. It's tight and uncomfortable, but my body adjusts as he kisses me.

"Good?" he asks, voice strained with the effort of holding still.

I breathe, experimentally moving my hips. It's still tight, but easing up. I nod.

He groans and begins to move, setting a slow rhythm that

sends shockwaves through my entire body. I never imagined it would feel like this—so full, so connected.

"Tell me how it feels," he whispers against my ear, his voice strained with the effort of maintaining control.

"Incredible," I gasp, easing my legs around his waist instinctively. "I never knew—oh god, Ewan."

He grunts, swearing in Gaelic.

Each movement creates friction in places I didn't know could feel this good. The initial discomfort fades into pure pleasure as he moves gently.

"You're so tight, so wet," he groans, his cheek pressed against mine. "Made for me. You feel amazing."

My body responds to his increasingly urgent rhythm. I can feel something building inside me again, different from before but just as overwhelming.

"Faster," I beg, surprising myself with my boldness.

"Aye, love, anything you want," he pants, picking up the pace. His breathing becomes more ragged as he moves deeper, hitting spots that make me cry out. "You're so beautiful like this, taking me so well."

The tension coils tighter with each thrust, each whispered praise, each kiss he presses to my throat. I can feel his muscles trembling.

"Let go, Hazel," he urges. "I want to feel you come around my cock."

Two more thrusts and my climax hits with earth-shattering intensity that leaves me gasping and clinging to him. My pussy convulses around his length as he growls, then roars, following me with his orgasm.

"Still think I'm faking?" he asks softly, once the aftershocks subside.

I trace the fluttering pulse at his throat with my tongue. "The data's compelling. But I might need more of it."

His laugh rumbles through me. "I'll give you as much data as you need, however long it takes."

CHAPTER 6
EWAN

I wake with Hazel's dark hair tickling my nose and her long legs tangled with mine.

For a minute, I forget that today she goes back to Boston.

She's curled against my chest like she belongs there, one hand splayed over my heart, breathing soft and even. In sleep, all her anxiety melts away, leaving just the smart, beautiful woman who trusted me with her first time.

Christ, I'm lost.

I've had my share of lasses over the years, but none of them ever made me want to wake up early just to watch them sleep. None of them made my chest hurt with the thought of saying goodbye.

Her presentation starts in four hours. Her flight leaves in eight. The numbers glare at me like a countdown to heartbreak, but I shove them aside.

Right now, she's here—soft, rumpled, and utterly delicious in my arms.

"Mmm," she murmurs. She blinks up at me, green eyes still hazy with sleep, and smiles. "I'm glad you're still here."

"Aye. Couldn't leave if I tried."

"What time is it?"

"Early," I whisper, pressing a kiss to the top of her head. "Your presentation isn't until two."

She goes rigid in my arms. "Oh god. The presentation—"

"Hey." I tilt her chin up to meet my eyes. "None of that. Yesterday you were networking with the best of them, industry professionals hanging on your every word. Today you're going to blow them away."

Her green eyes search my face. "What if I choke? What if I make a complete fool of myself?"

"Then you'll remember that you're Hazel bloody Phillips, and you know more about actuarial risk assessment than anyone else in that room." I stroke her cheek with my thumb. "Or I'll storm the podium and flip up my kilt. Distract everyone while you escape."

A laugh bursts out of her—startled and bright. "You're a goofball."

I chuckle. "Actually, I've already told you about the secret weapon I have for you."

"Secret weapon?"

"Aye. Highland storytelling techniques, perfected over centuries of keeping drunk Scotsmen entertained around campfires."

She laughs despite her nerves. "Right. But I'm not sure statistical models translate to Highland folklore. And I don't think most of them will be drunk."

"Even numbers tell a good story, mo chridhe." I sit up, pulling her with me.

"What does 'mo chridhe' mean, anyway?"

"My darling. Haven't you watched Outlander?"

She chuckles. "Haven't had the chance. But I guess I'll have to make the time."

"No. I'd rather teach ye all the romantic words without you swoonin' over that bloody Sam Heughan."

"You're the only Scot for me, Ewan."

My heart twists and I kiss her again.

Later, we're back in Graham's workshop, but this time I've rearranged things properly. The workbench is cleared, giving her space to move around, and I've positioned myself where she can practice making eye contact without feeling trapped.

"Right," I say, settling onto a sawbench. "Show me your opening again."

She clears her throat and launches into the same dry recitation from yesterday.

"Wait." I stand and walk over to her. "You're doing it again."

"Doing what?"

"Hiding. You're reciting facts like you're apologizing for your existence. But this is *your* moment, lass. Own it."

"I don't know how to own it."

"Start with your posture." I position myself behind her, and slide my hands up her spine to her shoulders. "Stand tall. You're six feet of gorgeous woman. *Use. Every. Inch.*" I grin. "That's what she said."

She giggles and straightens, and I can feel some of the tension ease in her back.

"Better. Now, instead of telling them what you're going to discuss, tell them why they should care." I step around to face her. "Like we said before. Real people, real consequences."

I watch her present, adding what I can to help, until she finishes.

I applaud. "Captivating, Hazel. You're going to kill it."

Her face glows. "You think?"

"They'll be handing you Nobel Prizes by suppertime." I pull her close, unable to resist kissing her. "I'm so proud of you."

She beams at me, then sobers. "Will you...sit in the front row?"

"Of course I will."

She smiles and melts against me, and for one reckless second, I consider bolting the door. Skipping the conference. Driving her up into the highest peaks of Deepwood Mountain and keeping her forever.

"Ewan," she says softly, "what happens after today?"

My idealistic plan fades, replaced by the question I've been dreading. I stroke her hair, buying time.

"What do you mean?"

"Don't be coy. You know what I mean. I'm leaving today. You have your life here. This whole thing...it feels like a fantasy."

My voice comes out rougher than intended. "Feels pretty real to me."

She pulls back to look at me. "Long distance, different worlds, different—"

"Different everything," I finish. "Aye, I know."

The silence stretches between us, heavy with everything we can't say.

"I won't ask you to give up your career," I say finally. "Won't ask you to stay somewhere that doesn't make you happy. You've worked too hard for this."

"And I won't ask you to leave Timber Run. This place is part of who you are. And honestly, the camp wouldn't be as wonderful without you. You're a star."

We stand there, holding each other and trying not to think about the impossible math of love and logistics.

"Maybe," she says hesitantly, "maybe we could figure something out. Eventually."

"Maybe," I agree, though my heart is breaking. "But today, we focus on your presentation. The rest... we'll face it when we have to."

She nods, but I can see the sadness in her eyes that matches what I'm feeling.

"Come here," I murmur, pulling her back against me. "One more practice run, and then we're going to get you ready to conquer the world."

As she launches into her presentation again, I memorize everything about this—the way she moves her hands when she gets excited about the data, the flush in her cheeks when she hits her stride, the sound of her voice growing stronger with each word.

Tomorrow she'll be gone, back to her spreadsheets and her orderly life in Boston. But right now, she's here, she's radiant, and she's *mine*.

"Dazzling," I tell her when she's done. "You're going to be absolutely perfect."

And as she beams at me with confidence and joy, I realize that's exactly the problem. She is perfect—for me, for a future I can't figure out how to build.

But I'll be damned if I let my broken heart ruin her triumph.

"Right then," I say, forcing my voice to stay steady. "Let's get you ready to slay."

Because that's what love is, isn't it? Wanting someone to succeed so badly that you'll let them go if that's what it takes.

Even when it kills you.

CHAPTER 7
HAZEL

I stand outside the event center, clutching my presentation materials like they're the only things keeping me tethered to reality.

Through the glass doors, I can see the packed room—every seat filled with insurance professionals, safety consultants, and outdoor industry representatives who've heard whispers about my research.

No pressure at all.

"You've got this, lass," Ewan murmurs beside me, his presence steady and reassuring. "Just remember what we practiced. It'll be a breeze."

I nod, trying to channel the confidence I felt in the workshop this morning. Ewan's storytelling techniques have been a godsend, transforming my presentation into something that actually feels... compelling. Who knew actuarial models could have narrative arc?

"What if they ask questions I can't answer?"

"Then you'll dazzle them with your brilliant mind until they forget what they asked." His blue eyes crinkle with warmth. "But you know this stuff better than anyone in that room. Trust yourself."

Dr. Morrison appears beside us, beaming. "Hazel! Ready to revolutionize the industry?"

I manage a smile. "As ready as statistical analysis can make me."

"Excellent" His white mustache ripples. "Your reputation precedes you—we've got representatives from major adventure tourism companies, three different insurance firms, and even some folks from the National Park Service. Word travels fast in our little world."

My stomach does a gymnastics routine that would impress Olympic judges. "That's... a lot of people."

"All eager to hear what you've discovered." Dr. Morrison checks his watch. "See you inside."

Ewan squeezes my shoulder. "I'll be right down in front. Go show them what you're made of my warrior queen."

I nod and take a deep breath before following Dr. Morrison into the room.

The introduction feels like it happens to someone else. I hear my name, my credentials, the importance of my research, but all I can focus on is the sea of expectant faces. Then I'm behind the podium, looking out at eighty-plus industry professionals who represent everything I've worked toward.

For a second, panic threatens to overwhelm me. These people could make or break my career. One fumbled answer, one statistical error, and—

Stop. I glance at Ewan and he winks—then makes a funny face.

I smile and hear him say: *Tell them your story.*

I straighten to my full height, shoulders back, chin up...and begin.

"Two years ago, I was reviewing incident reports for a

client when I noticed something disturbing," I say, abandoning my prepared opening. "Traditional risk models were failing to predict accidents that should have been preventable. People were getting hurt because we were calculating risk incorrectly."

The room goes quiet, attentive.

"That's when I realized we weren't just looking at statistical probabilities—we were looking at real people whose lives could be saved by better data."

For the next twenty minutes I walk them through my research using every storytelling technique Ewan taught me. I explain how temperature coefficients create exponential rather than linear risk progression. I show them how equipment maintenance variables dramatically alter safety calculations. I demonstrate how my models could have prevented specific accidents by accounting for variables traditional assessments missed.

When I reach my conclusions, the room is dead silent.

"The implications for adventure tourism safety aren't just significant—they're revolutionary," I conclude, gesturing to my final slide. "We're not just calculating risk anymore. We're redefining it." I pause. "Thank you."

The applause starts slowly, building as Ewan puts his fingers in his mouth and whistles, then cheers.

Soon, everyone is clapping and cheering.

During the Q&A, something magical happens. Instead of stammering through answers, I find myself energized by their questions. A consultant from Colorado asks about applying my models to high-altitude scenarios. An insurance executive wants to know about implementation timelines. A National Park Service representative asks if my research could be adapted for wilderness permits.

Each question validates that my work isn't just academically interesting—it's crucial to so many industries in numerous ways.

"One final question," Dr. Morrison announces. "From our hosts at Timber Run."

Brady stands up, and I'm surprised to see him in the audience. "Ms. Phillips, how would you assess the safety protocols here at Timber Run using your new models?"

I smile, remembering all the conversations I've had with the camp staff about their procedures. "Actually, Timber Run's safety protocols align remarkably well with my risk assessment framework. Their equipment maintenance schedules, environmental monitoring, and instructor certification requirements create what I'd classify as an optimal safety environment. They're already implementing many of the principles my research validates."

The room murmurs appreciatively, and I catch Brady's slight smile.

As the session ends, I'm immediately surrounded by people wanting to discuss consulting opportunities, speaking engagements, and collaboration possibilities. Business cards appear in my hands faster than I can process them.

"Hazel, that was extraordinary," says a woman from a major insurance firm. "We'd love to discuss implementing your models across our adventure tourism policies."

"The Park Service needs someone exactly like you," adds the federal representative. "Would you consider a consulting position? It would require some West Coast travel, but the impact could be national."

West Coast travel. My heart jumps at the geographical implications.

"I run adventure tours in Montana," says another man. "Your research could transform how we operate. Any chance you'd consult for smaller operators?"

Montana. The same state as Timber Run!

"I'd be interested in discussing all of these opportunities," I hear myself saying. "Let me get your contact information."

Twenty minutes later, I finally escape the crowd, my bag full of business cards and my head spinning with possibilities I never imagined.

Ewan is waiting outside, leaning against the wall with a grin that warms my soul.

He reaches for me and I rush to him as he sweeps me into a bear hug that lifts me off the ground.

He spins me around, laughing. "You were magnificent, he murmurs against my hair. "Like watching a goddess claim her throne."

"You're biased," I say, but my heart soars.

"Biased? Aye. Never." His hands settle on my hips.

"Ewan, they want me to consult. Multiple companies. The Park Service mentioned West Coast travel, and there were adventure tourism operators from here in Montana, and—" I stop, suddenly realizing what I'm saying.

His expression grows cautious. "That's wonderful, Hazel. Everything you deserve."

"Don't you see?" I grab his shirt. "Montana's part of the West Coast region for federal lands. And those Montana operators—they're all within driving distance of Timber Run."

His blue eyes widen. "You're saying..."

"I'm saying there's a way for me to have both my career and...us." I stroke his jaw. "I could base myself here, consult remotely for the East Coast clients, travel to Montana operators, and work with the Park Service on Western region implementations."

"Hazel," he says carefully, "that's a huge risk. Leaving Boston, changing your whole life—"

"You know what the biggest risk is?" I interrupt. "Calculating my way out of happiness. Choosing safety over the best thing that's ever happened to me."

His hands frame my face. "Are you sure? *Really* sure?"

"I've spent my entire life minimizing risk. But some risks are worth taking." I meet his eyes. "I want all of it. You. The camp. My research. I want to revolutionize this industry *and* wake up in your bed. You're worth it. If you want me."

"Mo chridhe," he growls. "I want you more than anything in this world." And he crushes his mouth to mine right there in the hallway, with such passion I forget who I am.

When we break apart, I'm breathless and grinning. "Think Timber Run could use a consulting actuary?"

"I think Timber Run could use you in any capacity you want," he says.

I look at this man who saw past my anxiety to my potential, who coached me through my biggest professional triumph, who makes me feel beautiful, brilliant, brave, and oh so sexy.

"The statistical probability of finding someone like you again?" I shake my head. "Let's just say those odds are not in my favor."

"Smart woman."

As he spins me around the hallway, both of us laughing, I know I've finally made a calculation that has nothing to do with risk assessment and everything to do with my heart.

And it feels amazing.

EPILOGUE - EWAN

ONE YEAR LATER

The sound of Hazel's laughter drifts across the camp as she explains statistical modeling to a group of wide-eyed tourists, and I have to stop mid-swing to just watch her work.

"So you see," she's saying, gesturing to the chart she's set up near my sawing demonstration area, "Ewan's accident probability actually decreases with audience size because he shows off less when there are more witnesses."

The crowd chuckles, and I call out, "Oi! That's classified information, woman!"

She grins at me, all confidence and sass in her Timber Run polo shirt and hiking boots. A year ago, she could barely speak to five people without hyperventilating. Now she's running statistical analysis workshops for our guests and loving every minute of it.

"Plus," she continues, "his extensive experience and High-land stubbornness create what we call 'positive risk variance.'"

"Meaning I'm too bloody-minded to get hurt?" I wink at the tourists.

"Meaning you're a show-off who's very good at what he does," she retorts, and the crowd laughs again.

Christ, I love this woman.

"Alright, you mathematical minx," I say, hefting my axe. "Let me show these good people how it's really done."

I line up my shot, feeling Hazel's eyes on me as I bring the blade down in a perfect arc. The log splits cleanly in two, and the tourists applaud.

"Impressive, Mr. MacLeod," calls out Dr. Morrison, who's back for his third visit this year. "Though according to Ms. Phillips' data, that was a statistically probable outcome."

"Was it now?" I glance at Hazel, who's trying not to smile. "And what do your numbers say about this?"

I grab her around the waist and dip her dramatically, planting a kiss on her that makes the tourists cheer and whistle, while some of the ladies, *and men*, fan themselves.

When I pull her upright, she's flushed pink and breathless. "That wasn't in my calculations," she admits.

"The best surprises never are, mo chridhe."

Later, as the afternoon demonstrations wind down, I find Connor and Teagan by the main lodge, watching their two-year-old son toddle around the deck while chasing a butterfly.

"Jamie's getting quick," I observe, settling onto the bench beside them.

"Too quick," Connor grumbles, but his eyes are soft as he watches the lad. "Yesterday he tried to climb the water tower."

"He gets that from his father," Teagan says, dryly. "Absolutely no fear."

"Hey now," he interjects. "I just don't let fear run my life."

Teagan glances meaningfully toward where Hazel is

packing up her presentation materials. "Remember when she wouldn't even attend a conference mixer?"

I follow her gaze, watching my lovely wife—the word still giving me a thrill—efficiently organizing her charts with the same precision she brings to everything else.

"Hard to believe it's only been a year," I admit.

"Best year of your life though, right?" Connor claps me on the shoulder.

"Aye. Best year of hers too, I'd say."

And it has been. Hazel's consulting business is thriving —she splits her time between remote work for her Boston clients and on-site consulting for Western adventure tourism operators. The Park Service contract alone keeps her busy three days a week, and she loves every minute of it.

But more than that, she's bloomed. The anxious, hiding woman I met has transformed into someone who leads work-shops, gives presentations at industry conferences, and just last month, delivered the keynote address at the International Adventure Tourism Safety Summit.

"Speak of the devil," Teagan murmurs as Hazel approaches, charts tucked under her arm.

"How'd the workshop go, love?" I ask, making room for her on the bench.

"Brilliantly. Three new consulting contracts...and one date request." She settles beside me with a grin.

"Excuse me?" Connor raises an eyebrow.

"From the tourism board representative. He said anyone who could make risk assessment sexy was clearly wife material."

I growl low in my throat. "Hope you told him you're taken."

"I told him my husband was the jealous type and happened

to be very good with sharp objects." She pats my knee. "He backed off quickly."

"Smart man," Connor chuckles.

Just then, Graham and Sky appear from the direction of the workshop, both covered in wood shavings and looking thoroughly pleased with themselves.

"How's the new cabin coming along?" Teagan asks.

"It's coming...slowly," Sky says, pulling wood chips out of her blonde curls. "Because my husband is a perfectionist who's redone the window frames three times."

"They have to be right," Graham protests, crossing his arms over his chest. "It's our first home."

"Everything's your first with Sky," I tease. "First viral video, first social media campaign, first time letting someone reorganize your workshop..."

"First time being truly happy," Graham says simply, and even I want to swoon. It's still shocking to hear the big grump talk like that.

Sky's face goes soft. "You romantic sap."

"Only for you, sunshine."

Before the moment can get too sentimental, Brady appears from behind the lodge, moving stiffly and rolling his shoulders.

"You alright there, mate?" I ask, noticing his careful gait.

"Just a twinge," he mutters, stretching his neck to one side. "Nothing serious."

"That's not nothing," Connor observes. "You're moving like an old man."

Brady's jaw tightens. "I'm fine. Just pulled something during yesterday's demonstration. Had to catch a guest who lost his grip about twenty feet up."

"Hero complex will get you every time," Graham says, but

there's concern in his voice. "How long's your back been bothering you?"

"It's not bothering me."

"Brady," Hazel says gently, "you're literally wincing every time you move."

"I said I'm fine."

"Stubborn arse," I mutter. "When's the last time you took a proper break? Or saw someone about that back?"

"I don't need to see anyone. It'll work itself out."

"You know what would help?" Sky suggests. "A good massage. I could help you find a place—"

"I don't need a massage," Brady cuts her off sharply.

"Why not?" Teagan asks. "Massage therapy is incredibly effective for muscle strain and—"

"I don't like strangers touching me, alright?" Brady's voice has an edge now. "I'll ice it, stretch it out, and it'll be fine in a few days."

Connor and I exchange glances. We all know Brady's history with trusting people, but this is ridiculous. And he rarely lets anything put him in such a bad mood.

"It's not 'strangers touching you,'" I point out. "It's medical treatment."

"Same thing."

"It's really not," Hazel says. "Therapeutic massage is a legitimate treatment modality with proven efficacy for muscular injuries. The practitioners are licensed professionals who—"

"I said no." Brady's tone brooks no argument. "I'll handle it myself."

Rourke jogs up to our group with his usual energy. "What's everyone talking about? Please tell me it's something scandalous because I've had the most boring day demonstrating log rolling to a church group."

"Brady's got a sore back and won't do anything sensible about it," Sky informs him.

"Ooh, that sucks. You should totally get a massage."

"Not you too," Brady groans.

"What?"

"Rourke," Graham cuts him off. "He's not interested."

I watch Brady's shoulders tense even further at all the unwanted attention, his usual zen gone when it comes to taking care of himself.

"Look," I say, taking pity on him. "Your back, your choice. But if you can't climb safely because you're hurt, you shouldn't be doing demonstrations."

Brady's expression tightens. "I can climb just fine."

"Can you? Because from where I'm sitting, you look like you can barely walk."

"I'm perfectly capable of—"

"Brady," Connor interrupts gently. "We're not questioning your abilities. We're worried about you. Take a few days off, let it heal properly."

"I don't need time off. I need everyone to stop treating me like an invalid."

Hazel reaches over and gently touches Brady's arm. "We're not treating you like an invalid. We're treating you like someone we care about who's clearly in pain."

Brady's expression softens slightly at her words, but his jaw remains set.

"Fine," he says finally. "I'll take it easy for a few days. But I'm not getting a massage, so stop suggesting it."

"Deal," Connor says. "But if it's not better by next week—"

"It will be."

"It better be," I add. "Because if you hurt yourself worse trying to prove a point, we'll all feel terrible, and then we'll have to take you down stream and put you out of your misery."

Despite everything, Brady's mouth twitches. "Understood."

As our little group disperses—Connor and Teagan chasing after Jamie, who's discovered the flower beds, Graham and Sky heading back to work on their cabin, Rourke off to find his next meal—I find myself alone with Hazel on the deck.

"Penny for your thoughts?"

She leans into me, sighing contentedly. "Just thinking about how much has changed. A year ago, I was hiding in my cabin, terrified of talking to anyone. Now I'm part of a lumberjack family."

"And running statistical analysis workshops. And consulting for the Park Service. And married to a devastatingly handsome Scottish lumberjack."

"That last part was definitely the biggest surprise," she says, tilting her face up to mine.

"Good surprise though?"

"The best surprise." She kisses me softly, and I taste the sweetness that's become as essential to me as breathing. "Though I have to say, the statistical probability of everything working out this perfectly was remarkably low."

"But not impossible."

I gather her closer, my warrior queen who's made me the happiest I've ever been. "Come on then, wife. Let's go home and I'll show you some new risk assessment data."

"Is that what we're calling it now?"

"Among other things."

Her laughter echoes as I sweep her off her feet, carrying her over my shoulder like the good Scottish rogue I am. She protests that she's perfectly capable of walking.

"Aye, but where's the fun in that?" I say, smacking her sexy ass and grinning like a fool.

CLIMB ME MAYBE

CHAPTER 1
IMOGEN

B*ehold the land of sexy mountain men...*
I park in the lot near the main lobby at the *Timber Run Eco-Historical Lumberjack Camp*, and my composure takes a nosedive straight into a pool of inappropriate comments. Followed by a *Beavis and Butthead* chuckle.

The place is crawling with ridiculously attractive men doing smoking hot things with axes, chainsaws, and enough flannel to single-handedly revive the grunge movement.

One guy's in a sleeveless shirt that shows off biceps that could crush beer cans. Another—*sweet baby Jesus*—is hefting an enormous log over his shoulder like it's a bag of cotton balls.

"Imogen...you're here for business," I recite to a chipmunk staring at me from a stump.

Right. Business. The kind that involves keeping my hands strictly professional and my panties firmly in place while I provide massage services to stressed-out lumberjacks for a week.

Yikes.

The camp worked out a deal with the Serenity Springs Wellness Center, a resort and spa currently under construction in Deepwood Mountain, Montana, where I'll be interviewing for Managing Massage Therapist.

That is…if I don't let one of these lumbersnacks whisk me away forever to the top of a mountain.

I shake off the fantasy and head toward the lobby office. I'm attempting to look competent and self-assured instead of someone whose brain just short-circuited. Because a bearded giant across the way just split wood with a talent that makes me wonder what else those hands are good at.

Professional. Boundaries. Ethics.

The mantra works for approximately thirty seconds until I walk past the axe-throwing demonstration area and witness what can only be described as a tactical flannel situation. Three different lumberjacks, three different styles of devastatingly handsome, all wielding sharp objects with casual competence that should come with a warning label.

I mean, holy mother of forearm porn.

I'm so busy noting the various ways Montana has cornered the market on gorgeous outdoorsmen that I nearly walk face-first into the camp office door.

The door swings open just as I reach for the handle, and I find myself colliding with a towering slab of solid muscle wrapped in a navy flannel shirt.

"Whoa—" Strong calloused hands shoot out to catch my shoulders, steadying me before I can embarrass myself further. "Sorry about that. Are you okay?"

The voice rumbles through me before I see his face. I tilt my head back. Further. Further. Shit, is his hairline in *orbit?*

Striking midnight blue eyes blink down at me, his salt and pepper hair styled with careless perfection…like it's saying "I fell out of a tree and somehow this happened." His square-jaw could be chiseled from stone, and I watch his throat bob as my gaze lingers on the ink peeking from his collar—traditional

Japanese waves or something, ancient and beautiful against his lightly tanned skin.

My brain promptly forgets how to speak.

"I—yes. Sorry. I wasn't watching where I was—" I pat his rock-hard pec and he jolts like I tasered him. Then I gesture at the door, at him, at the general concept of spatial awareness that's abandoned me. "You're very big—uh, tall."

Brilliant opening line, Imogen. Really showcasing your communication skills.

A flush creeps up his neck and his mouth quirks up on one side.

I figure he's probably in his forties, with the kind of mature handsomeness that suggests he's figured out exactly who he is and gotten comfortable with it. There's something quietly magnetic about the way he carries himself—controlled, refined, like every movement is deliberate.

Also, his hands are still on my shoulders, and the heat is doing illegal things to my core.

"I'm..." Seems I'm *still* having trouble forming complete sentences. "Yes. I'm okay. How about you?"

"I'm fine," he says, and there's something almost shy in the way he's looking at me. His gaze travels over me, but instead of judgment, like I often get with my pink hair, piercings, and tattoos, I see what looks like curiosity.

"I should—I need to get going," he says suddenly, dropping his hands and stepping back. But he doesn't actually move toward wherever he's supposed to be going.

"Right. Of course. Me too. I mean, I'm here for—business." I point at the door, trying to look like someone who definitely knows what she's doing and isn't completely flustered by a hunky lumberjack.

He nods, still not moving. "Good. That's...good."

That voice does things to me. *Filthy* things.

What is happening right now?

"Well," I say, finally taking a step toward the office. "I should probably..."

"Yeah. Yeah, me too." He turns to go, but I catch him glancing back over his shoulder. Once. Twice.

And then he stumbles on the bottom step of the boardwalk.

I bite my lip to keep from smiling as he recovers quickly, pretending nothing happened, and disappears around the corner of the building.

Interesting.

As I walk into the office, the woman behind the desk looks up with a warm smile. She's pretty in that outdoorsy, no-makeup-needed way that I simultaneously admire and resent.

"You must be Imogen! I'm Teagan Leigh, co-founder. We're so excited to have you here." She shakes my hand enthusiastically. "The crew is practically fighting over massage appointments."

"Nice," I glance toward the door where Mr. Tall-Dark-and-Adorably-Awkward disappeared. I *really* hope he's part of the crew.

Teagan's smile turns slightly conspiratorial. "Most of them, anyway. One of our guys is a little... resistant to the idea of therapeutic touch."

"Oh?"

"Our high-rigger, aka tree climber. Incredible body, but he's got some...issues with strangers touching him."

"I find that resistance usually comes from unfamiliarity," I say. "A lot of people think massage is just spa fluff, but therapeutic work is actually pretty intense. Deep tissue, trigger point release, myofascial work—it's more like physical therapy than a spa treatment at times."

"Exactly," Teagan agrees.

"I specialize in working with athletic populations," I add.

"Climbers, especially, tend to develop very specific muscle tension patterns. I'd be happy to do a consultation for him—no pressure, just education about what therapeutic work involves."

"That sounds perfect," Teagan says warmly. "He mentioned some back tension after yesterday's demonstration, but getting him to actually do something about it..." She shakes her head with fond exasperation.

"Ah, the classic 'I'll walk it off" type," I say with a knowing smile. "I see that a lot. They'll push through pain that would have most people flat on their backs."

"I could see him favoring his left side yesterday, walking like his spine's made of Legos. But he's too stubborn to admit he needs help."

I perk up at the challenge. "I'll keep that in mind," I say, accepting the cabin key Teagan hands me. "If he—or any of the guys—wants to reach out, just have them text me. Sometimes it's easier for them to ask for help when they don't have to do it face-to-face."

"Smart," she says.

"Thanks, Teagan. I'm looking forward to working with your team."

"Our pleasure...*literally!*"

She waves as I head toward my cabin with a head full of questions about midnight blue eyes, sexy hair, and massive pecs.

The way my pulse kicked up when those firm hands steadied me suggests I might be in trouble.

But this gig with Serenity Springs is my golden ticket—full-time position, health benefits, and someplace stable to call home. No more freelance hustle.

The spa manager wants testimonials from the guys here before my interview. And yet the thought of touching every inch of the lean, muscled body on that sexy lumbersnack is driving me a little crazy.

Professional boundaries, I remind myself firmly as I unlock my cabin door.

Right. Those.

CHAPTER 2
BRADY

I stare at my phone, my stomach knotting up each time I read the text Teagan sent me yesterday:

> Imogen Navarro, LMT. Really nice, specializes in athletes. Just a consultation. And if you don't get your keister over there, Connor plans to drag you over himself. Her number: 406-555-0187.

I huff.

The rational part of my brain knows I need help. My back's been spasming since yesterday's demo where I did an extra long drop with the rig, showing off, trying to prove I could still climb like I was twenty-five instead of forty-three.

My muscles pulse in disapproval. Sharp. Insistent. *"Old man,"* it mocks.

The irrational part of me keeps flashing back to that much-too-young woman I bumped into with sexy pink hair and whiskey-brown eyes—some random visitor passing through who keeps popping into my fantasies.

Damn, she was beautiful.

My phone feels like a brick in my hand.

Teagan's been trying to get me to see a massage therapist for weeks, and suddenly there's one on site? Coincidence? Doubtful. More like suspicious.

A stranger's hands on my body.

I shudder, thumb hovering over the text box. Twenty-five years of logging, climbing, hauling timber, and the idea of lying still while someone pokes and rubs at my muscles makes my shoulders creep toward my ears.

Traditional Japanese stoicism runs deep—my grandfather's voice echoes in my head:

Endure. Adapt. Do not show weakness.

But Teagan's right. The crew needs me functional.

> This is Brady. Teagan said you might have time for a consultation about my back.

I hit send before I lose my nerve.

Imogen's response is almost immediate.

> Absolutely! I'm free this afternoon if you'd like to stop by Cabin 7. We can just talk - and only hands-on diagnostics if you're comfortable.

The word "hands-on" makes me pause. But "diagnostic" is a clinical word. A safe word...and it brings me back to reality.

I have to get over this.

> 2 PM work?

Pride will not intervene.

> It does. See you then, Brady.

I shove the phone in my pocket and try to focus on this tree health assessment I'm supposed to be doing. Instead, I'm worried about someone who's supposed to make me feel better.

Zen, Tanaka.

But when 2 PM rolls around, I'm standing outside Cabin 7 wondering if I've made a mistake in agreeing to this.

I knock twice.

"Come in!" her voice calls from inside.

I push open the door and freeze.

Recognition hits me like a felled tree.

It's her.

The little sprite from yesterday—all cotton-candy hair and dark eyes and the soft *'oh'* when my hands gripped her shoulders to steady her. The woman who's been haunting my periphery for hours, smirking at me.

She's sitting cross-legged on the couch, laptop balanced on her knees, wearing ripped jeans and an oversized T-shirt that's sliding off one sexy shoulder. Her pink hair is cropped short except for the bangs that flop into her eyes when she looks up.

"Oh geez, it's you." She closes the laptop and uncurls from the couch in one fluid motion. "The guy from yesterday. The one I made a complete ass out of myself in front of." Then her cheeks turn as pink as her hair. "And you're Brady."

"Yeah." My voice comes out rougher than intended. "And you're the massage therapist." I take a deep breath. "You know, I should probably go. I think this is a mistake."

"Wait," she says, and I stop despite every instinct telling me to go. "Why? Because we bumped into each other? Surely we can get past that."

I rub the back of my neck, trying to find words that don't make me sound like a basket case. "It's just...complicated."

"How so?" She tilts her head, studying me with the kind of

attention that makes my skin feel too tight. "Is it me? Am I not what you expected in a massage therapist?"

"No," I say quickly. "Nothing like that. Not really."

"Then what's complicated about a consultation? We're just talking." She gestures to the chairs by the window. "Come on. I may be clumsy, but I don't bite."

I swallow that image down, stepping inside.

The cabin's all soft lighting and linen sheets, earthy and feminine. She gestures to a chair. "Sit. Stand. Whatever's comfy. This isn't a dental exam."

I stand. Military stance. Shoulders back.

She tilts her head. "You're comfy like that?"

"Yes," I lie. As comfortable as I can be right now.

She shrugs. "So you're the mysterious high-rigger Teagan mentioned," she says, settling into one of the arm chairs. "The one who's too stubborn to admit he needs help."

My mouth twitches. "I'm here, aren't I?"

She accepts that. "Tell me about your back issues."

There's something about the way she asks: direct but not pushy, that makes it easier to talk than I expected. "Think I pulled something yesterday during a demonstration. Lower back. It's happened before."

She circles me slowly, and I swear I feel her gaze like sunlight through leaves—warm and persistent. "Which side do you favor when it acts up?"

"Left."

"Any numbness? Tingling?"

"No."

"How long have you been climbing?"

"Twenty-three years professionally. Longer if you count growing up around the family business."

Her eyebrows raise. "That's a lot of repetitive stress on your back. Do you do any regular maintenance? Stretching, strength training, bodywork?"

"Of course...some stretching, weight-lifting, calisthenics." I shift on my feet. "Look, I know you probably think I'm being ridiculous with being hesitant about the whole massage thing."

"Actually, I think you're being smart," she interrupts. "Therapeutic touch is intimate, even when it's professional. You should be comfortable with whoever's working on you."

The way she says 'intimate' sends heat shooting down my spine.

"The thing is," she continues, "climbers like you develop very specific tension patterns. Your lats, rhomboids, the deep muscles around your spine—they're probably locked up like Fort Knox. That demonstration yesterday probably just triggered something that's been building for months."

She's right, and we both know it. I've been waking up stiff for weeks, taking longer to warm up before climbs, favoring my left side without really admitting it.

She steps closer, and I register her height—or lack thereof. The top of her head reaches my sternum.

"What's this consultation involve?" I ask.

"Just assessment. I ask you to move in certain ways, maybe do some basic range of motion tests. If you're okay with it, I can do some diagnostic palpation—just feeling for areas of tension or restriction." She smiles. "No oils, or Enya, or pressure to do anything you don't want to do."

I smile, despite nerves.

"It's only to try to understand what's going on with your body."

What's going on with my body is that it's attracted to her in a way that goes beyond a professional consultation.

But I need help, and she clearly knows what she's talking about.

"Okay," I hear myself say. "What do you need me to do?"

Her face lights up. "Just some basic movement first."

She has me bend forward, twist left and right, reach overhead. Her eyes track every movement like the pro that she is, but I can't shake the feeling that she's seeing more than just muscle mechanics.

But that's probably just wishful thinking.

"Your left side is definitely restricted," she says. "Hip flexors are tight, probably compensating for whatever's going on in your lower back. Would you be comfortable if I did some light palpation? Just through your shirt?"

"Would it be easier if I took my shirt off?" I ask, then immediately wonder where that came from.

She blinks. "Yes, actually. But only if you're cool with that."

It's just a professional assessment, right?

Before I can reconsider, I pull the Henley over my head and fold it, setting it on the chair. When I turn back, I watch her gaze travel over my torso.

"Those tattoos are beautiful," she says, eying the traditional Japanese artwork that covers me. For a heartbeat, her lips part, fingers flexing like she wants to trace the ink curling over my shoulders.

Then she shakes her head, and it's back to business. "Okay, turn around for me."

I do as she says. The air's cold on my bare skin.

Her silence prickles.

"Holy shit," she breathes.

"What?"

"Your latissimus dorsi. They're…Jesus, they're *art*."

"They're muscles," I reply, but some pride creeps in.

"*Masterpiece* muscles. Development in those is really rare. Amazing work."

"Thanks," I say, unsure how to respond to that kind of compliment.

Her fingertips brush my trapezius, and I nearly gasp in a full-body shiver.

"Wow," she mutters. "You *are* wound tighter than a fiddle string."

"Duh." I chuckle, and she laughs. "Okay, wise guy."

Her following touch is warm and sure, fingers moving along the edge of my shoulder blade with practiced deliberation. I work to keep my breathing steady, to stay neutral, but there's something about her tiny hands on my back that makes it hard to think straight.

"Just breathe normally," she says, working down my spine. "Tell me if anything feels tender."

She begins rolling her thumbs into muscle knots I didn't know existed.

Pain blazes, sharp and bright, but her voice softens: "That's tender, huh? Tell me these things. Now, breathe into it for a second. Don't fight me."

Her hands are *strong*. Small but relentless, working a little deeper with each breath. My eyes drift shut against my will.

"There you go," she murmurs. "Your Erector Spinae are pissed. It's all these muscles that run along the length of your spine." She continues her movements. Her touch is clinical but reverent, tracing the topography of my back. "Your years of climbing show. The angular fibers here—" her thumb slides over a sensitive spot near my spine, "—indicate repetitive overhead engagement. Your rhomboids are compensating."

Her fingertips chart territories no one's mapped before.

I swallow hard.

She kneads a knot near my scapula. "Do you ever *stop* working?"

"No."

"Shocker." She prods a tender spot. "This hurt?"

"N-no." I bite back a groan.

Her hands still. "Hey." Softer now. "You're allowed to feel things, you know."

My jaw flexes. "I'm fine."

She spends a moment exploring the area, and every touch sends heat racing through me despite the professional nature of what she's doing.

"This is definitely inflamed. And these muscles up here—" her hands move to my upper back"—are doing double duty. You're probably getting headaches too."

I am, but I don't want to admit how right she is about *everything*.

She sighs but resumes working, quieter. Her thumbs press waves into my lower back, each stroke pulling tension like rotten roots from soil. Against my will, my body succumbs— shoulders dropping, breath deepening.

I panic.

Too intimate. Too close. *Too much.*

"I think that's enough." I step away abruptly out of her reach and turn to face her.

She blinks, hands frozen mid-air. "Did I hurt—"

"No, I…" I keep my head down and start pulling on my shirt. "Should get going."

Her brow furrows but she nods. "Okay, then."

She busies herself with notes while I dress, my fingers trembling on my buttons. My skin smells like her now—euca- lyptus and jasmine clinging to me.

When I'm dressed again, she turns to me. "You need help," she says simply. "The good news is that most of this is soft tissue restriction. Very treatable with the right approach."

"And the bad news?"

"It's going to get worse if you ignore it. You're already

compensating in ways that are putting stress on other areas. Give it another month and you'll be looking at more serious issues."

I believe her. Everything she's said so far has been dead-on.

She studies my face. "Look, I know this is...difficult. Knowing your body isn't functioning like it used to."

"You mean because I'm getting old," I say, with a huff.

"I didn't say that," she replies. "But with the wear and tear you've put your body through over your years of climbing, I really want you to think about all of this."

"Think about it," I repeat, and she gives me a smile.

"If you decide you want to work with me, we can set something up. If not, that's okay too. I can always recommend someone else."

The idea of someone else working on me doesn't appeal at all, but I appreciate she's giving me space to decide.

"I will," I say, heading for the door. "Think about it, I mean."

But as I walk back to my own cabin, I know I've already made up my mind...despite my fears.

CHAPTER 3
IMOGEN

Dinner in the dining hall is like stepping into a lumberjack convention where everyone hit the genetic lottery. It smells like cedar, marinara sauce, and testosterone.

I swipe a plate of lasagna and garlic bread from the buffet line and scan the room—log beams overhead, picnic tables packed with rugged men shoveling food into their faces like it's a competitive sport.

I'd like to find a place to sit that won't have me drooling over broad shoulders and corded forearms.

Ha! Good luck.

"Imogen!" Sky, the camp's social media manager and a sustainable travel influencer, waves me over to a table where she's sitting with her husband Graham, and Teagan. "Come sit with us!"

I settle in next to Sky, just as Connor, Teagan's husband, slides onto the bench across from us, biceps testing the seams of his shirt. At least he's taken. "Saw you worked on Ewan's rotator cuff this afternoon. Dude's tossing logs like he's going to compete for the Highland Games again."

Before I can answer, Sky launches into a detailed review of the massage I gave her this afternoon as well.

"Oh my god, you guys," she gushes, "I feel like I've been reborn. Like, completely reconstructed from the ground up." She rotates her shoulders demonstratively. "I didn't even realize how tight I was until Imogen got her magic hands on me."

Graham raises an eyebrow. "Better than *my* magic hands?"

"That's different." She winks at him. "Seriously, it was like she found muscles I didn't know I had and convinced them to work again." Sky turns to me. "Where did you learn to do that thing with the trigger points?"

"Practice," I say, stabbing a piece of lasagna. "And a lot of continuing education. Bodies are puzzles—you just have to figure out which pieces are stuck."

"Well, you definitely figured mine out," Sky says. "I'm booking another session before you leave."

The conversation flows easily around the table, and I find myself relaxing despite the intimidating concentration of attractive men.

Connor and Graham have that easy camaraderie of people who've worked together for years, while Teagan and Sky clearly adore their husbands in a way that's sweet without being nauseating.

Suddenly, I look up and Brady appears in the doorway holding his dinner tray. My pulse jumps when our eyes meet across the dining hall. He hesitates for a moment, then heads toward our table. He's got that controlled grace that I'm beginning to recognize as his armor, carrying his tray like it's a ceremonial offering.

"Brady!" Teagan calls out. "Come sit. Imogen was just telling us about trigger point therapy."

He slides into the chair directly across from me, and I catch his fresh, rich scent that had me holding back from burying my face against his shoulder during his consultation.

"How was your meeting with Imogen?" Connor asks through a mouthful of cornbread, and I watch Brady's jaw tighten slightly.

"Informative," he says, glancing at me. "She knows what she's talking about."

"Of course she does," Sky chimes in. She rolls her shoulders again. "I feel like I could climb a mountain right now."

"So what's your secret?" Connor asks. "Witchcraft? Dark rituals."

"Swedish techniques and spite," I say, watching Brady methodically dissect his baked potato like a surgeon. "Sky is a champ at taking direction, also."

"Who?" Graham chuckles as Sky swats his arm.

Sky preens. "She told me to breathe into the pain and I literally cried on her table."

Brady's fork pauses mid-air. "You…cried?"

"Happy tears!" Sky insists. "The cathartic kind."

He blinks at me like I've performed actual sorcery. "That sounds…intense."

"Occupational hazard." I shrug, but heat creeps up my neck when his gaze drops to my hands. "Sometimes the body needs to reset. Doesn't make you weak."

His jaw tenses, but he nods—once, sharp—before retreating into silent potato annihilation.

Brady stays quiet, but I notice him watching me when he thinks I'm not looking. There's something different about his posture, less rigid than this afternoon, but still guarded.

Teagan finishes her lemonade, crunching on the ice. "Are you going to let Imogen work her magic on you, too, Brady?"

Brady shifts in his chair. "Still thinking about it."

"What's to think about?" Connor says.

"Connor, it's a big decision. Some people need time to feel comfortable with the idea," I say, deciding to rescue Brady from the well-meaning interrogation.

Connor raises his hands in surrender. "Fine."

"No pressure." I turn to Brady and put a hand on his forearm. It flexes under my touch.

But the gratitude in his expression makes my chest warm.

After I finish eating, I excuse myself and say goodnight before cleaning up my dishes. Walking back to my cabin, I hear my name.

Brady's voice pins me in place. I turn to find him under a flickering light near the path, hands jammed in his pockets like he's containing a live grenade.

"Hi. Escape the inquisition?"

His mouth quirks up. "Something like that. They mean well, but..."

"But pushy friends are still pushy, even when they're right."

"Exactly." He clears his throat a little. "I've been thinking about this afternoon. What we talked about, I mean."

I bite back a smile.

"Tomorrow, if you're not booked. Could you...?"

"Squeeze you in?"

A muscle jumps in his jaw and he nods.

My heart does a little skip. "Of course. When were you thinking?"

"After lunch?"

"How about two o'clock again?"

He nods stiffly, turning to leave, then hesitates. "Sky said something. Earlier. About breathing into the pain."

"Yeah?"

"What was she talking about?"

The question feels bigger than anatomy.

I step closer, tilting my head back to hold his gaze. "One of my massage mentors taught me that pain's a conversation. If you fight it, it screams louder. If you breathe *with* it, you can negotiate, and work on relieving it."

He swallows hard. "How should I dress…or what do I need to do…logistically?"

The nervousness in his voice is endearing. This big, capable man who scales trees is anxious about a massage.

"It's pretty straightforward," I say gently. "Wear whatever is easiest to remove. You'll undress to your comfort level and lie on the table under a sheet. I'll only uncover the area I'm working on at any given time."

"Okay."

"I promise I'll take good care of you." The words come out more intimate than I intended, and I see his cheeks go pink before he looks away.

He nods and starts to walk away, then pauses. "Imogen?"

I turn back to him.

"Thank you. For being patient with me about all this."

"Of course, Brady."

He gives me a smile that makes my knees weak, then disappears into the pines like a shadow.

I spend the next morning massaging Hazel, Ewan the sawyer's wife, then preparing the room for Brady.

Fresh linens, the right lighting, my selection of more robust-scented oils within easy reach. I want Brady to feel as comfortable as possible for what's clearly going to be a big step for him.

He arrives five minutes early, knocking like he's interrupting a funeral.

"Come in!" I call, wiping my suddenly damp palms on my yoga pants.

He steps inside, shoulders nearly spanning the doorway. It's as if he's entering a minefield, gaze darting to the table, the oils, the Himalayan salt lamp casting a warm glow over his inked forearms.

He glances around. "This looks..."

"Professional?"

"Relaxing," he finishes. "Very relaxing."

"I'm glad." I gesture to the massage table dominating the center of the room. "That's the idea. How are you feeling? Nervous?"

"Yeah, maybe," he admits.

"Completely normal. Your first massage can be intimidating." I hand him a towel. "Okay, so here's how this works. I'm going to step out while you get comfortable. Most people undress down to their underwear, but it's all up to you. There's nothing I haven't seen before. Then lie face down on the table and pull the sheet up to cover your lower half."

His Adam's apple bobs as his fingers hover over his shirt buttons. "Is this usually..."

"Awkward?" I shrug. "Maybe at first, but soon you'll be a pro," I tease. "Take your time getting situated, then just call out when you're ready."

I retreat to the bathroom, giving him privacy while my heart hammers against my ribs. The rustling of fabric makes me very aware of Brady Tanaka stripping twenty feet away from me.

Professional. Boundaries. Ethics.

"Ready," he eventually calls out, slightly muffled.

I open the door and nearly forget how to breathe.

He's a mountain under crisp white linens, positioned perfectly on the table, face buried in the cradle. The sheet clings to his hips and glutes like it's begging for mercy.

Jesus Christ.

His entire back is exposed, the tattoos I saw yesterday displayed in their full glory: traditional Japanese waves and clouds, and vibrantly colored dragons, flowers, and koi fish flowing across his shoulders, arms, and down his back—a storybook on skin.

But it's the musculature underneath that has me speechless.

As I told him yesterday, years of climbing have sculpted him into a work of art. His lats create this beautiful V-shape that narrows to his waist, while his rhomboids and traps are defined in a way that speaks to serious strength. Every muscle group flows into the next with the kind of development you only see in athletes who've dedicated decades to their craft.

"Everything all right?" he asks, and I realize I've been staring.

"Sorry, just...admiring your artwork again." I approach the table, warming oil between my palms. "Your tattoos really are incredible. How long did they take?"

"About five years, on and off," he says. "My grandfather's designs, mostly. Stories from our family history."

"They're stunning," I reply. "I'm going to start with some general warming strokes, then work deeper into the problem areas. Let me know if anything feels too intense."

The moment my hands make contact on his upper back, his entire body tenses.

"Try to breathe normally," I murmur, beginning with long, flowing strokes across his shoulders. "I know it might be weird having someone touch you like this, but I promise it'll feel better once you relax into it."

My thumbs sink into corded muscle, and I swear the

room's oxygen evaporates. He's radiating heat like a forge—and the low groan he muffles into the cradle makes my knees weak.

"Breathe," I remind him again, but as I work down his spine, I wonder if *I* need reminding, too.

Gradually, I feel some of the tension ease out of his shoulders. His breathing deepens, and I catch the occasional soft sound when I hit a particularly tight spot.

He gasps when I hit a knot near his scapula. *"Fuuuuck."*

"You okay?" I ask, grinning when his shoulders inch down.

"Yeah," he groans when I work a knot near his shoulder blade. "That hurts in the best way."

Heat swirls low in my belly.

Watch it, Imogen.

I work systematically down his back. His body tells a story of hard work and dedication, but also of accumulated stress and compensation patterns.

"Your right side is definitely overworking," I tell him, pressing my thumbs into his erector spinae. "Compensating for whatever's going on with your left side."

He lets out a sound that's almost pornographic when I hit a particularly stubborn knot. "Sorry, I—"

"Don't apologize. Your body's releasing tension it's been holding onto for a long time. Those sounds tell me I'm doing something right."

The next hour is equal parts torture and revelation. His body speaks in shudders and hitched breaths—resistance melting into surrender beneath my hands. I map every ridge of scar tissue, every ripple of ancient tension, and when I work the oil into his lower lumbar region his choked noise has my lower parts clenching.

"You're...thorough," he rasps, voice wrecked.

By the time I finish, he's putty...cheek smushed against the cradle, fingers limp near the floor. I cover him with a heated blanket and step back, dizzy from whatever pheromone cocktail his unbelievably hot body excretes.

"How do you feel?" I ask, stepping back.

"Like I've been taken apart and slowly rebuilt," he says, his voice drowsy and content. "I had no idea how much tension I was carrying."

"Most people don't, until it's gone." I wipe my hands on a towel. "Now stay there for five minutes," I order, fleeing to the bathroom.

I run the water and wash up, taking my time. I splash water on my face, staring at my flushed reflection.

My god, this man.

I want to climb up onto the table naked and just rub my body all over him while biting, kissing, and licking every inch of his skin.

Massage him with my *mouth*.

He's a client. He's a client. He's a—

"Imogen?"

I jump. Brady's leaning against the doorframe, sheet wrapped around his hips like a bath towel. His hair's mussed, eyes heavy-lidded, and his chest—*Lord*—I'll never get over that roadmap of ink and muscle I want to explore with my teeth.

"You're supposed to be horizontal," I manage to say. "I said five minutes."

He rubs his neck, adorably sheepish. "It's been eight minutes and…I forgot where I put my shirt."

I walk out to the main room with him and point near his boots.

I should turn to give him privacy, since he hasn't finished changing. He shrugs on his flannel as he looks at me with something like awe. "That was…incredible. Thank you."

"Good. You did great."

Finally, I turn to clean up my supplies, and let him get dressed properly.

I know this was about more than just professional obligation. There's something about him that gets under my skin.

"Could you do the same time tomorrow?" he asks, after he's clothed and tying his boots.

I check my schedule.

Hallelujah, I'm open.

"I'm free. But are you sure?" I chuckle. "You might need a week to recover."

He looms in my space with that crooked smile that hits me lower than it should.

His gaze drops to my mouth.

A loud knock on my cabin door makes us both jump.

"Imogen! I have a tension emergency!"

Oh geez.

"Come in," I tell her, smiling at Brady.

Sky opens the door and freezes, seeing us standing close together. "Oh. Should I come back...*after* the sexual healing?"

Brady's entire face, including his ears, turns crimson. "I was leaving."

He brushes past me, all heat and shame, leaving me alone with Sky's shit-eating grin.

I stomp my foot and give her a friendly swat on the butt. "You scared him away. He was doing so well."

She smiles and flops onto the table. "He'll be back."

God, I hope so.

Even if my professional boundaries are eroding faster than a clearcut hillside.

Because Brady Tanaka, half-naked and wrecked under my hands, is impossible to ignore.

CHAPTER 4
BRADY

I can't think straight.

That's the only explanation for why I'm standing outside Connor's cabin at seven in the morning like a spooked animal.

The door opens before I can knock.

"Brady?" Connor's holding a steaming mug of coffee, looking confused. "Everything okay?"

"I need to ask you something," I say, then immediately regret it. "Actually, forget it. This is stupid."

"Hey, wait." He steps aside, gesturing me in. "Come on in. Coffee?"

I follow him into the kitchen, where Teagan's feeding their son Jamie in his high chair. She looks up with a smile that falters when she sees me.

Damn, I must look like hell.

"Everything all right?" she asks.

Ugh. No way am I talking to Connor with Teagan and their baby right here.

"I'm just going to..." Connor jerks his thumb toward the door. "We'll be on the porch."

I blow out a breath. *Thank god.*

Outside, Connor settles into one of the rocking chairs and waits. The morning air is crisp, pine-scented, and normally calming. Today it does nothing for my nerves.

"What's up?" he says after a long moment. "This about your massage yesterday?"

Heat crawls up my neck. "How did you—"

"Heard you sharpening axes by the equipment shed at the break of dawn. Probably murdering the whetstone in the process."

I shrug. "Don't worry, I didn't decapitate any axes."

"Sky mentioned you looked like you'd been hit by a truck after you emerged from Imogen's cabin." His mouth quirks up. "In a good way."

I scrub my hands over my face. "This is embarrassing."

"What is?" he asks. "You know, you can talk to me about anything. I guarantee I've been through worse."

I doubt that. Sure, Connor has been around. But a guy like him would have plenty of experience with women before Teagan.

And I'm...a virgin.

"Fine. Yesterday, during my massage. I...reacted."

Connor's eyebrows climb toward his hairline. "Reacted how?"

I'm *not* spelling it out. "You know how."

Understanding dawns on his face, followed by what looks suspiciously like relief. "Jesus, man. You pitched a tent? *That's* what this is about?"

I make sure no one else is around that heard him, then glare. "Shit. Keep your voice down. I'm supposed to see her again today, and I—"

"Got hard during a massage," Connor finishes. "Welcome to being a red-blooded male, Brady. It happens."

"Not to me it doesn't." The words come out sharper than intended. "I don't...I'm not used to..."

"To what? Attractive women putting their hands all over you?" Connor's grin is merciless. "Yeah, that'll do it."

My jaw clenches. "She's a professional. I don't want to make her uncomfortable."

"Did she seem uncomfortable yesterday?"

I think about Imogen's easy confidence, the way she handled everything without judgment. "No, but she didn't see it. I was face down. Today, I might be—"

"You're overthinking it. Like you said...she's a professional. I'm sure it happens all the time." Connor leans forward. "Look, if you're really worried, take care of business beforehand. Takes the edge off."

"Take care of—" I stare at him. "You mean..."

"Rub one out, Brady. Whack off. Dammit, do I have to draw you a diagram?"

I nearly choke, my face going up in flames. "I can't believe I'm having this conversation."

"You're a forty-three-year old virgin, not a Catholic school-boy. Welcome to a healthy sexual discussion," Connor says cheerfully.

"Why does it seem like you're enjoying this?" I ask.

"Because I am." He chuckles. "It's kinda fun to see the 'zen master' getting all flustered. Oh, how the tables have turned."

I huff loudly. "Whatever. Just promise me you won't tell Teagan we talked about this."

He snorts. "Like I want to talk about *your* boners with *my* wife. Your secret's safe."

∽

Back at my cabin, my grandfather's proverb curdles in my throat: *Discipline shapes the man.*

Somehow I don't think he was talking about...*this*. But who knows anymore. These days all I do is question myself.

Then Connor's advice pushes its way through.

It makes sense, in a mortifying, practical way. If I'm going to lie on that table again and let Imogen's incredible hands work my body into submission, I need to have some semblance of control.

I grab my phone and find Imogen's website photo—pink hair, sexy smile, nose stud. I imagine her biting that sweet lower lip.

This feels so dirty...forbidden even.

Tearing off my clothes, I set the phone down and head to the shower.

The hot water eases the morning stiffness from my muscles. I soap my chest, thinking about yesterday, and how Imogen's fingers explored my back, the little sounds of concentration she made when she found a particularly stubborn knot.

Her low, soothing voice haunts me. "Breathe into it..."

My cock stirs, and I wrap my hand around it almost without thinking. The soap makes my palm slick, and I stroke slowly, letting myself remember the heat of her touch, the scent from the oils she used.

God, the way she looked at me.

I think about her hair falling into her eyes, the way her small hands glided over my skin. Those strong fingers that could find every hidden tension and coax it into surrendering.

What would those hands feel like on my cock?

The thought has me trembling.

My thumb swipes the slit, fantasizing it's her tongue darting out to taste me. Her fingertips trail down my chest, nails dragging over my inner thigh, lips grazing my ear.

I lean against the shower wall, stroking faster as I imagine Imogen's whiskey-brown eyes watching me as she straddles the massage table, light reflecting off a sexy shoulder I want to bite. That confident smile spreads across her face as her hands slide lower, whispering…

"That's it. You're doing so good…don't fight it."

"Fuck, Imogen," I grit out, hips jerking. Muscle memory betrays me—every stroke synced to yesterday's whispers of *"you're so tight here…let me…"*

Reality and fantasy blur as I explode with more curses and a groan that echoes off the tile, my release washing away with the shower spray.

I stand there breathing hard, letting the water cascade over my shoulders.

Better. Definitely better.

Later, I'm standing outside her cabin again, feeling more centered. The edge is gone, replaced by something that feels almost like anticipation instead of dread.

I knock.

"Come in!"

Imogen's voice pulls me inside like a magnet. She's wearing yoga pants and a fitted tank top that shows off her toned arms and pretty tattoos.

"How are you feeling today?" she asks, her smile bright. "You definitely look more relaxed."

Because I came all over myself thinking about you.

"Yep." My voice cracks, but I press on. "I'm feeling good. Really good, actually." I gesture to my back. "Whatever you did yesterday is working."

Her face lights up. "I'm so glad. Any soreness?"

"Some, but it feels like proper soreness. Like I actually

worked out instead of carrying tension around."

"Excellent." She moves to the massage table, smoothing the fresh sheet. "Ready to go a little deeper today?"

The way she says it makes my pulse react, but I'm able to keep it under control. For now at least. "Yeah."

"Great. Same routine—undress to your comfort level, face down on the table, sheet over your lower half."

She disappears into the bathroom, and I strip faster than dignity allows, folding my clothes neatly on the side table, noting exactly where they are this time.

The padded massage table feels familiar now, welcoming instead of intimidating. I bury my nose in the cradle inhaling the fresh scent of the room.

"Ready," I call out.

I hear her come back in and pump oil into her hands.

"I want to work your back again, but also spend some time on your legs if that's cool," she says.

"Whatever you think is best."

Her hands settle on my shoulders, and I let out a long breath. Yesterday's magic happens again—tension melting under her touch, muscles surrendering to her skilled fingers.

"Tell me more about your tattoos," she says as she works down my spine. "You mentioned they were your grandfather's designs?"

"Mostly, yeah." Her thumbs dig into a knot near my shoulder blade, and I pause to breathe through it. "He was a master tattoo artist in Japan before he came to America. Traditional irezumi style."

"They're beautiful." Her fingers trace the edge of a dragon that curls around my ribs. "What do they mean?"

"Each symbol's a story." I find myself talking as she works —about my grandfather's stories, the symbolism of the koi swimming upstream, the cherry blossoms that represent the beauty and fragility of life.

Her touch makes the words flow easier, like she's massaging my lungs along with my muscles. "Hammer waves for resilience. Peonies for prosperity. Kintaro battling the koi—tenacity."

Her finger lingers on the warrior's face. "And this?"

"Strength beyond brute force." I swallow as her hand drifts away. "Wisdom."

"Your grandfather sounds like an amazing man," she says, rolling her fingers into my lower back.

"He was. Taught me that the body tells stories, even when we don't mean it to."

She huffs out a chuckle. "That's so true. He taught you climbing, too?"

"Yeah. Found himself at a logging camp when he first came over here...and thoroughly embraced it. Loved nature."

She hums. "Fascinating."

Her hands move lower, working the muscles near my hips. "These are definitely tight. I'm going to work down the backs of your legs now, okay?"

"Okay," I reply, and she adjusts the sheet, exposing my legs while keeping everything else covered. Her touch on my hamstrings is firm and purposeful, but there's something sensual about the way she works—the glide of her hands over my skin. The care she takes in making sure her touches don't stick or snag.

"Let's stretch this hip flexor out." She rests her hand on the back of my knee. "I want you to pull your knee up and out to the side. I'll have my hand under it so you don't need to hold it up. Just let me take the weight. I'll pull the sheet down as you do to keep your lower half covered."

I do as she says. The stretch is good, and she rocks me slightly, pushing gently on my thigh.

I groan into the stretch.

"Your flexibility is incredible for a man your age," she says, continuing to hold my knee and press downward on my thigh, stretching my hip. "Most guys are locked up like Fort Knox by their forties."

"Climbing keeps you limber," I manage, trying not to think about her innocent, yet backhanded compliment. Yeah, I'm old. Probably too old for this beauty with her hands all over me.

She does the same thing to my other side, then works my calves, my feet, finding tension in hidden places. By the time she's massaging my toes, I'm floating in that same blissful haze as yesterday.

"Ready to turn over?" she asks.

This is the moment I've been dreading.

Even relaxed, just being near Imogen makes me half-hard. Despite Connor's advice, despite taking care of business this morning, I'm still nervous.

But I nod and flip over, settling onto my back with the sheet across my lap.

The first thing I notice is how different this feels—being able to see her face, watching her as she moves around my body. She starts with my arms, working my shoulders and biceps with the same focused intensity.

I relax into it, listening to her breath.

"Your range of motion is amazing up here," she says, manipulating my shoulder joint. "No real restriction at all."

I try to focus on her words instead of the way her tank top gapes slightly when she leans over me, or how her hair slides over her cheek. I wonder how soft those pink strands are…?

Then she moves to my chest.

Her palms press against my pectorals, fingers finding the tight spots where my harness sits during climbs. The touch is professional, therapeutic, but being able to see her face while she works adds an intimacy that makes my heartbeat speed up.

"This okay?" she asks, seeming to notice my tension.

"Yeah," I say, voice rougher than intended. "Just nice, being able to see you."

Such a smooth talker, Brady.

She smiles and works around my chest muscles methodically, but she's carefully avoiding my nipples. Part of me wishes she'd touch them. What would her skilled fingers feel like there? Would she use the same firm pressure or something softer, more teasing?

Christ, Brady. My nipples are definitely stiff now.

"Your pecs are pretty tight," she murmurs, working deeper into the muscle. "All that rope work and reaching overhead."

Her hands move lower, pressing into my ribs, then lower still to my stomach. I suck in a breath as her fingers find the ridges of my abs, working the muscles with slow, deliberate strokes.

"Breathe," she reminds me softly. "Don't hold your breath."

But it's hard to breathe when her touch feels this good, when every stroke sends heat shooting through my body. She works my obliques, the muscles along my sides, and I can feel my body…*responding.*

No. Not now.

But my body doesn't listen. Blood rushes south, and I feel myself getting hard beneath the sheet.

I try to think about anything else—tree climbing techniques, safety protocols, my to-do list—but her hands inching down my stomach are undoing all my control.

"Shit," I breathe when I realize there's no hiding it. "I'm sorry. I—"

"Hey." Her hands still, and she smiles at me with those warm brown eyes. "It's completely normal. Please don't worry about it."

My face burns with embarrassment. "I'm not usually—I mean, I don't—"

"Brady." Her voice is gentle, reassuring. "It's a physiological response to touch. There's nothing to be embarrassed about."

The matter-of-fact way she says it, without judgment or awkwardness, makes some of the tension leave my shoulders.

"You sure?"

"Positive." She gives me another soft smile. "Can I finish up here?"

I nod, and she continues working my stomach muscles, her touch professional, but somehow more intimate now that the…er…*elephant* in the room has been acknowledged.

When she's finished, I feel boneless and energized at the same time. She covers me with the sheet and steps back, and I have to resist the urge to pull her down onto the table with me.

Oh man, I'm toast.

I get dressed and stare out the window of the cabin.

"Same time tomorrow? I left it open for you," she asks when she comes back in, and there's something in her tone that tells me the earlier situation didn't change anything between us.

"Yeah," I say, probably too quickly, then clear my throat. "Yes. I'd like that."

Her smile is warm and genuine. "Good. I'll see you then."

As I walk back to my cabin, I'm wondering why I wish something *had* changed.

CHAPTER 5
IMOGEN

I'm trying to concentrate on refilling my oils, but every scent carries traces of him.

I'm losing my damn mind.

Three days of Brady Tanaka on my massage table, and I'm about as professional as a cat in heat.

Every time those blue eyes meet mine, every breathy sound he makes when I work his muscles, every glimpse of those incredible tattoos—it's like my body's staging a revolt against my brain.

My professional boundaries are fraying faster than cheap massage table linens.

If these massages had been for actual money, I'd have dumped Brady as a client by now…and done his work for free to protect my reputation.

I mean, I've had thoughts about my clients, especially all these rugged, muscled lumberjacks here. But I know how to keep myself in check. If I ever felt I was crossing a line, I'd bail.

That's why this whole thing with Brady is killing me.

Since tonight's Heritage Night, I hope to let off some steam.

170

The whole camp's gathered around the fire pit for Ewan's storytelling. But it's more like Mardi Gras for lumberjacks.

Twinkle lights zigzag between the trees as Connor mans the whiskey barrel punch. Fiddle music tangles with laughter as guests weave around displays of antique logging tools and family heirlooms.

Teagan shoves a mason jar into my hand, moonshine sloshing. "Drink. You look like you need it."

"Thanks," I say, sipping cautiously—sweetness masking a kerosene kick.

I really should be networking, making connections for my Serenity Springs interview in a couple of days. Instead, I'm focused on Brady sitting across the circle from me, firelight dancing across his cheekbones.

He's had a couple beers. I can tell because his usual rigid posture has relaxed into something more natural—more approachable. And he keeps catching my eye with these little smiles that make my panties damp.

"SUPREME LORDS OF TIMBER!" Rourke, the log-roller, bellows from the ale cask, shirtless and glistening. "Guests go home with a free bottle of our signature punch if you beat the staff in arm wrestling!"

Chaos erupts. Guests cheer as a couple of beefy Canadian men challenge Rourke and Connor.

Teagan slaps her head. "Oh no. Not again. Rourke, we can't do that!" She heads toward them as I chuckle.

When the challenges die down, Ewan kicks off an animated tale about selkies and lost love, his Scottish brogue thick.

Brady gets up and moves around the fire.

"Mind if I sit?" he asks, even though he's already settling onto the log bench right next to me. "I wanted to hide until the arm wrestling was over."

"Oh, darn," I say, watching the way his flannel shirt pulls

across his shoulders. "I was hoping you'd want to arm wrestle me."

"Hell no. You'd take me. Easily."

I giggle like a silly girl talking to her crush.

Oh geez, Imogen.

"Great story," he says with a smile, nodding toward Ewan.

"Mmm, yeah," I reply, but I'm too distracted by his proximity to follow the plot. He smells like the smoke from the fire, and I'd like to lick him to see if he tastes like it, too.

The story ends to applause, and Ewan launches into a haunting melody on his fiddle. Couples start pairing off—Connor pulling Teagan closer, Graham's arm around Sky's shoulders. The atmosphere turns intimate and romantic.

Brady shifts beside me, his thigh brushing mine. "Want another drink?" he asks, gesturing to my empty jar.

"I'd love a beer. This moonshine is crazy strong."

"You got it." He returns with two fresh beers and he sits as close to me as before, close enough that I can count his long eyelashes.

"So," he says, taking a sip of his beer. "Your interview with the spa's coming up soon, right?"

"Uh-huh." I take a drink.

Something flickers across his face. "How are you feeling about it?"

"Confident. But still nervous."

"Why? You're a shoe-in. You know your stuff, have excellent skills, and are great with people."

I smile. "Well, thank you for that, Brady." I sigh, looking out at the fire. "I'd love to stick around here, put down some roots." I glance at him sideways. "This place is growing on me."

"The camp?"

"The camp. The people." I pause meaningfully. "The scenery."

His cheeks flush, and he looks down at his beer. "Montana's beautiful."

"It is." I'm not just talking about Montana, and I hope he knows that.

The evening progresses with more music, more drinks, more stolen glances. Brady's quiet laugh becomes more frequent, his smiles lasting longer. When Sky drags Graham up to dance to Rourke's guitar playing, Brady shakes his head in amusement.

"Never seen him dance this much before," he says.

"Before when?"

"Before Sky."

"They're cute together." I watch the couple swaying to the music, completely absorbed in each other. "How long have they been married?"

"About a year. Ewan and Hazel have only been married a few months. They're both in that honeymoon phase. It's kinda annoying."

I laugh. "Cynical much?"

"Realistic." But his expression softens. "But Teagan, Sky, and Hazel, have been good for the guys. They're a nice balance to each of them."

"Is that what you think makes a good relationship? Balance?"

He considers this, rolling his beer bottle between his palms. "Maybe. Or maybe it's finding someone who sees your broken pieces and stays anyway."

The words hang between us. I turn to study his profile, the way the firelight plays across his features.

"You're not broken, Brady."

He meets my eyes, and something stirs in them. "I'm heading that direction."

"Oh come *on*," My voice comes out on a groan. "You're in excellent shape for your age. *Outstanding* shape. Better than any man I've ever worked on. Strong, inside and out."

His jaw tics. "Imogen, you really don't know me."

"Hmm, well, from what I've seen so far...you're kind, thoughtful. You care about your work, your friends, and preserving your family's legacy."

He rubs the back of his neck, and I press on.

"You make these sexy little sounds when I work the knots out of your muscles that make me think incredibly dirty thoughts."

His face flames red. "Christ."

"And I know that despite what you think, you're not too old, or too set in your ways, or too *anything* to deserve good things."

The music around us fades to background noise. Brady's staring at me, his breathing slightly uneven.

"You should stop," he says quietly.

"Stop what?"

"Looking at me like that."

"Like what?" I touch my face, wondering what it's doing besides heating up.

"Like you want to climb me like a tree."

Did he just say that? In that low, rough-edged voice that has my belly somersaulting?

He grins and I laugh, pushing at his rock hard bicep. "Is that some liquid courage?"

"Maybe." He chuckles and sets down his beer with deliberate care. "It's getting late."

The party's still going strong, but I nod anyway. "Yeah. Another long day tomorrow with more massages."

We wave to the group, Brady's hand finding the small of my back as we walk toward the cabins. The touch is light, probably him being gentlemanly, but it still gives me goosebumps.

The forest path swallows night sounds—our footsteps crunching pine needles the only rhythm. Fireflies blink between trees like wandering stars.

"I'll walk you back," he says when we reach the fork.

My cabin's only fifty yards away, perfectly safe, but I don't argue. We walk in comfortable silence, the sounds of laughter and music fading behind us.

On my porch, I turn to face him. The moon's bright enough to see his expression clearly—conflicted, held back by something I can't quite identify.

"Thanks for the escort," I say.

"Of course."

He should leave. Because I don't know how much longer *I* can hold myself back.

And yet, he lingers, wrapping an arm around the porch post, looking at his feet.

"Brady," I say softly.

"Yeah?" He raises his eyes to meet my gaze.

"What are you afraid of?"

The question clearly catches him off guard. He opens his mouth, closes it, and then runs a hand through his hair. "I'm not afraid."

I step closer. "No, you're terrified. Why?"

He looks down again and shakes his head. "Of everything...fucking this up," he admits. "Of being too old for you, too inexperienced, too—"

"Too inexperienced?" I interrupt.

His jaw tightens. "With relationships. And with..." He gestures vaguely between us.

Oh. *Oh.* I had no idea.

I climb up and sit on the porch railing, bringing us closer to eye level, my legs dangling. "The superficial stuff doesn't matter to me."

"You're this incredible woman—confident, successful, edgy. I'm just some guy who climbs trees and overthinks everything." His voice is rough, vulnerable.

"You're not just some guy." I reach out, my fingers finding the front of his flannel shirt. "You're the guy who's been driving me completely insane for three days."

His eyes darken. "Imogen..."

"Whose smile makes my stomach do flips. Whose body responds to my touch like you were made for it."

"You gotta stop." But he doesn't step away. If anything, he moves closer.

I tug gently on his shirt, pulling him between my knees. "Because it scares you? Or because you want it too much?"

"Both," he groans, one hand on the post beside my head, the other caging in my hip.

He crowds me, his breath hot against my face.

Then his gaze drops to my mouth, and I see the exact moment his control starts to fray.

"I want to kiss you," he whispers.

"Why don't you then?"

"Because we shouldn't—"

"I know." I slide my hands up his chest, feeling his heartbeat thundering beneath my palms. "Do it anyway."

For a heartbeat, he hesitates. Then he mutters something in what sounds like Japanese and his mouth crashes into mine.

And holy shit.

If I thought Brady was intense during massages, it's nothing compared to this. He kisses like he's been starved for it, like he's memorizing the contours of my mouth and the taste of me. His fingers thread through my hair with a desperate groan that steals my breath.

I moan into his mouth, my legs wrapping around his waist to pull him closer. He's all heat and lean muscle and barely restrained power. His tongue slides against mine, and I want to devour him whole.

This is what I've been craving—not just the physical contact —though I can't complain about *that*. But this raw and real connection. The way he clings to me like I'm precious and dangerous at the same time.

I bite his lower lip gently, and he growls, the sound vibrating through both of our bodies. His hips thrust forward, and I feel his thick, hard cock against my inner thigh.

"Fuck," I breathe against his mouth, and he immediately stiffens.

"Shit. Shit." He jerks away from me like I've burned him, stumbling backward. "I'm sorry. I shouldn't have—we can't—"

"Brady, wait."

"This is wrong." He's backing away, shaking his head. "You're too young, too sweet, and I'm your client, and I just— god, I'm sorry."

"You don't need to apologize."

"Yes, I do." His voice is thick with self-contempt. "I completely crossed the line. I shouldn't see you for massages anymore."

He's spiraling, right before my eyes.

The kiss that felt like coming home to me has apparently spooked him into full retreat mode.

"Brady, please, listen to me."

"I need to go." He's already turning away. "I'm sorry, Imogen. Really sorry."

And then he's gone, disappearing between the cabins,

leaving me sitting on my porch railing with kiss-swollen lips and a heart that feels like it's been put through a blender.

I sit there for a long time, replaying every second of that kiss, trying to understand how something so perfect could end so badly.

The taste of him lingers on my lips, the memory of his hands in my hair making my entire body tingle.

But the look in his eyes when he pulled away—panic, regret, shame—that's what I can't shake.

I should be focused on preparing for my interview, getting a good night's sleep.

Instead, I'm obsessing over a man who just ran away from the best kiss of my life like his hair was on fire.

Professional boundaries. Right. Those things I used to have.

I laugh at the ridiculousness of it all.

But as I lie in bed staring at the ceiling, all I can think about is the way Brady said my name against my lips, like a prayer and a curse all at once.

And how badly I want to hear it again.

CHAPTER 6
BRADY

I spend half the night pacing my cabin like a caged animal, replaying that kiss over and over until I want to punch something.

I can still taste her, the memory of her legs wrapped around my waist making my cock throb with want.

What the hell was I thinking?

She's a professional. She came here to do a job, to interview for a position that could change her life, and I... I mauled her on her porch like some desperate teenager.

Sunrise finds me hacking at a fallen log with all the subtlety of a chainsaw murder. Graham wanders by with a coffee mug full of steaming judgment, telling me I look like something Rourke will probably cough up this morning, and I wince before telling him to get lost.

But two hours of chopping firewood hasn't done much but give me something to do while I think about her sexy mouth and her breathy "do it anyway" as it snarls through my skull.

The rational thing to do is stay away, let her finish her week here without me complicating it. But the thought of leaving things like this—with her thinking I ran because I didn't want her—makes my chest ache.

I have to apologize. Again. Face to face.

The walk to Imogen's cabin feels longer than my first solo climb. My knock cracks the silence like dropped kindling.

"Who is it?" she calls.

"Brady," I answer, my palms sweating.

She opens the door, wearing pajama pants and a *Namaste in Bed* T-shirt, pink hair sleep-mussed. She looks *gorgeous*.

"I wasn't sure you'd—"

"I came to apologize," I interrupt, the words rushing out.

She opens the door wide and turns to walk back inside.

I close the door and follow her. "Last night was completely out of line. I took advantage of the situation, of your kindness, and I'm sorry."

She tilts her head, studying me. "Took advantage how?"

"You've been nothing but professional with me, and I..." I scrub my hands over my face. "I shouldn't have kissed you. It was wrong."

"Was it?" She moves closer to me. "Because I'm pretty sure I kissed you back."

"That's not the point—"

"What *is* the point, Brady?" She asks, crossing her arms over her chest. "Because from where I'm standing, two consenting adults shared a kiss. Nothing wrong with that."

I shake my head. "You're here for work. I don't want to mess that up for you."

"You won't." She reaches out, her fingers brushing my forearm. "Look, I have a rule about not getting involved with clients. But since you're not technically paying me..."

My stomach drops. "I really shouldn't get massages from you anymore. It wouldn't be right."

"So you don't want massages either? Why not?"

"Because...of what happened. Because I obviously have a hard time controlling myself around you and I can't promise it won't happen again."

Her lips curve into a small smile. "I don't want you to promise that."

The words confuse me. "What?"

She huffs. "Sure, it wouldn't be right for you to give me a testimonial for the spa interview. That's not ethical. But there's no payment involved here, no professional conflict." She steps closer. "You were just starting to trust me, to let me *help* you. I don't want you to lose that progress because you're over-thinking this."

"I'm not overthinking—"

"You are." Her smile widens. "It's kind of adorable, actually."

I stare at her, stunned. "You're not upset?"

"About the kiss? Brady, that kiss was...*mind-blowing*. I can't stop thinking about it." Heat creeps up my neck as she continues. "I'm only upset that you ran away afterward."

"I didn't know what else to do."

"You don't give yourself enough credit. Next time, stick around and see what happens." Her fingers trace along my forearm, and I shiver.

She said 'next time.'

"So, do you want to skip today's session?" she asks. "Or can we be adults about this?"

I should probably say yes, skip it, and maintain some distance.

Instead, I hear myself asking, "What time?"

She grins. "Two o'clock?"

I nod, not trusting my voice.

∾

When I arrive at her cabin later, I'm not prepared for Imogen answering the door in tiny cutoff sweat shorts that show off her toned legs and a baby tank that barely covers her sweet breasts.

"Hi," she says, stepping aside to let me in, and I try not to stare at the way those shorts cling to her plump little ass. Or how the thin fabric of her top does nothing to hide her stiff nipples.

"H-hey." My voice comes out rougher than intended.

The room's set up as usual—massage table, soft lighting, the scent of eucalyptus in the air. But something feels different. Maybe it's how Imogen is eyeing me.

"Same routine," she says, as her eyes drag down my body slowly. "But leave the boxers off this time. Get comfortable."

Naked? I gulp.

I strip down and position myself face down on the table, pulling the sheet over my lower half.

"Ready," I manage to croak out.

I hear her enter the room, warming oil in her hands. She settles her palms on my shoulders and begins those long, flowing strokes across my back. I immediately let out a breath. Damn, how did I already miss this?

"You okay?" she asks.

"I'm confused," I admit. "About last night. About this."

"What's confusing about it?"

Her thumbs swirl around a knot near my shoulder blade, and I groan. "Everything. I don't know how to *do*—whatever this is."

"Maybe you don't have to *do* anything." Her hands work down my spine. "Maybe you just let it happen."

"That's not how I work. I like to have a plan."

She laughs softly. "How's that working out for you right now?"

Despite everything, I smile. "Point taken."

She moves over the familiar territory of my back and shoulders, but her touch feels different—slower, softer. Every stroke lingers, and she's using her nails over my skin, alighting my nerve-endings.

Oh god…

"Let's talk more about this fear of yours," she says.

"About what fear?"

"About you being afraid to take what you want."

I blink, trying to understand what she's saying. "I don't…"

She sweeps down to my legs. "You want something, but you're convinced you don't deserve it. Or that you're too old, too inexperienced, too whatever."

The words hit closer to home than I'd like. "Okay."

"You think your grandfather would want you to be hiding from life? That he'd want you to shy away from experiences… from people?"

"No," I say quietly. "He always said life was meant to be lived fully."

"Then maybe it's time you listened to him…and to your heart."

When she asks me to turn over, my heart hammers against my ribs. I flip onto my back, adjusting the sheet across my hips, and watch as she moves around the table.

Her nails skate over the sheet, dangerously close to my stiffening cock, and I gasp. "And you should definitely start listening to your body," she says, climbing up onto the table and straddling my hips.

"What are you—" I begin, but the words die as she settles her weight on top of me, the heat of her body pressing against mine through the sheet.

My cock goes rock hard under her instantly.

"Working on your chest," she says innocently, but there's

nothing innocent about the way she sinks down onto my groin, or the way her hands press against my pectorals.

"Imogen..."

"Just relax." Her fingers trace the lines of my tattoos, following the curves of dragons and waves across my chest.

Her touch is firm but teasing, working the muscles of my chest with slow, deliberate strokes. When her thumbs brush across my nipples, I gasp, my hips jerking.

"Sensitive," she murmurs, doing it again, and I bite back a groan.

"This isn't—" I swallow hard as she circles my nipples with her fingers then drags her nails over them. "*Fuck*....this isn't therapeutic massage." I'm writhing, it feels so good.

"No," she agrees, leaning down until her breath is hot against my ear. "It's not."

Before I can respond, she sits back and pulls her tank top over her head, revealing perfect, round breasts with dusky nipples.

My mouth waters.

"Touch me," she whispers, guiding my hands to her breasts.

They fill my palms like heaven, soft and warm, and when I brush my thumbs across her nipples, she arches into my touch with a soft moan that makes my trapped cock throb against her molten lava center.

"You're so beautiful," I breathe, stroking her sweet curves and velvety skin as she gasps.

She lifts up and I immediately miss her heat. She moves lower on the table, her hands sliding down my abs.

"Can I touch you here?" She trails a finger along my hips at the edge of the sheet, making my skin flutter.

"Yes, please…" I nod enthusiastically, and she pulls the sheet away, exposing me completely. My cock is already so hard and desperate.

She just stares for a moment, her lips parting.

"God, your cock is magnificent," she breathes, then wraps her oil-slicked hand around me.

"Holy shit," I gasp, my entire body jolting at the contact. Nothing—*nothing*—has ever felt like this.

"Wow," she purrs, her grip firm but gentle as she explores me. "I love how you react to my touch."

I have to get up onto my elbows to watch. Her thumb swipes across the swollen head, collecting the bead of moisture there, and my toes actually curl. A shudder racks my entire body as she spreads the slickness around the sensitive crown. My head goes back with a loud groan.

"Mmm, you like that," she whispers, her voice husky. "Leaking for me already."

"I won't last," I rasp, as she strokes down to the base, then back up, her fingers learning every ridge and vein.

"I'm aware," she replies, as she bites her lower lip.

She works me over with agonizing patience, my body riding a fine, maddening edge.

When she draws her fingers into a twist at the top, focusing on the spot just beneath the head, I buck.

"Oh Christ," I groan, my hands clawing at the vinyl table.

"That's the spot, isn't it?" She does it again, her smile wicked as she watches me fall apart. "Right here on your sensitive cock?"

Her other hand cups my balls, rolling them gently as she continues that electrifying twist of her oiled fingers. The sensation makes my vision blur.

"Imogen, I can't—" My voice breaks as she varies her rhythm, sometimes stroking slow and deep, sometimes quick and light across the head.

"Can't what, baby?" she teases, using both hands now—one working my shaft while the other focuses on the swollen tip.

"Can't handle how good this feels? Can't believe someone's touching you this way?"

She's destroying me. Every nerve ending is on fire, every muscle taut with pleasure I never knew existed.

"You're shaking," she observes with obvious delight. "Your whole body's trembling for me. I bet you never imagined it could feel like this."

She's right—I'm shaking like a leaf, my hips bucking helplessly into her touch as she works me with devastating prowess. When she leans down to kiss the tip, her lips glistening with my precum, I nearly black out.

"That's it," she murmurs, stroking me with slow, firm pressure. "Let it happen, Brady."

I groan. "I've never…been touched like this."

She presses a soft kiss to my lips. "I'm honored to be your first."

The tenderness in her voice, combined with the exquisite torture of her hand on my throbbing cock, has me ready to blow.

"I'm going to—" I start, then she circles her fingertip on that spot and I'm suddenly coming. "Fuck!" I shout, my release painting my stomach as pleasure crashes over me.

"Yes…feel it everywhere," she whispers, as she works me through it. I jerk and convulse, unable to control myself. But moreover, not wanting to control it.

When I can finally breathe again, I realize she's watching me with something like awe, her slick touch soothing me through the aftershocks.

"Watching you climax is so special." She grabs a wet cloth near the table, and begins cleaning me up with gentle care. "I can't wait to do that again..."

"Oh god…" I breathe, struggling for words.

I sit up, pulling her into my arms, and capture her mouth

in a kiss that's hungry and full of hope. She melts against me, her hands fisting in my hair as I devour her mouth.

I'm not done. Not even close. If this is happening—if she's giving me this gift—then I want to give her something in return.

"I want to taste you," I growl against her lips, maneuvering her so that she's now laying back on the table.

I kiss down her body, sucking on her sweet nipples, savoring the flavor of her skin, nipping at her stomach as she moans under me.

"Tell me if I do anything wrong," I rasp.

"You won't...but I understand," she says, tugging at my hair as I peel off her shorts. She's completely bare underneath, all smooth skin, soft curves, and delicate folds like petals of a flower.

I press wet kisses to her inner thighs, working my way higher. When I drag my tongue through her glistening pussy, she moans. She's a mix of tang and salty musk, and the sound she makes when my tongue rolls over her tender flesh makes my spent cock ache.

I explore her with my mouth, kissing, licking, and suckling, feeding off her gasps, and growling when she arches off the table.

"Yes, Brady, Oh god...yes," she pants, and I find the bundle of nerves that makes her whole body shudder.

I groan, working her with everything I have until she's trembling and chanting my name.

"You're going to make me come, baby," she breathes.

Those words are music to my ears.

"Yes," I rumble against her pussy, not stopping. She arches with a yell, her hips grinding upward, her release flooding my mouth.

I lap her up, feeling like I've conquered a redwood.

She pulls me up and I give her all of me in our kiss.

When he finally break apart, she's breathing hard, her eyes glazed with satisfaction.

"How…that was amazing. You didn't need my direction at all."

I smile, proud.

"I had a lot of years to study," I tease, and she laughs.

"Just wow." She traces one of my tattoos with her fingertip. "I have my interview tomorrow morning, but then I want to watch your climbing demo in the afternoon."

"Yeah?" …is all I can manage, as I lay there.

"Yeah." She presses a soft kiss to my lips. "I want to see you in action."

I arch a brow at her.

"A *different* kind of action," she clarifies, chuckling.

As I hold her against me, skin to skin, I'm content. Whole.

I'm experiencing life to the fullest.

And hell, I'm falling in love as I do it.

CHAPTER 7
IMOGEN

I practically float across camp toward the climbing demonstration area.

My interview this morning went even *better* than I'd hoped —the spa manager loved me, said the glowing reviews from the Timber Run staff had sealed the deal, and offered me the position on the spot.

I'll have to give them all a proper thank you.

But more importantly, I get to stay.

And build something here with Brady.

The thought of him makes my skin tingle with memories of last night...the way he kissed me and held me like I was the most precious thing in the world, the sounds he made when I took him apart with my hands, the reverent way he worshipped my body with his mouth.

I'm getting wet just thinking about it.

I find a spot near the demonstration platform where Brady's setting up his climbing gear. He's all business— checking his harness, testing his ropes, adjusting his helmet. But when he spots me in the crowd, his entire face lights up with a smile that makes my heart skip.

"Ladies and gentlemen," Connor's voice booms across the assembled group of guests, "prepare to witness Brady Tanaka, our resident high-rigger, show you why he's considered one of the best climbers in the business."

Brady scales the massive tree with fluid grace, his movements smooth and steady. I watch, mesmerized, as he navigates the branches with the confidence that comes with years of experience.

When he reaches a particularly challenging section near the top, he glances down to make sure I'm watching before attempting a complex maneuver that has the crowd gasping in appreciation.

He's clearly performing for me, taking more risks than necessary, climbing higher than usual.

Show-off.

That's when it happens.

His foot slips on a wet branch, and he catches himself awkwardly, his thigh slamming against a thick limb. Even from the ground, I know that *had* to hurt.

He's definitely favoring his left leg now.

By the time he rappels down, his jaw is tight with obvious pain and something else—embarrassment, frustration, maybe even shame, if I know him well enough.

"That was incredible!" one of the guests gushes as Brady unclips his harness. "How long have you been climbing?"

"Too long, apparently," he mutters, avoiding my eyes.

The crowd disperses, praising his skill, but I can see the way he's holding himself, the careful way he's moving. More concerning is the look on his face—like he's just confirmed his worst fears about himself.

"Brady," I approach him carefully. "Come to my cabin. Let me look at that thigh."

"I'm fine." His voice is clipped, distant. "Just need to ice it."

"You're not fine. You're hurt, and you're being stubborn about it."

He finally meets my eyes, and what I see there breaks my heart. "I'm forty-three years old, Imogen. I just nearly fell out of a tree because I was showing off for a woman young enough to be my—"

"Don't you start with that," I interrupt. "You slipped on a wet branch. It happens to climbers half your age."

"Does it?" His laugh is bitter. "Because right now it feels like my body's betraying me. Maybe I am too old to be taking these kinds of risks."

"Brady—"

"You should be with someone who doesn't need to prove he's still capable of doing his job."

I stare at him, anger and hurt warring in my chest. "Is that really what you think? That I care about you because of some misguided hero worship?"

He doesn't answer, just starts limping toward his cabin.

"Fine," I call after him. "But when you're done feeling sorry for yourself, I'll be in my cabin."

An hour later, I can't take it anymore. If Brady won't come to me, I'll go to him.

I march across camp to his cabin and knock firmly on the door. "Open up, Brady."

There's a few moments of silence then: "Please go away, Imogen."

"No way. I'm not called 'The Five-Foot-Three Menace' for nothing." I try the handle and find it unlocked. "I'm coming in."

His cabin is sparse but comfortable, all clean lines and rugged simplicity. Brady's sitting on the edge of his bed, in just boxers, pressing an ice pack to his thigh, his face a mask of stubborn misery.

"You shouldn't be here," he says without looking up.

"Too bad." I close the door behind me and go over to him. "Want to tell me what this is really about?"

"I told you. I'm too old for this. Too old for you."

"I'm not buying that." I sit down on the floor in front of him.

His jaw tightens, and he looks away from me. "Well yeah. I'm old, Imogen. Today proved it. I'll keep slowing down, aching more—"

I sigh. "Nope. There's more. Tell me."

He closes his eyes and takes a deep breath. "I don't know who I am if I'm not climbing. It's part of me. How can I give all of myself to you, when I'm losing everything I know."

"Hold up," I say, crawling over to him. "You're just getting older. You can still climb, you just need to take better care of yourself in order to do it. I have news for you. You're going to be climbing for decades."

"It doesn't feel like that right now."

"Hmm...well, maybe you should start getting more massages. From a very specific therapist, of course."

He smiles at that.

"But I think we need to focus on why you're so convinced you're not enough as you are that you're willing to throw away what we're building?"

He looks up at me then, his midnight blue eyes filled with pain. "Imogen, you're beautiful, successful, full of life. You could have—"

"I want you." The words come out fierce and uncompromising. "Not some theoretical perfect man, not someone younger or more reckless. You, Brady Tanaka. With your magnificent mind, your incredible skill, your gentle hands, and yes, your forty-three-year-old body that drives me absolutely insane with lust."

He stares at me like I'm speaking a foreign language.

I reach for the hem of my shirt and pull it over my head, watching his eyes widen.

"I see a man who's lived long enough to know exactly what he wants." My bra joins the shirt on the floor. "Who's patient enough to learn my body instead of just using it."

His breathing grows ragged as I continue undressing, my shorts and panties pooling at my feet.

"And I see someone who's smart enough to recognize love when it finds him." I stand naked before him, vulnerable but unashamed. "The question is, will you take it?"

For a long moment, he just stares at me, his expression cycling through disbelief, wonder, and something that looks like hope.

"Imogen," he breathes.

"Show me that you want this," I whisper. "That you want *me*."

Something breaks in his expression, and he surges to his feet, pulling me to him as he kisses me with wild hunger. I taste his fear and his longing, his doubt and his desire, and I pour everything I have into kissing him back to show him I'm not going anywhere.

"I love you," he gasps against my lips. "Christ, I love you so much it makes me crazy…in good and bad ways, as you've witnessed."

"I love you too." I start pushing down his boxers, needing to feel skin against skin. "So stop being scared and let me love you properly."

When he's naked, I push him gently back onto the bed, mindful of his injured thigh.

"I need you," I murmur, straddling his hips carefully. "All of you."

I start with his thigh, my hands gentle as I massage around

the area. He hisses at first, then relaxes as my touch eases the tension.

"Better?" I ask.

"Everything's better when you touch me," he admits, his voice rough with emotion.

I lean down to kiss him, slow and deep, as my hands continue their exploration. He's already hard beneath me, his cock hot and thick against my belly.

"I want to feel every inch of you inside me," I whisper against his lips.

His hands stroke up my back, fingers tracing the curve of my spine. "I don't have any—I mean, I'm not prepared for—"

"I'm on birth control," I assure him, then smile.

"You have to tell me what to do," he says.

"Just...love me, baby." I rise up on my knees, positioning myself over him, and slowly sink down onto his thick length. We both groan at the sensation—he's big, and thick, filling me completely.

"Jesus," he breathes, his hands gripping my hips as I take him deeper. "You feel spectacular."

"So do you."

His first thrust is clumsy, all nervous strength. So I adjust the angle and start moving, rolling my hips in slow circles that have him panting beneath me. "God, Brady, I could come at any moment you feel so good inside me."

His responses are pure instinct...the way his hips buck up to meet mine, the sounds he makes when I clench around him, the adoring way he touches every inch of skin he can reach.

"I've never felt anything like this," he gasps as I pick up the pace, riding him with increasing urgency.

"Neither have I," I admit, because it's true. Sex has never felt this right, this perfect.

When I feel my climax building, I lean forward, bracing my

hands on his chest as I move faster. The new angle has him hitting that delicious spot inside me with every thrust.

His rhythm steadies as his confidence builds—deep, aching rocking movements that have me on edge.

"Come with me," I plead, feeling my body coiling tight. "I want to feel you come inside me."

That breaks his control completely. His hands grip my hips, helping me move as we chase our release together.

My orgasm hits me, white-hot and endless. "Brady!" I cry out.

"My god, Imogen," He follows immediately, his body arching beneath mine as he pumps me full of liquid heat.

We collapse together, breathing hard, hearts racing.

"Imogen..." he starts, then trails off, trying to find the words. "You make me better in so many ways."

"You're perfect the way you are. I fell in love with the man you are right now," I finish, pressing a soft kiss to his chest. "Even the part that's a stubborn ass sometimes."

He laughs, holding me close while his fingers scratch patterns on my back.

"I got the job," I tell him eventually.

His hand stills. "The spa position?"

"Mm-hmm. I start next month." I lift my head to look at him. "You okay with me staying?"

The smile that spreads across his face is adorable. "I want you to stay more than I've ever wanted anything."

"Good." I settle back against his chest, content. "Because I'm not going anywhere."

"Even when I'm an old man who falls out of trees?"

"You won't be falling out of trees, so hush." I chuckle and trace one of his tattoos with my fingertip. "Your grandfather was right, you know. About the body telling stories."

"Yeah?"

"Yours tells the story of a man who's dedicated to a full life, loving deeply, and creating new chapters." I press a kiss over his heart. "And I want to be part of those new chapters."

His arms tighten around me. "All of them?"

"All of them," I confirm. "Starting right now."

As the afternoon light fades outside his window, we make love again—slower this time, savoring every touch, every kiss, every whispered endearment.

And when we're finally spent, wrapped around each other, I know I've found something special with this lumbersnack.

Not just great sex or professional fulfillment, but a true partnership. The kind where two people complement each other's strengths and shore up each other's weaknesses. The kind where age becomes an asset rather than an obstacle, where experience trumps youth, and where love grows deeper with understanding.

Brady's breathing evens out as he drifts toward sleep, and I smile against his chest.

Tomorrow I'll start planning my move to Montana.

But tonight, I'm exactly where I'm supposed to be…in the arms of a man who's finally learned that aging doesn't mean losing anything.

It means gaining the wisdom to recognize when the best things in life climb right into your lap.

EPILOGUE - BRADY

SIX MONTHS LATER

I 'm standing in the kitchen of our cabin watching Imogen make coffee in nothing but one of my flannel shirts...and I'm positive this is what happiness looks like.

The shirt barely covers her ass, and every time she reaches for something in the upper cabinets, I get a glimpse of pink lace panties that makes my mouth water. She's humming some pop song under her breath, completely unaware that she's giving me the best show on earth.

"Stop staring at my butt and help me with this breakfast," she says without turning around.

"How did you—?"

"Because you're *always* staring at my butt. Not that I'm complaining." She glances over her shoulder with a wicked grin. "But I need you to flip the pancakes before they burn."

I move behind her, pressing myself against her back as I reach around to handle the spatula. She melts into me with a soft sigh, and I can't resist nuzzling her neck.

"Brady," she warns, but there's no heat in it.

"What? I'm flipping pancakes."

"You're also getting me all worked up before breakfast."

"Good." I bite gently at the spot where her neck meets her shoulder, and she shivers. "I like you worked up."

She turns in my arms, her hands sliding up my bare chest. "Keep that up and these pancakes are going to burn while I climb you like a tree."

"I'm okay with that."

She laughs and pushes me away. "Food first. *Then* climbing."

Six months of living with Imogen, and I'm still amazed that this is my life—that this incredible, young, sexy woman chose me. That every morning I wake up next to her and every night I fall asleep with her curled against my body.

The transition wasn't seamless. Her moving into my cabin, learning each other's habits, figuring out how to share space; it all took adjustment. But the foundation we built during that first week at camp has only gotten stronger.

"I have news," she says, as she settles onto my lap at our small kitchen table.

"Good news or bad news?"

"Good news."

I take a bite of my pancakes.

"The spa's been so successful that they want me to hire three more therapists. And because I've done such a great job bringing in business from the camp, they're giving me a raise."

Pride swells in my chest. "That's awesome, babe. You deserve it."

"I know, right?" Her smile is brilliant. "It seems like just yesterday I was a freelancer without steady income or any kind of benefits, and now I'm building something real."

"You've always been building something real. Now you just have the recognition you deserve."

She kisses me softly, and it tastes like maple syrup and coffee . "I love how you see me."

"I love everything about you."

It's true. Even the things that drive me crazy—like how she leaves wet towels on the bathroom floor, or how she steals the covers every single night—I adore because they're part of her.

"What are you thinking about?" she asks, studying my face with those perceptive eyes.

"Just...this. Us. How different everything is now."

"Different how?"

I consider how to put it into words. "Before you, I thought my life was shrinking. Getting smaller as I got older. But now..." I shrug. "Everything feels bigger. Like there are more possibilities instead of fewer."

Her expression softens. "That's the sweetest thing you've ever said to me."

"I was just...existing. Going through the motions. Now I feel like I'm actually *living* my life."

She slides her arms around my neck. "You were living before. You just needed someone to remind you that life doesn't end at forty-three, you silly man."

"Little did I know it actually gets better."

She smiles up at me, like I'm serenading her with my words. Me. The quiet one.

We finish breakfast and get ready for the day. Imogen has appointments at the spa, and I've got a climbing demo for a group of outdoor education instructors. But before we leave, she corners me in the bathroom while I'm brushing my teeth.

"I've been thinking about something," she says, leaning against the doorframe.

"Mm?" I rinse and spit, then turn to face her.

"The future. Our future."

My stomach clenches. "What about it?"

"We've never really talked about what we want long-term. Besides the obvious staying together forever part."

I dry my hands slowly. "What do you want to talk about?"

"Kids."

"Kids," I repeat, blinking.

She swallows. "I know you're older, and maybe you think you've missed that window, but—"

"I want kids," I interrupt, the words rushing out before I can second-guess them. "With you. I want *everything*."

Her face lights up like the sunrise. "Really?"

"Really. I've been thinking about it too. What it would be like to have a little girl with your feisty attitude or a little boy with your stubborn streak."

"Me?" She swats my arm. "You're the stubborn one."

"Babe, you once spent three hours trying to work a knot out of my shoulder because you refused to admit it might need a different approach."

"That's persistence, not stubbornness."

"Same thing." I grin.

She laughs and launches herself into my arms. I catch her easily, spinning her around our small bathroom.

"So we're doing this?" she asks when I set her down. "The whole domestic bliss, babies, mini-van thing?"

I shake my head. "I draw the line at mini-vans."

"Fine. But I want the rest of it. With you."

"Even when I'm fifty and you're thirty-four?"

"Especially then. You'll be even sexier and so distinguished, and I'll be in my prime. Perfect combo."

I kiss her hard, pouring all my love into it. "I love you," I murmur against her lips.

"I love you too."

Later that afternoon, I run into Teagan at the main office while she's juggling Jamie and what looks like three different phone calls.

"Brady!" She hangs up and shifts Jamie to her other hip. "Perfect timing. I need someone to tell me I'm not insane."

"What's going on?"

"My sister Opal is flying to Vegas this weekend for some architecture conference, right? And Rourke's there too for his friend's bachelor party."

I nod, waiting for the punch line.

"Same weekend. Same city. And..." She gestures vaguely. "You know how they are."

I think about party-loving, chaos-creating Rourke and quirky, up-for-anything Opal. "Yeah, I can see how that might be interesting."

"Interesting is one word for it. I'm half-worried they'll either become best friends or burn down the entire Strip."

"My money's on both."

Teagan laughs. "That's exactly what Connor said. I guess we'll find out Monday when they both get back."

I grin, thinking about the potential for disaster. "Vegas won't know what hit it."

When I get home that evening, Imogen's already there, curled up on our couch with a book and a glass of wine. She looks up when I walk in, her smile bright.

"How was your day?" she asks, marking her place and setting the book aside.

"Good. Yours?"

"Exhausting but satisfying. I worked out some serious knots in a software developer's neck. Poor guy spends twelve hours a day hunched over a computer."

I settle beside her, pulling her feet into my lap. "Well, I'm sure he'll be back. You are magic at working out knots."

"Flattery will get you everywhere." But she melts when I start massaging her feet. "Mmm, *that* will get you anything you want, too."

"Anything, huh?"

"You heard me." She chuckles, then lets out a sigh.

I reach into my pocket and pull out the small velvet box I've been carrying around for a week, waiting for the right moment.

Imogen's eyes go wide as she spots it, her wine glass slamming down hard on the coffee table. "Brady...what is that?"

"I know we just talked about kids this morning, but—"

She launches herself at me before I can finish the sentence, knocking us both sideways on the couch. "Yes!"

"I haven't asked you anything yet."

"I don't care. Yes to whatever you're about to ask."

I laugh, rolling us so she's beneath me. "Imogen Navarro, will you marry me and put up with all my silliness and stubborn streaks for the rest of our lives?"

"Only if you promise to keep climbing trees and letting me massage your sexy body until we're both too old to care about anything except each other."

I bark out a laugh. "Deal."

I slip the ring onto her finger—a simple solitaire that catches the light like a captured firefly.

She stares at it for a long moment, then looks up at me with tears in her eyes.

"I love it so much."

"I'm so happy."

"Me too," she says, pulling me down for a kiss that I'll remember forever.

"So," I say, as we come up for air. "When can we start working on those babies?"

"How about right now?" she replies, getting up from the couch.

I laugh, and stand with her. "I love your work ethic."

I squat down so she can climb up on my back and then I carry her to the bedroom.

And as I make love to my fiancée that night—this little pink menace who saw past my fears and convinced me that the best chapters of my life were still being written—I think about how wrong I was six months ago.

Getting older isn't about losing yourself.

It's about having the confidence and the courage to reach for what you want.

And if this is what forty-three looks like, I can't wait to see what fifty has in store.

∼

LOG IT LIKE IT'S HOT

CHAPTER 1
OPAL

The first thing I register when I wake up is that my head feels like a construction site...complete with jackhammers, bulldozers, and buzzsaws.

The second thing? A man-shaped lump is snoring on the other corner of the bed.

My eyes snap up to a ceiling fan spinning lazily, its blades carving the sunrise into fractured stripes. I don't remember ceiling fans. Or velvet drapes the color of a bruised plum.

"Oh no," I croak, throat raw. This isn't my hotel room! "*No no no—*"

I jerk upright, and the world tilts violently.

My head protests with a stab of nausea, as I glance at my hand. There's a ring on my wedding finger. A chunky silver band with Celtic knots that glint mockingly in the harsh Vegas sun.

My clothes are still on, *thank Christ*, but the Greenbuild Conference badge clipped to my shirt stares back at me.

OPAL KENT, KEYNOTE SPEAKER screams the lanyard, now tangled with a gauzy white veil knotted in my bird's nest of hair.

The ring wasn't there yesterday afternoon. Which means it was probably put there sometime after the Elvis officiant started singing "Love Me Tender."

Oh God.

The man sprawled across the king-sized bed is face-down in a pillow, one muscled arm hanging off the edge. His hair is copper under the sunlight, and even asleep, he radiates the kind of rugged confidence that I'm sure gets him in trouble on a regular basis. His contoured back is bare, revealing a landscape of tattoos with freckles in between, across broad shoulders. The sheet is tangled around his waist, but miraculously he's still in his jeans.

I *know* this man.

Rourke Fogerty. The log-rolling expert from my sister Teagan's lumberjack camp with the Irish accent and a grin that melts your panties right off. The one who's been flirting with every female guest for the past three years, according to Teagan's exasperated updates.

And apparently, if the matching silver band now visible on his left hand is any indication…*my husband.*

"Holy shit," I whisper, my voice sounding like I've been gargling gravel.

Rourke stirs at the sound. He groans as he turns his head toward me, his beard a glorious mess of auburn, gold, and a hint of gray. When his eyes open—green as the Irish countryside, naturally—they focus on me with the same dawning horror as mine.

"Please tell me, lass," he says, his accent thick and rough, "that you're just a very vivid dream brought on by too much tequila and whiskey."

"Sorry to disappoint," I croak, holding up my left hand to show him the ring. "But I think we have bigger problems."

He squints, then looks at his own hand. The color drains from his face, which is impressive considering he already looks like death warmed over.

"Jesus, Mary, and Joseph," he breathes, running a hand through his hair. "We couldn't have..."

"I'm afraid we did." I spot my purse on the nightstand and reach for it, ignoring the way the movement makes my stomach lurch.

My phone has seventeen missed calls from Teagan, but more importantly, tucked into a side pocket is a piece of paper that confirms my worst fears.

"Certificate of Marriage," I read aloud. "Issued by the Little Chapel of Everlasting Love."

Rourke's head falls back into the pillow. "This is exactly the kind of shit Teagan lectures me about avoiding."

Wait. "Teagan lectures *you* about avoiding this crap? She lectures *me* about creating it."

"Aye, well." He looks up, and despite everything, he grins. "Takes one to know one, I suppose."

The Greenbuild International architecture conference ended yesterday with a celebration lunch. I'd been the hit of the weekend—my presentation on sustainable resort design had gone over so well that three different companies wanted to hire me on the spot. I was feeling invincible, celebrating with an enthusiasm that would make Teagan roll her eyes and my brother-in-law, Connor, shake his head.

Then there was the bachelor party. A group of guys had crashed our event when we moved out to the hotel bar, and I recognized their leader—tall, charming, with an accent that scrambled my insides—from Timber Run.

Small world.

Flashes erupt in my head like firecrackers.

Rourke leaning across the bartop, rolling a lime wedge between his fingers like a dare. "You drink like you design buildings, lass—all flair and no foundation."

Me slamming back my fourth shot, the room spinning in a kaleidoscope of conference badges and bachelor party beer steins. "Says the man in a feather boa. I bet I can outlast you."

His grin, sharp and delighted. "Careful, architect. I'm Irish, the closest to a professional you can get."

The clink of glasses.

"Your friend's bachelor party," I say to him slowly. "You bet me I couldn't out-drink an Irishman."

He snorts "And then you proved it by putting away half the bar and still being coherent enough to suggest we find somewhere 'more festive.'"

My head throbs. "Jesus…"

"We hit the town. I remember riding a mechanical bull, winning at roulette, and volunteering at a magic show." He chuckles. "I proposed in front of a crowd after you sang "Luck Be a Lady" at a karaoke club better than Frank Sinatra."

My face heats up. I barely remember any of this. Just moments. Happy moments… but… "We found the rings and this," I yank the veil from my hair, "at a pawn shop."

Rourke nods. "Then it was off to the wedding chapel."

The chapel. I remember the neon signs, the plastic flowers, the way Rourke had looked at me when the Elvis impersonator asked if we were sure we wanted to do this. There had been something in his eyes, not just alcohol and attraction, but something I'd never seen before in a man's eyes. Something that made me say yes instead of laughing it off.

"We were completely plastered," I say, suddenly disappointed that I don't remember our kiss.

"Aye," he agrees, but there's something careful in his voice. "Completely pissed."

Getting drunk and marrying someone I barely know in Vegas is excellent evidence for my sister's treatise on "Opal makes terrible decisions."

At least Rourke isn't a *total* stranger. I've met him a couple of times at the camp. And I've been hearing about him for a while now. How he makes the guests laugh during log-rolling lessons. How he playfully banters with Ewan, the Scottish sawyer, at Heritage Nights. How he's always been the life of every party.

"We should figure out how to fix this," I say.

"Right," he confirms, nodding. "Should be simple enough, considering..."

He doesn't finish the sentence, but he doesn't need to. I swear this is the kind of mistake that only happens in romantic comedies, not to real people. Right?

"We just need to keep it quiet until we can get it sorted out." I try to ignore the twist in my stomach. "No need for anyone to know we screwed up this badly. Especially my sister."

"Agreed." He's already reaching for his phone. "The crew would never let me live it down. Shite, I'm supposed to be the fun one, not the—"

"Disaster?" I suggest helpfully, and he lets out a laugh that's only slightly strained.

"Isn't that usually you?"

"Hey!" I protest, then wince because talking loudly makes my head pound. "I prefer *spontaneous*."

"Is that what we're calling it?" But he's smiling now, and I'm reminded of why the female population swoons over him. It's not just the accent or the muscles...or the height—though those don't hurt at all. It's the way he focuses all his attention on you, even when you're discussing what a terrible mistake you've both made.

"Look," I say, forcing myself to be practical. "We're going back to Timber Run anyway. I have a week before I head back to London. We can figure out the legal stuff together once we're there."

"Right. Together."

There's something odd in his green eyes that makes my pulse quicken despite my aching head.

"I should go back to my own hotel," I say, more to break the tension than because I'm in any hurry to move. "I need to shower and pack."

"Aye, wait a second and I'll get you a cab." He sits up and stretches, and I watch as those decadent abs flex and bunch. I have to tear my gaze away before I do something even more impulsive than marrying him.

"I'll be fine," I say, my mouth watering. I grab my purse and stand carefully, gaining my balance.

"Are you sure? I don't want you meeting another man on the way and having two marriages to annul."

My mouth drops open, then my eyes narrow. "You're funny."

"Just playin', Opal." He laughs. "Come on, let me walk you down to the lobby."

I shake my head, and instantly regret the motion. "No, please. I'd like to be alone for a little while."

He gets up and studies me, tilting his head. Or maybe that's still my hangover. "I'm assuming we're on the same flight to Bozeman at twelve-thirty. How about I have my cab swing by your hotel and pick you up at..." he glances at his phone... "Eleven?"

I nod. "Yes, that'll work. Thank you."

He smiles.

And as I walk out of the room, I try to convince myself that this is just a crazy story I'll tell at parties someday. It's just a wild weekend in Vegas that doesn't mean anything beyond a temporary lapse in judgment.

The problem is, I've never been very good at convincing myself of things I'm not one hundred percent sure of.

CHAPTER 2
ROURKE

I'm Irish. We're known for being able to handle our liquor. It's practically written into our genetic code, passed down through generations of pub philosophers and hard-working fellows alike.

So waking up married to the gorgeous woman I've been crushing on for years now should feel like a victory, not a mistake.

But *she* thinks it's a mistake.

So I feel like I've been kicked by an arse and then trampled by the rest of the herd.

I'm standing outside her hotel with a cab idling behind me, fighting the urge to pace. When she emerges from the lobby, she's made an attempt at pulling herself together, but it's distinctly Opal-style. Her wild curls are twisted into a messy bun, and she's wearing worn paint-splattered jeans and a vintage *Clash* T-shirt under an oversized cardigan.

The only sign of our Vegas adventure is the way she's gripping her coffee cup like it's keeping her upright. And maybe a few specks of glitter on her face.

"Morning, Mrs. Fogerty," I say with a grin, taking her bag before she can protest.

She shoots me a look that could melt steel. "Don't you dare start with that."

"Just trying to lighten the mood." I open the cab door for her, catching a whiff of her subtle flowery-sweet perfume as she slides past me. "We're going to be stuck on a plane together for three hours. Might as well make the best of it."

By the time we're through security, she's gone three shades paler and is swaying slightly on her feet.

"When's the last time you ate something?" I ask, steadying her with a hand on her elbow.

"I don't remember." She closes her eyes.

I recall more than I'm willing to admit. The way her laugh made every other sound in that karaoke bar fade to background noise. I remember how her body felt pressed against mine when we were dancing, all soft curves and fiery energy.

And I remember the exact moment when joking about getting married stopped being a joke...how she stared at me right before we kissed at the altar—like she was seeing something in me that I could no longer hide.

I buy her a breakfast sandwich and a ginger ale, watching as she picks at the food. When she finally takes a real bite, some of the color returns to her cheeks.

"Better?" I ask.

"Marginally less like death." She takes another bite, then studies me curiously. "You're being very..."

"Very what?"

"Considerate. I wasn't expecting that."

For some reason that stings more than it should.

"Maybe I'm full of surprises," I say lightly.

"That's what I'm afraid of," she mutters.

On the flight we strategize about our story.

"Different hotels, different parts of the strip," I say. "Never crossed paths until the airport this morning when we happened to be on the same flight."

"Exactly. Pure coincidence that we ended up traveling together." She plunks her chin into her hand on the middle arm rest between us. "Think Teagan and the rest of the camp crew will buy it?"

"Why wouldn't they?"

"Yeah." She doesn't sound entirely convinced. "What if they ask about why we both look like we've been through a blender?"

"Vegas does that to people," I say with a grin. "Specifically. Us."

"Speak for yourself. I was completely professional the entire time." But she's near laughing as she says it, and I catch a glimpse of the woman who put half the bars in the entire city under the table last night.

Feck, this woman...

I've spent countless nights lying awake thinking about her since the first time we met the summer the camp opened—her sexy smile, her wild creativity, the way she makes everything around her more...everything. The *only* reason I never made a move was because she's Teagan's older sister, and I didn't want to mess up the close-knit friendship I have with her and Connor. They're the only family I've got.

Plus, I'm not exactly relationship material. I've never been good at that stuff.

I'm Mr. Right Now, not Mr. Forever.

And Opal deserves forever.

Connor's waiting at baggage claim with three-year-old Jamie bouncing at his side.

"Well, well," he says, pulling me into a one-armed hug. "Look what Vegas dragged in. You look like s-h-i-t, man," he says, spelling it out to make sure Jamie doesn't understand the word.

"Aye, thanks," I say, scratching at my beard. "I appreciate the ride."

"Had to be here anyway for this one." He gestures toward Opal.

"Uncle Roke!" Jamie interrupts, hugging my leg. He can't seem to say my name quite yet, so 'Roke' it is.

I ruffle his light hair. "Hey, laddie. You miss me?"

"Yeah!" he says, smiling up at me.

"Hi Connor." Opal kisses Connor's cheek, then immediately crouches down to Jamie's level. "Oh my God, you've gotten so tall, sweetie! What's that you've got there?"

Jamie holds up a small toy truck, chattering excitedly. "Auntie Opal! I got a new truck and Daddy says we're gonna build roads for it at camp and Mama said you were coming to visit!"

"Did she now?" Opal grins, and I watch as she gets completely absorbed in him, asking serious questions about the truck's capabilities and nodding at his explanations.

And I'm standing there like a fool, watching her with my best friend's kid trying not to think about how she'd be with our kids one day.

Christ. *Where did that come from?* This whole situation is messing with my head.

"Teagan's in the car," Connor says. "She's not feeling well today."

"That sucks. But I know how she feels," Opal replies, standing up. "I feel like I've been hit by a truck."

Connor glances at us, his expression unreadable, as he swings Jamie up into his arms to walk.

"Ditto," I say weakly.

At the car, we pile in as Connor straps Jamie into his car seat. Teagan turns to look at Opal from the front.

"Honey, you look as terrible as I feel." Then she juts her chin toward me. "You too."

"I'm fine," Opal says. "Just a little too much fun in Sin City."

"Uncle Roke and Auntie Opal both have glitter on them!" Jamie announces excitedly.

Opal and I exchange a look. Hush kid!

I'm crammed into the back seat of Connor's truck next to Opal, closer than we were on the plane. She's telling Teagan about her conference presentation, all animated and brilliant, and I find myself hanging on every word.

This is the Opal I remember from her previous visits— passionate about her work, quick-witted, completely unafraid to take up space. But there's something different now. A new confidence, maybe, or just the way she keeps smiling my way.

Which I don't mind one bit.

When we finally pull through the camp gates, she falls silent. I'm sure she's taking in the changes since her last visit. It all looks more established, more permanent.

"Wow," she breathes. "The camp is really transforming."

"Connor and Teagan have big plans," I say. "Always expanding, always improving."

"What about you?" she asks, turning to face me. "What are your big plans?"

It's an innocent question, but something in her tone makes it feel loaded.

I shrug. "I take things as they come." Which is the truth, but sounds more like a cop out.

The crew descends on us the moment we get out of the truck. Everyone wants to say hello to Opal, to hear about her trip, catch up. And she throws herself into it with the same energy she brings to everything else, charming everyone within thirty seconds and making them all feel like they're her favorite person in the world.

Connor calls everyone together for an impromptu welcome dinner. Which means I'm about to spend the next several hours trying to act normal while my wife—*Christ, my wife!*—sits across from me and pretends nothing's changed.

It's going to be a long night.

Dinner is held in the main lodge, everyone gathered around the long pine table that Connor built himself. Teagan's made her famous chili, and there's fresh bread from the local bakery, and enough beer to float a boat. It should be relaxing, familial, the kind of evening I usually love.

Instead, I'm on edge.

Opal's sitting between Teagan and Sky, telling stories about London and making everyone laugh with her descriptions of pretentious clients. Her hands move constantly as she talks, painting pictures in the air, and I'm mesmerized by the graceful dance of her fingers.

The same fingers that wore my ring this morning.

Why can't I get that outta my feckin' head?

Jamie tugs at her sleeve. "Aunt Opal! Build the napkin castle again!"

"Your wish, my command!" She snatches every linen in reach, folding towers like it's second nature. "This," she declares, planting a fork banner atop the highest turret, "is where the soup dragon lives. He guards the mashed potato moat."

Jamie's eyes go saucer-wide. "But what about the pea knights?"

"Obviously, they're staging a coup. *But*—" She drops her voice, dramatically. "The broccoli trees have *allies*."

The kid's enraptured. Hell, *I'm* enraptured. My chest does this daft tightening thing.

Then I notice Connor watching me watch her.

Shite.

"Any new projects on the horizon?" Ewan asks when Opal has successfully led the troops into battle for Jamie to proceed.

"Actually," Opal says, glancing quickly at me before looking away, "I'm not sure what's next. My lease in London is up soon, and I've got options."

The words are carefully neutral, very unlike her.

"Really?" Teagan's voice is controlled, but I can see the hope in her eyes. "What kind of options?"

Opal shrugs, suddenly fascinated by her beer bottle. "I got a lot of offers after my presentation. Just...keeping my mind open to possibilities, you know? Sometimes you need to be willing to change course."

Her eyes flick to mine again, and this time she doesn't look away.

"Well," Connor says, raising his beer, "to keeping your options open."

Everyone drinks to that, but I barely taste the beer. I'm too busy trying to figure out what's going on behind those pretty eyes of hers.

After dinner, people start drifting away. Teagan and Connor take Jamie home to their cabin. Graham and Sky follow. Ewan heads to his cabin to video call his wife, Hazel, who's still in Boston wrapping up some consulting project. Brady and Imogen walk off hand in hand, talking quietly about their wedding plans. Opal heads to her guest cabin to get settled.

I should go get some sleep, maybe work on figuring out how to approach the annulment process. Instead, I grab my guitar and sit at the fire pit, tuning the strings by feel and start picking out a melody my da used to play...something old and Irish and melancholy.

The music helps sooth the restless in my chest. This is what I do when I can't sleep, when my thoughts are tangled up like fishing line—I play until everything makes sense again.

Tonight, though, the playing just makes me think about Opal more.

I'm so lost in the music that I don't hear anyone approaching.

"You play it slower than Nan used to."

I look up to find Opal standing at the edge of the firelight, wearing an oversized sweater and leggings that hug her curves in such sinful ways that I'll be thinking about her long into the night. Her hair's down now, wild and beautiful in the light, like copper sparks.

"Nan?" I keep playing, but my fingers stumble slightly on the next chord.

"My grandmother used to sing it every Sunday." She steps closer, close enough that I can smell her perfume again. "Nan MacBride."

"Aye, MacBride's a good Irish name," I say, finding my rhythm again. "She teach you the words?"

"Some of them." Opal sits down on the log bench next to me. "I probably don't remember them right."

"Give it a try."

She's quiet for a moment, listening to the melody, then starts to sing. Her Irish is rusty, but the Gaelic pronunciation is good enough that I can tell she learned it young. And her voice...god, her voice is gorgeous. Clear and sweet with just enough roughness around the edges to make it interesting— just like everything about her.

I sing along, filling in the spaces between verses. Just our voices and my guitar and the crackling fire painting us in shades of gold.

When the song ends, the air feels different somehow.

"Beautiful, Opal," I say finally. "I can see why I proposed right after you sang karaoke."

She laughs, and gives me a shove, her cheeks flushing. "Stop it." She smiles, and it's different from her earlier smiles—softer, more real.

"These songs keep me connected to my Irish roots."

"You miss it? Ireland?" she asks.

"I miss my ma and da, but they died long ago. The rest isn't as important." I tap my chest. "Everything's still in here."

"Nan used to tell me that home wasn't about the place, but about the people who made you feel like you belonged."

I nod, understanding more than she probably realizes.

"Let's work on that annulment tomorrow," she says quietly, and something catches in her voice.

I glance up sharply, wishing I could hold her when she sounds so vulnerable like that. Tell her it'll be alright.

She leans forward, bringing us closer.

The fire pops, sending sparks spiraling up into the dark sky, and I can see her freckles and the sparkle of Vegas glitter that lingers. She puts a hand on my knee and I hold back a gasp.

"Opal," I whisper.

And then footsteps crunch on the gravel behind us.

We spring apart like we've been doing something unsavory, just as Connor's flashlight beam cuts through the dark and he appears in the circle of firelight.

"Sorry," he says, but there's an odd glint in his eyes. "Just doing my evening rounds. Making sure the…fire's safe."

"Safety first," I manage, my voice rougher than I'd like. Jerk.

"Everything okay?" he asks.

"Peachy," I rasp, guitar twanging as I fumble it. "Singin' and stargazin' is all."

Connor nods. "You two have a good night. Don't stay up too late."

He disappears back into the darkness, leaving us there alone.

"I should really go," Opal says, standing up.

"Yeah," I agree.

She takes a shaky breath. "Good night, Rourke."

"Good night, lass."

She walks quickly toward the guest cabins without looking back and I watch until she's gone, strumming a few chords on my guitar.

What would've happened if Connor hadn't interrupted?

Damn, I've got a problem.

But the problem isn't wanting her. Hell, I've wanted her since the first time she careened into camp like someone had just shaken a bottle of champagne and watched it explode.

My problem's the *aching* want, the kind that doesn't fade with the sunrise.

The kind that makes a man reckless. The kind that makes forever sound less like a trap and more like a future.

CHAPTER 3
OPAL

"So then the client says, 'But can we make it more...*architectural*?'" I wave my hands dramatically as Sky and Imogen laugh at my impression. "I mean, what does that even *mean*? It's already a building!"

I've been like this all morning—talking too much, flitting between different groups at the camp like a hummingbird on espresso. It's a nervous habit when I get anxious, words spilling out of me like I'm a broken faucet.

All to avoid Rourke.

Which is ridiculous because he's impossible not to notice. His booming laugh carries across the grounds, and I hear his accent thicken when he's explaining something he's passionate about, and those big, brawny shoulders...

Heaven help me.

"Earth to Opal," Sky waves a hand in front of my face. "You were telling us about the Dubai project?"

"Right, sorry." I drag my attention back to the conversation, but not before I catch Rourke watching me from across the yard.

The bastard actually winks at me.

My stomach does a back flip.

And suddenly there he is, materializing beside our picnic table like he's been summoned by my wayward thoughts. "Ladies, sorry to interrupt. Opal, Connor was wondering if you had a moment to look at the site on the west ridge? Something about future cabin placement."

Huh? Connor didn't mention anything to me before. But it's not like I've been paying close attention to anything else except the flannel-clad flirt in front of me.

"Um, okay." I stand up, nearly knocking over my mug. "I'll catch you both later," I say to the girls.

As soon as we're out of earshot, I hiss, "Does Connor really want to see me?"

Rourke grins, and scratches his beard. "Not at the moment. But it's a good excuse to talk about...*you know*." He taps his left ring finger. "The annulment."

I figured. "Good thinking." I glance around, paranoid that someone might overhear us. "Where should we go?"

"How about the log rolling pond? We don't have anything scheduled there today."

"All right then."

We walk side by side, careful not to touch.

The log rolling pond is tucked behind a stand of pines, out of sight from the main camp. It's really just a small, partially man-made pool with several massive logs floating in it, tethered so they rotate in place rather than drifting.

I take a seat on a bench at the edge of the water. Rourke sits beside me, leaving a few inches between us. "I did some research last night," he starts. "Nevada has a pretty straightforward process. We'd need to file a joint petition citing that we were, well..."

"Completely trashed?"

"I was going to say 'impaired,' but aye, trashed works too."
His smile makes the corners of his green eyes crinkle.

"So we just file the paperwork, and that's it?"

"I'll text you the link to the application. But essentially, yes,
that's all there is to it."

I nod, a strange twinge of disappointment in my chest.
"Great. That's...great."

We sit in the awkwardness for a moment, and I gaze out at
the pond, listening to the gentle lapping of water.

"Wanna try it?" Rourke asks suddenly.

"Try what?" I jump at the question, my eyes wide. He
couldn't possibly mean staying married?

He chuckles. "Log rolling."

"Oh!" I let out a choppy breath, as I look at the logs floating
in the water. "Is it difficult?"

"For some. Not for me." There's a challenge in his voice that
pricks at my competitive side.

"Are you suggesting I couldn't do it?"

"I'm suggesting," he says with a slow grin, "that maybe we
get you a little wet."

Oh my...

Before I can formulate words, he's pulling his T-shirt over
his head, revealing that brawny body that should come with
hazard lights. I can't get enough of those tattoos that sweep
across his chest and down his arms—Celtic knots intertwined
with natural elements, all flowing across the landscape of thick
muscle.

"Coming?" He's already stepping out of his boots, and slipping on aqua socks from a chest near the water.

"I'm not dressed for swimming," I protest weakly. "Clothes
optional?" I joke.

His eyes darken. "Only if you're lookin' to consummate our marriage."

The air goes thick and I'm suddenly burning up.

He reaches into the chest and lobs a wadded towel at my face. "You're wearing shorts, a T-shirt, and canvas shoes. They'll all dry." He chuckles and jumps into the pond. "Unless you're afraid of some water?"

I've never been able to resist a dare.

"Fine. But when I master this in ten minutes, you have to admit I'm better at it than you."

His laugh is a deep rumble that I feel much too low in my belly. "Deal."

The water is cool but not cold as I wade in, grateful that at least I'm wearing a sports bra under my shirt. Rourke is already standing on one of the logs, balanced perfectly as it spins this way and that under his feet.

"The trick," he says, helping me up, "is to keep your center of gravity low and your eyes forward. Don't look at your feet."

His hand is warm and rough against mine as he pulls me onto the log. I immediately start wobbling, and he steadies me with a firm grip on my waist.

"Bend your knees a bit. Shift your weight, don't fight the spin. That's it."

I'm acutely aware of his big body behind mine.

"Now, small steps. Keep it turning under you."

I try to follow his instructions, moving my feet in tiny, shuffling steps. For a second, I think I've got it—and then the log rolls sharply, and I'm airborne, flailing before splashing into the water.

When I surface, sputtering, Rourke is still on the log, laughing.

"That was...impressive," he says, eyes dancing.

"Shut up," I splash water at him, but I can't help but laugh, too. "Let me try again."

The next attempt is better—I manage three whole steps before toppling sideways into the pond. And the next, and the next. Each time, Rourke is there with a steadying hand, patient instructions, and increasingly creative encouragement.

"You're getting it! Just a wee bit more...oh, there you go. Swimming again."

"You're enjoying this too much," I accuse after my seventh dunking.

"I'm enjoying the view," he admits shamelessly, helping me back onto the log.

This time, when he positions himself behind me, he keeps one hand on my waist, the other holding my arm out for balance. "Move with me," he murmurs, and suddenly we're stepping in unison, the log spinning smoothly beneath our feet.

"I'm doing it!" I exclaim, wishing I could jump up and down.

"Aye. you're doing it," he confirms, his voice low.

We move together for several revolutions, his body guiding mine, our rhythm spot on.

His solid strength is keeping me balanced.

And then he lets go, stepping back slightly, and I'm doing it on my own. One step, two steps, three—

"Rourke!"

"You're a natural," he says.

I feel him moving closer behind me, one hand reaching to settle on my waist. His chest presses against my back. We move together, finding that same rhythm again, but this time I'm focused on every point where our bodies connect. His thighs behind mine, his hands guiding my hips...

I'm so distracted that I miss a step, the log shifting sharply beneath us. I yelp, sliding backward against Rourke.

We both hit the water with a splash.

I land in his lap and he wraps his arms around me from behind.

I go to turn, but he holds me in place, letting us float there for a minute.

"Sorry," I gasp.

"Don't be," he says, voice rough right at my ear. "I wish every fall was like this."

He nuzzles my neck and I push forward. "I should try again," I blurt, panicking. "One last time."

I turn and see him moving over to the log, pushing it toward me, expression unreadable. He helps me back onto it.

Now, I'm even more determined. I plant my feet, bend my knees, and start the shuffling steps he taught me. To my surprise, it works. I'm actually doing it completely on my own, the log spinning steadily beneath me.

"Look at you go!" Rourke calls from the water, followed by a loud whistle. "You're a pro!"

I laugh, exhilarated by my success. "I told you I'd master it!"

"Never doubted you for a second, lass."

But again the log shifts and I stumble on a piece of bark. I fall—not into the water this time, but onto the log itself, my shin scraping painfully against the jagged surface before I slide into the pond.

"Ow! Shit!" The water stings the fresh scrape.

Rourke is at my side instantly. "You alright?"

"Just scraped my leg," I say, wincing as I try to stand. "It's nothing."

But when I look down, there's a nasty gash running along my shin, already starting to bleed.

"That's somethin'," Rourke says firmly. "Come 'ere, we need to clean that."

He helps me out of the pond, and before I can protest he's lifting me into his arms. "I've got a first aid kit in my cabin."

I should tell him I can walk, but instead, I lean my head on his beefy shoulder.

His cabin is cozy and neat, with flannel shirts hanging by the door and books stacked on the coffee table. He sits me on the edge of the couch.

"Be right back," he says, heading to the bathroom.

I look around, noting the log-rolling trophies on his mantel, a vintage Irish music festival poster on the wall, and a photo of him and the crew on his side table. There's a distinct scent of cedar and spice that fills the room.

He returns quickly with a towel and a well-stocked first aid kit.

"This might sting a bit," he warns, kneeling in front of me.

His touch is incredibly gentle as he cleans the scrape, his big hands moving with surprising deftness. I watch his handsome face as he works...the furrow of concentration between his brows, the way he bites his lower lip, the careful attention he pays to every detail.

This isn't the rowdy party guy everyone sees at the camp. This is someone else entirely—someone sweet, nurturing, and intensely focused on me. The man I saw glimpses of in Vegas.

"Almost done," he murmurs, applying antibiotic ointment. "You're being very brave."

"It's a minor abrasion, not a gunshot wound," I say, but my voice comes out soft.

He looks up, a half-smile playing on his lips, as he affixes a small bandage. "Still. *Very brave*, lass."

Our eyes lock, and suddenly I'm aware of our...position. Him kneeling between my legs, his hands on my calf.

Water drips from my hair onto his couch, his floor.

Without a word he lifts my calf higher, so I have to lean back a little. I watch as he lowers his mouth to my skin next to the bandage...

...and kisses it.

I gasp. "What are you doing?"

"Kissing it better," he says, his mouth pressing against another spot on my calf.

Oh.

But he doesn't stop there. His hands glide up my calf to my knee, then higher, resting on my thigh. His touch is feather light, caressing more than anything else, and it's wreaking havoc on me.

He moves up to kiss the inside of my knee, and I bite back a moan.

I want to tilt my head back and let my legs fall open.

He starts up the inside of my thigh with his mouth, his beard rough and thrilling, making my breath stutter.

Now, I'm trembling like crazy.

When he reaches the hem of my shorts, his tongue slides against my skin and I whimper.

His answering groan rumbles through me.

I can see his pulse fluttering in his throat, matching the frantic beat of my own heart.

"Feck, Opal," he says roughly. "Why can't I control myself when I'm around you?"

"Rourke, wait," I say, pushing forward to sit up.

He moves back and looks up at me with those emerald eyes, pupils large and black.

"I can't remember our kiss," I say, breath heavy.

He furrows his brow. "What—?"

"Our wedding kiss," I say. "It's killing me that I can't remember." I glance down and shake my head.

"Then maybe I can jog your memory." And suddenly he surges upward, capturing my mouth with his. The kiss is hungry and desperate, like he's been starving for the taste of me.

I respond in kind, my hands tangling in the damp strands of his hair. He groans into my mouth, the sound igniting a primal heat in my core.

His beard brushes against my face as he deepens the kiss, his tongue sliding against mine, teasing and claiming all at once. I may not be able to recall this kiss in Vegas, but I know with absolute certainty that it couldn't have been this good.

Because this? This is transformative.

His hands move to my waist, pulling me closer to the edge of the couch, pressing me against the hard planes of his chest.

His heart thunders against mine as I run my hands down his back, feeling the shift of muscles under wet skin.

He moves to trail kisses over my jaw, then lower, licking and sucking on my neck. I tilt my head back, and moan as he bites down on my shoulder.

"Yes," I breathe, as his hands slip under my T-shirt to touch the bare skin of my belly.

"You're so soft, lass," he whispers, his fingers caressing me.

His kiss is slower now, but no less intense, as he pushes my shirt upward. I pull back just long enough to raise my arms, letting him peel the wet fabric away. His eyes darken further at the sight of me in my sports bra, his hands sliding up my ribs.

"Beautiful," he breathes, and the raw heat in his eyes sends a shiver through me.

He leans in again, pressing open-mouthed kisses along my shoulder, as he slides the strap of my bra down.

I clutch at his thick arms and back, nails digging into skin as my belly clenches.

He pulls down the other bra strap, following it with kisses—

A thunderous BANG shakes the cabin, a loud crash sounding from outside.

We freeze, both panting, staring at each other with wide eyes.

"What was that?" I whisper.

There's shouting, closer now, and Rourke reluctantly pulls away, moving to the window.

"Raccoons in the trash cans again!" Connor's voice booms.

"Everyone's running to help," he says, peering through the blinds.

Reality crashes back into the room like a bucket of ice water.

What am I doing?

Why am I making out with Rourke when we're supposed to be planning our annulment? When anyone could walk in and discover us?

"I—" I start, suddenly frantic, grabbing my shirt and pulling it over my head despite it still being soaked. "I need to...go."

Rourke turns back to me. "Opal, hold on."

"This was a mistake," I say, even as every cell in my body screams that it's a lie. "We're supposed to be ending our marriage, not...*this*."

"Then why doesn't it feel like a mistake to me?" he asks.

My eyes go wide. What is he even saying?

"We should talk," he says, quietly.

"Should we?" The question comes out sharper than I wanted. "Or should we stick to the plan? Annulment, clean slate, pretend this never happened?"

The look in his eyes—hungry and vulnerable and so damn...*I don't know*—nearly undoes my resolve.

"If that's what you want," he says.

"It's what makes sense," I reply, but my voice wavers as I back toward the door.

"Right. Makes sense," he echoes, and I can't tell if he's agreeing or mocking the very idea.

I flee before he can say anything else that might change my mind.

Because that's what I do. I run when things start feeling too real....and too much like something I might actually want.

CHAPTER 4
ROURKE

"Rourke!" Connor's voice breaks through my thoughts as I'm chopping firewood. "Need you for something."

I bury the axe in the chopping block and wipe sweat from my brow. "What's up, boss?"

"We're doing a site walk. Need your input on the activity areas."

My stomach drops. "With who?"

Connor gives me a confused look. "Just me and Opal."

Of course. Because the universe has a wicked sense of humor.

"Give me five to clean up," I say.

By the time I join them at the west ridge trail, Opal is deep in conversation with Connor, gesturing at blueprints that somehow make sense of the landscape around us.

She's wearing those paint-splattered overalls that shouldn't be so hot but are, with her hair up in a brightly-colored scrunchy, and a measuring tape dangling from her pocket.

All business. Feckin' sexy business.

It's a stark contrast to yesterday's soaking wet T-shirt and trembling kisses.

Stop thinking about that!

"—so if we nestle the new guest pods *here*," she says, jabbing a finger at the map, "they'll have sunset views through the pines without disturbing the barred owl nesting grounds. And *this*—" She flips to a page of swirling, organic shapes"—is a hybrid sauna and rainwater collection system. Aesthetic *and* functional, just like your lumberjack darlings."

Connor chuckles and strokes his beard, obviously impressed with her plans. Then he turns his attention to me. "You know, this guy knows the terrain better than anyone. He's been scouting potential activity locations for months."

Opal's eyes meet mine briefly before darting away. "Great."

"I was thinking," Connor continues, oblivious to any tension, "we could also expand the log rolling area over here, maybe add some demonstration platforms on this slope."

Opal shifts into professional mode so completely it's fascinating to watch.

"The grade is too steep," she says, evenly. "You'd need significant excavation, which undermines your sustainability goals."

She moves with purpose, taking measurements, making notes in a small leather-bound book. It's like watching a different person—still Opal, still vibrant, but channeled into something altogether extraordinary.

"What about over there?" I suggest, pointing to a flatter area to the east.

She looks where I'm pointing, her brow furrowed. "Better topography, but you'd lose those old-growth hemlocks."

"And the shade they provide in summer," I add.

She gives me an approving nod that makes me puff out my chest a bit. "Exactly."

For the next hour, we hike the property, discussing potential building sites. I find myself completely captivated by this side of Opal—the architect with an eye for both beauty and function. She asks questions about visitor flow, activity logistics, seasonal considerations.

"The problem," she says, crouching to examine the soil composition, "is balancing expansion with preservation. You want more capacity without losing the intimate connection to nature that makes this place special."

"That's exactly it," Connor agrees, his eyes lighting up.

Opal stands, brushing dirt from her hands, and turns to me. "What do you think, Rourke? Where do the guests naturally gravitate?"

The fact that she's asking my opinion, that she values my experience, feels good. I'm typically seen as the entertainment, not someone with valid input.

"They love the ridge views," I say with a smile. "But they also need gathering spaces that feel enclosed, protected. Like that natural amphitheater by the old cedar."

Her eyes sparkle. "Ooooo...show me."

I lead them to my favorite spot on the property—a gentle depression surrounded by towering cedars where the acoustics are perfect for storytelling or whittling demonstrations. Opal walks the perimeter, muttering to herself, occasionally scribbling in her notebook.

"This is perfect," she finally announces. "We could create a tiered seating area that follows the natural contour, minimal disruption to the root systems, excellent sight lines..."

She's pacing now, ideas flowing faster than she can articulate them. "Sustainable materials, reclaimed timber, maybe a retractable canopy system for weather... Connor, this could be Ewan's new Heritage Night venue, with proper lighting and sound."

Her enthusiasm is contagious. I find myself jumping in with suggestions about stage positioning and audience flow, which she incorporates seamlessly into her rapidly evolving vision.

Connor watches us ping-pong ideas with a half-smile on his face. "I'll leave you two to work out the details. I need to check on Jamie—Teagan has that women's wellness workshop today over at the spa."

As he walks away, the air between us grows heavy.

I clear my throat. "I need to tell you...you're, like, *crazy* talented, lass."

She shrugs as she tightens her ponytail. "It's my job, but I do love it."

"You see things differently."

"Is that your way of calling me weird?" But she's smiling now.

"It's my way of saying you're brilliant, Opal."

Her cheeks flush pink, and she busies herself with her notebook. "Well, you surprised me too. You actually have quite the spatial awareness."

"Don't sound so shocked," I laugh. "I do more than just fall off logs for applause."

"Could have fooled me," she teases, and this...is much more comfortable. Something that feels dangerously like friendship.

Or maybe more...

We're discussing potential building sites when we hear it— the unmistakable wail of a toddler mid-meltdown through the trees.

Jamie comes tearing around the bend in the path, face red and streaked with tears, Connor jogging behind him looking harried.

"Sorry," he calls. "Teagan's still busy, and this little guy's having a rough day."

Jamie spots me and charges, wrapping himself around my leg. "Uncle Roke! The blue truck is GONE!"

Connor sighs. "We've looked everywhere. I think it might have fallen into the creek or something."

Jamie's wail reaches new decibel levels.

I glance at Opal, who looks concerned, then back to the distressed toddler.

I crouch down to his level. "This sounds like a job for...Rescue Rangers!"

His sobbing hiccups to a stop. "What's dat?"

"Only the most elite team of rescue experts in all of Timber Run," I say, lowering my voice conspiratorially. "And you're just the right size to be our newest recruit."

He sniffles as he looks up at me. "Me?"

"Absolutely." I tap his nose. "But Rescue Rangers need special equipment. Connor, we'll need the walkie-talkies."

Connor, the smart man that he is, immediately catches on. "I'll grab the kit."

"Auntie Opal, we'll need your expertise for this mission," I say. "That creek has dangerous...currents and things."

Her lips twitch. "Good thing I brought my special creek-mapping tools." She pats her measuring tape.

Jamie's tears are completely forgotten now, replaced by wide-eyed excitement as Connor returns with the kit and a small backpack.

We stage an elaborate "rescue operation," complete with code names (Jamie insists on being "Thunder Ranger") and strategic search patterns. Connor slips away at some point to actually try and find the truck, while Opal and I keep Jamie entertained with increasingly ridiculous rescue scenarios.

Finally, Connor alerts me to where he's cleverly wedged the truck between some rocks in the creek, making it look partially submerged. Opal, Jamie, and I form a human chain and edge toward the creek.

"Almost there, Thunder Ranger," I encourage. "Steady now."

Jamie leans forward, straining toward the truck. Opal and I exchange glances over his head, both biting back smiles at his intense concentration.

"Got it!" he crows triumphantly, holding the truck up. "Blue Truck is saved!"

"Mission accomplished, Rangers!" I high-five him, then Opal. "That was some expert rescuing."

Jamie beams, clutching his recovered treasure. "We're the best team ever!"

"The very best," Opal agrees, ruffling his hair. When she looks up at me, my heart beats faster.

By lunchtime, word has spread about our heroic rescue mission, thanks to Jamie's enthusiastic retelling. I'm grabbing food from the buffet when I feel a tap on my shoulder.

"So you're the famous log roller," purrs a voice that's trying way too hard to be seductive.

I turn to find a guest—Melissa? Melanie? Or Mindy, was it? —from the morning's demonstration group standing next to me, her hand lingering on my arm.

"That would be me," I confirm, taking a subtle step back.

"I was hoping to get some...private instruction." Her emphasis on "private" is long and drawn out as her fingers trail up my sleeve.

In the past, a woman coming on to me like this would be a done deal. I'd always oblige the needs of a pretty guest.

But today, it's just making me uncomfortable.

"All our classes are listed on the schedule board," I say, looking around for an escape route.

"I was thinking of something more...*hands-on*." She's practically on the plate I'm holding in front of me.

Over her shoulder, I spot Opal entering the dining hall, stopping dead when she sees us. Something flashes in her eyes —annoyance? She marches toward us with purpose.

"Rourke!" she says, slightly too loud. "Thank goodness! We have an emergency with the, um, log-rolling pond! Something about...excessive rotation!"

I bite the inside of my cheek to keep from laughing.

"Sorry," I tell the guest, not sorry at all. "Duty calls."

Opal grabs my arm and pulls me away, her grip tight enough to leave marks. "It's very urgent," she tells the woman with a forced smile. "Technical lumberjack stuff. You understand." The woman seems to be too confused about what's happening to be upset.

Once we're outside, I burst out laughing. "Excessive rotation? Really?"

"Shut up," she mutters, her cheeks flaming. "It was the first thing that came to mind."

"Jealous, huh?" I say, unable to resist teasing her. "Can't stand to see your *husband* getting hit on by other women?"

I take a big bite of the roll on my plate.

"Oh please!" she groans, but she won't meet my eyes. "I was...*rescuing* you."

"My hero," I say, placing a hand over my heart dramatically. "Saving me from the clutches of aggressive flirtation."

She shoves my shoulder. "You looked uncomfortable."

The fact that she noticed, and cared enough to intervene, stirs something deep inside. "I kinda was."

She blinks. "That's kind of your thing, isn't it? You could've had her in two shakes of your Irishman's ass."

I chuckle. "Maybe I don't want it to be my thing."

And as she stares at me, the sky opens up.

The rain comes suddenly and violently, a classic summer storm that turns the sky dark and the ground to mud in seconds. People scatter from the outdoor areas, running for shelter.

I grab Opal's hand, pulling her toward the equipment shed where we store the tools for demonstrations.

We burst through the door, already soaked to the skin, laughing breathlessly as thunder cracks overhead. Lightning follows, illuminating us for a split second.

I'm still chewing as she pushes the wet hair from her face.

"Why am I always getting wet around you?" she says, innocently.

"No comment," I say, flipping on the single overhead light.

The shed is small and crowded with extra axes, saws, climbing gear, and various lumberjack paraphernalia. There's barely room for both of us to stand without touching.

Opal shivers in her wet clothes.

I set the buffet plate down and grab a clean towel from the shelf, draping it around her shoulders. "Here. You're freezing."

"Thanks," she whispers, smiling up at me with lips parted.

We're standing too close in the dim light, the rain hammering on the metal roof.

"Opal," I begin, my voice rough. "About yesterday..."

"We don't have to talk about it." She clutches the towel tighter.

"What if I want to?"

Her eyes darken as she gazes up at me. "What if talking isn't what I want right now?"

I blink. "What do you…want?" I ask, slightly confused.

Instead of responding with words, she grabs the front of my shirt and pulls me down, pressing her mouth against mine.

And everything inside me ignites into flame.

I grasp her face, angling her head to deepen the kiss. Her moan goes straight to my already raging hard cock.

Pressing her against the wall, my hands slide down to lift her so our bodies align. My cock grinds against her hips and she wraps her legs around my waist.

Her hands are everywhere—in my hair, on my shoulders, sliding under my shirt to touch bare skin.

I shudder. "Feck, Opal," I groan as she rocks against me. "Your touch drives me mad."

Her head falls back as I trail hot, wet kisses down her neck. "I've been thinking about this since yesterday. Since Vegas, really."

I pull back to look at her, not sure I'm in my right mind.

She claws at my face, fingers threading through my beard. "I want you, Rourke. Right now. Here."

I don't know the full scope of what that means, but...I'll take it. Hell, I'll take any part of her I can get.

I capture her mouth again as my hands delve under her wet tank top. She gasps at my touch, shivering, but definitely not from cold this time.

Between desperate kisses, we peel away our sodden clothes. Her overalls puddle at her feet, while my shirt lands over a nearby buzzsaw. When I finally get her down to just her bra and panties, I move back to take her in, all soft sexy curves and pale creamy skin.

"You're a dream," I breathe, running my hands along her thighs as I move down.

I reach around and unclasp her bra, gliding it off and tossing it over my discarded shirt. "Jesus, your tits are glorious."

She blushes but doesn't shy away from my gaze, and I lean in to press my face between those soft mounds of flesh. I kiss and lick each one, taking extra time to taste her sweet velvety nipples, reveling in her gasps and moans.

"I can't take much more of that," she whispers, reaching for the waistband of my jeans. "I need you now."

I'm so wrecked already, unable to protest as she undoes my fly and shoves my jeans down my thighs.

She reaches into my boxers to pull out my aching cock.

"Damn, you're big...and hard," she says, stroking me.

I'm squirming under her touch. "For you lass, but if you keep that up with those silky little hands, I'm done for."

She grins, teasing me by sliding her fingers over my leaking tip. My stomach muscles clench.

Feck! "You devil," I gasp.

She places a kiss on my lips. "Protection?"

"Back pocket," I manage, and she reaches around to grab my wallet, finding the condom and unwrapping it.

She gives my cock one last sinful caress before she slips the condom on, squeezing my length tight as she cups my balls for good measure.

"You're lethal, woman," I rasp, wrapping my arm around her and yanking her to me.

She yelps as I slide my hand down into the front of her panties.

"Goddamnit, you're wet, love," I murmur, my fingers finding her slick, tender flesh.

"Oh god, Rourke," she moans, biting her lip as I tease and stroke her pussy.

"Feel good?" I whisper in her ear, as she trembles and gasps.

She moans. "Too good. I...I'm going to—"

"Come? I can't wait." I draw soft circles around her sweet clit.

"But—*oh fuck*—I want you to come with you inside me." She breathes.

I chuckle huskily. "Oh, you will. But why not both?"

She drags her nails down my chest, as I continue to discover what makes her gasp, moan, and shudder. She's so feckin' responsive.

"That's it…" I say, feeling her muscles clench. "Take it like a good girl."

"Oh god!" Her legs start to shake uncontrollably. "Rourke, my legs are going to give out."

"S'okay, I got you, lass. Let go."

And she does, on a loud wail, as I continue to rub her through her convulsions, wringing every last bit of pleasure from her pussy.

"Rourke," she whispers, coming down and sagging against my arm. My cock still rages watching her come undone. *Because of me.*

Before she can say anything more, I lift her up and push my hard length into her, using the wall behind us for stability.

I fight the intense, overwhelming sensation of her slick pussy gripping me, as her eyes go wide with surprise.

"Holy fuck, you feel good," she says on a groan, head falling back.

"Likewise, sweetheart," I reply, trembling as I start to move inside her. "This okay?"

"Yes," she whimpers. "It's fantastic." She rolls her hips against mine, erasing another shred of control. "More," she gasps.

"Yes, ma'am," I obey, thrusting into her harder, making the shed walls creak.

We find our rhythm quickly, urgent and primal. The storm rages outside while we create our own inside. Her nails dig into my shoulders and back, scoring my skin with marks I'll wear proudly tomorrow.

"I'm going to come again," she whines, and I almost lose it right there.

"Yes, lass. I want to feel your sweet pussy milk my cock."

"Oh god—*Rourke!*" she cries out as her climax rips through her, body jerking and spasming.

And with the grip of her muscles, I'm coming, too.

I shout my release as I pump into her, gripping her to me, burying my face in her neck.

"Feckin' hell, Opal," I say, breathing hard.

This didn't feel like just sex. It felt like claiming, possessing…proving something to ourselves and each other.

And I'm certain we've crossed a line we can't uncross.

CHAPTER 5
OPAL

I 've finished filling out the annulment application I found on the Nevada state website. It sits there staring back at me on my laptop, all bold text and official-looking boxes.

I take another sip of my coffee, which has gone cold.

Why am I hesitating?

I groan and push my computer away, flopping back onto the bed.

"This is stupid," I tell the ceiling. "You don't actually want to stay married to the man."

But after yesterday, I feel like I'm getting to know the *real* Rourke. The one who handles a crying child with infinite patience. Who plays haunting melodies on his guitar by fire-light. Who has a ton of hidden knowledge about the hospi-tality business.

And well, the one who ravaged me against the equipment shed wall, whispering deliciously filthy things to me as I came apart in his arms. Twice.

After we'd cleaned up and straightened our clothes, he'd walked me back to my cabin, our hands brushing but not quite holding, afraid to talk. Afraid of something we might say to ruin what we just shared.

Instead, we'd agreed to meet this morning to "discuss next steps."

And by "next steps," we both knew what we meant. *The annulment.*

I pull the laptop back over and attempt to focus on the form, trying to be sensible. But it's no use. I can't stop thinking about the big lumbersnack.

I slam the laptop closed. What is wrong with me? Why am I suddenly entertaining the idea of staying married to Rourke? We live on different continents, for God's sake. I'm based in London, with clients across the world. He's here, with his life built around Timber Run.

Not to mention that neither of us is exactly relationship material. I've never stuck around long enough to unpack my suitcase, let alone build a life with someone. And Rourke...his playboy mentality is more suited for a vacation fling.

But marriage?

I'm nuts!

I grab my jacket and head for the door. I need to talk to him. Tell him what drunk-me apparently knew all along: I don't want to end this.

The morning air is crisp and clean as I follow the path toward Rourke's cabin. Birds chirp overhead, and somewhere nearby a woodpecker, or maybe a lumberjack, is going to town on a tree. It's still stupidly quaint, like the universe is setting the stage for something sappy and romantic.

I'm so caught up in rehearsing what I'll say—*I was thinking, maybe we rushed the annulment idea. Maybe we should date? While married? Is that insane?*—that I almost miss the sound of a cabin door opening ahead.

I freeze mid-step.

A woman emerges from Rourke's cabin, quietly closing the door behind her. She's pretty in that wholesome way—blonde ponytail, yoga pants, softly flushed cheeks. She glances around furtively before hurrying down the path toward the main camp.

My stomach plummets to my feet.

You're such an idiot, Opal.

It's barely been twelve hours since we had sex in the shed, and he's already moved on to the next warm body. His next *conquest.*

I stumble backward and spin around, practically running back to my cabin. I grab my hiking gear and go.

I need space. Trees. A cliff to scream into. I need to get away from him and my own silly, romantic delusions.

The trail winds through the thick forest toward Timber Creek Falls. It's a two-mile hike from camp, but I'm practically jogging, propelled by a potent cocktail of hurt and embarrassment.

By the time I reach the falls, I'm sweating and out of breath. The water cascades over moss-covered rocks into a clear pool below, the sound drowning out my chaotic thoughts. I find a flat boulder at the edge of the pool and sink down, finally letting the tears come.

God, I'm such a fool. Thinking I could be different for him. Thinking he could be different for *me.*

I pull out the sketchbook, trying to lose myself in drawing. But instead of the waterfall, I find myself sketching Rourke's hands as he bandaged my leg, his smile as he held Jamie, the emerald color of his eyes just before he kissed me.

"Dammit," I mutter, ripping out the page and crumbling it into a ball. This is *exactly* why I don't do relationships. This *aching, desperate need* that tears at my heart when I let someone matter.

The sound of a twig snapping behind me makes me whirl around.

Rourke stands at the edge of the clearing, his thick hair wild, cheeks flushed from exertion. He's breathing hard, like he's been running.

"Opal," he says, relief washing over his face. "Thank Christ. I've been looking everywhere for you."

Whatever.

I stand up, shoving the sketchbook back into my bag. "I saw her, Rourke. This morning, leaving your cabin."

His brow furrows. "Her? Who—" Understanding dawns on his face. "You mean Kaylee? From registration?"

"I don't care what her name is. She was in your bed this morning. Talk about fast."

He looks genuinely baffled. "Kaylee wasn't in my bed. She came by to drop off some stuff for Brady's bachelor party. We're planning a surprise for him and Imogen."

I scoff. "Please. Mighty convenient story."

"Well, it's the truth!" His accent thickens with frustration.

"The truth is," I say, my voice rising, "I almost made a huge mistake. I almost convinced myself that what happened between us meant something. That maybe…" I sigh, shaking my head… "It doesn't matter now."

His eyes soften. "It did mean something."

"Save it." I turn away from him, fighting back fresh tears. "You have a reputation, Rourke. The sexy Irish flirt who makes all the female guests feel special…in *every* way possible. Well, I'm not going to be another notch on your belt."

"Is that really what you think?" His voice drops, hurt lacing his words.

I whirl back to face him. "What am I supposed to think? We got drunk in Vegas and got married as a *joke*. That's not exactly the foundation for happily ever after."

"Maybe not," he says, stepping closer. "But it's a hell of a story to tell our grandkids someday."

I gape at him. "Grandkids? Are you insane?"

"Aye, probably." He runs a hand through his hair. "But I know what I feel, Opal. And it's not something I've ever felt before."

"What about what I feel?" I snap. "Did you ever consider that maybe *I'm* not looking for forever? That maybe I'm just like you—looking for a good time, not a long time?"

He blinks. "Are you?"

I let out a frustrated yell. "You don't know me, Rourke. We've spent, what, a total of five days in each other's company over the past three years? You don't know that I've never stayed in one place for more than six months. You don't know that I've left every relationship the moment it got too real."

"And you don't know that I haven't been with anyone in over a year," he fires back. "That I've turned down more women than I can count because none of them were you."

That stops me cold. "What?"

"I've had a crush on you since the first time you visited the camp," he says, voice rough. "When you came whirling in like a tornado, turning everyone's heads, making everything brighter just by existing."

I shake my head, not willing to believe him. "That's just Irish blarney."

He takes another step closer. "Ask Connor or Teagan. They know who I spend my time with. Hell, they're probably sick of me always tagging along with them lately."

"Then why didn't you say anything? Why all the flirting with other women?"

"Because you were always jetting off to London or Dubai or wherever your next project was. And I was here, stuck in

Montana, watching you come and go like some mystical creature I could never catch."

"I'm not a creature to be caught," I say, but the heat has gone out of my words.

"No," he agrees. "You're a woman to be loved. Cherished. Every day, in every way."

I nearly sway on the spot. "Rourke, you can't just *say* things like that."

"Why not?" He's close enough now that I can see the seriousness in his green eyes. "It's how I feel."

"Because—" I falter, struggling to articulate the fear that's choking me. "Because what if it's not real? What if it's just the excitement of Vegas, or the novelty of being married, or the thrill of sneaking around?"

"Then we'll find out," he says simply. "But not by running away. Not by assuming the worst about each other."

I want to believe him. God, I want to believe him so badly. But the sight of that woman leaving his cabin is still burned into my retinas.

"I can't do this," I whisper, backing away. "I can't be just another woman who falls for your charm only to wake up alone." I sling my backpack over my shoulder. "I need to go."

"Opal, wait—"

But I'm already moving, darting down the trail that circles the falls. I hear him curse behind me, followed by the sound of his footsteps in pursuit.

"Opal!" he calls. "For Christ's sake, stop running!"

I bolt down the path, my heart pounding in my ears.

"Opal!" he calls out, voice echoing through the forest. "You can run all you want, but I'm not giving up!"

I duck under a low-hanging branch, veering off the main trail onto a narrower path that winds alongside the creek. The

roar of the falls grows louder as I race downstream, my breath coming in sharp gasps.

"I can do this all day, lass!" His voice is closer now, a dangerous rumble that sends an unwelcome thrill down my spine. "I'm a log roller, remember? I've got stamina for *days*."

The absolute nerve of this man.

"Leave me alone, Rourke!" I shout over my shoulder, but my voice lacks real conviction.

"Not a chance in hell," he calls back. "You're my wife, remember?"

"What I want," I pant, pushing myself faster, "is for you to take a hint and back off!"

"Nope." He growls. "I think you want me to catch you. To show you I'm not going down without a fight."

My treacherous body reacts to his words, as I keep running. *What is wrong with me?* I'm supposed to be furious with him, not turned on.

The path leads me to a small clearing beside the creek. I'm running out of places to go, the waterfall to my right, the steep hillside to my left.

"I'm gonna get you, a chroí," he calls, his voice a dark promise that makes me tingle. "You might as well stop."

"You wish!" I retort, but my pace slows as I reach the clearing. I spin around, ready to dart back the way I came, only to find him blocking the path.

He stands there, chest heaving, eyes wild and dark. *Fuck, he's sexy.*

"Nowhere left to run, lass," he says, taking a step toward me.

I back up, pulse racing. "There's always somewhere to run."

"Not from this, love." He smiles. "Not from us."

"There is no us," I insist, even as my body betrays me with a shiver of anticipation.

"Liar." He takes another step closer, and my heel hits the edge of the creek. "You feel it too. This thing between us."

"You don't know what I feel," I say, but my voice wavers.

His smile is slow and knowing. "I'd bet my left bollock that if I slid my hand into your panties right now, you'd be so wet for me."

My face flames with heat. "You're delusional."

I can smell the musk of his sweat. "Here I come, Opal. Whether you're ready or not."

I should push him into the creek.

Instead, I try to duck around him and make one last run for it.

CHAPTER 6
ROURKE

I grab Opal as she tries to brush past me.

She's mine now.

Opal squirms in my arms, her back pressed against my chest as I hold her tight around the waist. The roar of the waterfall nearly drowns out her protests, as she kicks and flails.

"Let me go, you big oaf!" She twists and writhes, all fire and fury.

"Not a chance, *a chroí*." I tighten my grip, lifting her so her feet barely touch the ground. "Not until you stop acting like a feral raccoon and listen to me."

"I've heard enough!" She kicks backward, narrowly missing my shin. "Your Gaelic endearments don't work on me."

I spin her around to face me. Her eyes blaze with anger and her wild copper hair escapes its tie to frame her flushed face.

Christ, she's a deranged beauty.

"Kaylee was dropping off bachelor party supplies," I tell her again, my voice low and insistent. "That's *all*."

"It doesn't matter," she spits, pushing against my chest.

"This whole thing was a mistake anyway. The marriage, yesterday in the shed, all of it."

"Bollocks!" I back her against a tree, caging her with my arms. "Look me dead in the eye and tell me you don't feel something for me."

She glares up at me, her breath coming fast. "I feel...*annoyed*."

"Feck, woman. Stop kiddin' yourself." I lower my head until our faces are inches apart. "You want me as badly as I want you."

"That's just...physical attraction." Her voice wavers as she presses herself back against the tree trunk. "Doesn't mean anything."

"Then why are you so upset about Kaylee?" I counter, watching her eyes widen. "If it's just physical, why do you care who comes to my cabin?"

"I—" she starts, then her eyes shimmer with unshed tears. "I'm scared, okay? Is that what you want to hear? I'm terrified of whatever this is."

The vulnerability in her admission knocks the wind out of me. I step back, giving her space, though every instinct screams to pull her close.

"I'm scared too, Opal." The words come out rough and raw. "I've never felt like this about anyone. Never wanted to try being more than just the fun guy who's only there for a good time."

She stares at me, eyes searching mine. "The camp Casanova suddenly wants to settle down? With me?"

"I didn't say anything about *settling down*," I counter. "There's nothing *settled* about you, lass. You're a feckin' tornado. And I love that about you."

A flicker of something—surprise, hope, desire, maybe—crosses her face before she masks it.

I sigh. "I don't want an annulment, Opal. I want you. *All* of you. The chaos and the genius and the way you make everything in my life more colorful."

Her breath catches. "Rourke..."

We stand frozen, staring at one another. I've never wanted anything as badly as I want her to believe me.

I grab her hand and press her palm to my chest where my heart's trying to punch through bone. "This is as serious as I get, lass."

She blinks. "Kiss me."

"What?" I ask, thrown by the sudden change.

"*Kiss me,*" she says again, though her hands are already fisting in my shirt, yanking me down.

My mouth crashes into hers, all hunger and hard edges. I groan into the kiss, relief and desire surging through me as I push her back against the tree. Her teeth scrape my lip as my tongue slides into her hot mouth.

"I hate that I want you so much," she gasps against my mouth.

"No, you don't," I murmur, kissing her jaw and neck. "You love it."

Her head falls back as she groans. "Smug bastard."

"*Your* smug bastard." I bite gently, making her gasp. "By legal documentation, even."

She chuckles, the sound transforming into a moan as my hands slide under her shirt to caress her. I rock my hips against hers so she can feel my raging cock, and she grinds back against me.

I kiss her slower, deeper, my tongue exploring her with deliberate intent. She melts into me as I slide my hands up her ribcage, brushing her tits through her bra. As I drag my fingers over the thin fabric of her already pebbled nipples, she shivers.

"God, Rourke," she whimpers.

But before I can continue, she's ducking down, dropping to her knees before me.

She pushes my shirt up and kisses my belly just about my waistband.

I let out a long groan.

The sight of her there, looking up at me with those seductive, mischievous eyes, nearly undoes me on the spot. She makes quick work of my belt and zipper, tugging my jeans and boxers down my thighs.

She licks her lips as my cock juts out through my boxer shorts. "Mmmm, impressive, husband."

"Jesus, when you call me that," I groan, threading my fingers through her hair.

She grins wickedly before taking me in her hand, stroking firmly from base to tip. "What? You like when I stroke your big, hard cock, husband?"

"You're evil," I gasp as she leans forward to lick a stripe up the underside of my cock.

"You have no idea," she murmurs, before taking me into her mouth.

The wet heat of her nearly buckles my knees. I brace one hand against the tree behind her, the other still tangled in her hair as she works me with her soft silky lips and velvety tongue. She takes me deeper with each slow bob of her head, her hand working what she can't fit.

"*Fuck*, Opal," I pant, watching her through half-lidded eyes.

She hums around me, the vibration sending shocks of pleasure up my spine. Her free hand cups my balls, massaging gently as she continues her sweet torture.

I'm so close already, and when I feel her tongue swirl cleverly around my tip, I gasp.

"Lass, if you don't stop..."

She pulls back just enough to say, "I'm not stopping..." before taking me deep again.

Those gorgeous lips stretched around me, those playful eyes so sultry as they glance up at me, combined with her talented mouth is too much. My climax hits me like a freight train, pleasure pulsing through me in waves as I empty myself down her throat.

She licks and sucks my cock through it all, swallowing everything I give her before finally releasing me with a satisfied smile.

"Christ on a bicycle," I breathe, trying to catch my breath and right myself. "Mrs. Fogerty, you are the best kind of trouble."

She laughs as I pull her up into my arms. "You better believe it, husband."

～

Back at my cabin we spend the next several hours relearning each other's bodies, taking our time in the privacy of my bed.

I worship every inch of her, memorizing the sounds she makes when I touch her just right, the way her body responds to my hands, my mouth...my cock.

Afterward, we lie tangled together in the rumpled sheets, her head on my chest, my fingers playing in her wild curls.

"I meant what I said, Opal. I don't want an annulment. I want to try—really try—to make this work."

Her expression softens. "Rourke..."

"I know it's crazy," I continue quickly. "We live on different continents. You're a globetrotting architect, and I'm a lumberjack in the middle of nowhere Montana."

"A very sexy lumberjack," she interjects.

"The point is," I say, pulling her bare leg across me. "I think we could be amazing together. If you're willing to give us a real chance."

She's quiet for a moment. "What would that even look like?"

"I don't know," I admit. "But there's no one else I'd like to figure it with."

Her hand slides over my chest. "And you'd be willing to try...what? Long distance? Me moving here? You moving to London?"

"Any of those." I brush my thumb down her cheek. "All of those. Whatever works for *us*."

She leans into my touch. "I'm not good at relationships, Rourke. I run when things get serious."

"I've noticed," I say playfully. "But maybe that's because you haven't found a man who'd run after you."

She glances up at me, eyes wide.

"No matter how many times I need to," I say. "This connection between us is special, Opal. Worth fighting for."

She takes a big breath. "It's still terrifying."

"Completely," I agree, tightening my arms around her. "But we can be terrified together. Until we're not anymore."

She burrows into me. "I'd rather be terrified with you than bored with anyone else."

I kiss her deeply, pouring every ounce of emotion I feel into it.

"Boring is something you'll never have to worry about with me, a chroí."

And as I drift off to sleep, I silently thank whatever Irish luck led me to that bar in Vegas and this beautiful woman.

CHAPTER 7
OPAL

I awake to warm, slick heat between my thighs and the soft scrape of Rourke's beard against my skin. My eyes flutter open to find him settled between my legs, his green eyes dark with mischief as his tongue slowly swirls through through my already aching pussy.

"Time to get up, Mrs. Fogerty," he murmurs against me, the vibration making me gasp and arch off the bed.

"Oh God," I breathe, gripping the sheets. "That's heaven."

"Mmm, thought you might like a nice way to wake up from your nap." His accent is thick and rough with sleep and arousal. "You taste divine, lass."

His lips tease my folds, tongue dragging lazy circles around my clit. I'm already on a delicious edge, my body humming with need.

"Rourke, please—"

He pulls back just enough to speak, his breath hot against my wet center. "Tell me."

"More," I whimper, my legs dropping open even wider. "Don't stop."

"Greedy little thing," he chuckles, but obliges, devouring me with relentless strokes.

I gasp, as pleasure shoots through me. His hands slide under my ass to tilt me toward his wicked mouth, as he holds my thighs open. He knows exactly how to alternate between broad, mind-scrambling strokes and featherlight teases that make my toes curl.

"That's it," he murmurs between licks. "Let me hear those pretty sounds you make."

I groan and pant, my hips rolling against his face.

"You like having your sweet pussy eaten out by your husband?"

"Fuck, yes," I moan loudly in response. "You're a master…"

The man really is a virtuoso. Every swirl, every nip, every rasp of his beard is calculated to dismantle me.

"Come for me, love," he commands, huskily. "Let me taste you completely."

His words push me over the edge and I come with a sharp cry, my body convulsing with white-hot bliss. He doesn't let up, working me through it until I'm a trembling, boneless mess.

"Bloody gorgeous," he breathes, pressing soft kisses to my inner thighs.

I reach for him, pulling him up my body until I can kiss him. "You're much too good at that, husband."

He grins like a wolf against my mouth. "It's because I love doing it."

"I'm one lucky woman," I groan.

We're basking in the afterglow, when a sharp knock at the door makes us both freeze.

"Rourke!" Teagan's voice carries through the cabin walls. "Are you in there?"

My eyes go wide with panic. "Oh shit."

Connor's voice joins Teagan's. "Your truck's here, and you missed breakfast and lunch. We're worried something happened to you."

Rourke checks his phone on the nightstand. "Christ, it's past three in the afternoon."

The knocking gets more insistent. "We're coming in!" Teagan announces.

"No!" I shriek, scrambling for my clothes as the door handle turns.

But it's too late. The door swings open just as I'm diving under the covers, and Teagan and Connor stop short in the doorway, taking in the scene—Rourke and I in his bed, our clothes scattered across the floor, the unmistakable smell of sex hanging in the air.

"Well," Connor says after a moment, his lips twitching. "This explains why neither of you answered your phones."

Teagan's mouth opens and then closes again. "What the hell, Opal?"

"Surprise?" I offer weakly, clutching the sheet to my chest.

Rourke, the bastard, has the audacity to look completely unbothered. "Good afternoon, you two."

"Get dressed," Teagan says, her voice dangerously calm. "Both of you. We're having a conversation. Now."

Connor tugs her arm. "Maybe we should give them a few minutes to—"

"No." Teagan's eyes blaze. "I've been worried sick thinking something happened to my sister. The least she can do is explain why she's screwing the Irish rogue."

"Hey!" Rourke protests. "That's a bit harsh, don't you think?"

"Is it?" Teagan crosses her arms. "How long has this been going on?"

Connor turns his back while I scramble into my clothes and Rourke pulls on jeans and a T-shirt. My hands shake as I try to finger-comb my sex hair into something presentable.

"It's...complicated," I say finally.

"Complicated how?" Connor asks, when he turns back around.

Rourke and I exchange a look. There's no way around it now.

"We're married," I blurt out.

The silence that follows is deafening.

Teagan blinks. Once. Twice. "Come again?"

"We got married," Rourke confirms, reaching for my hand. "In Vegas."

"You WHAT?" Teagan's voice cracks on the last word.

Connor, meanwhile, starts laughing. Actually laughing, doubling over with mirth.

"I knew it!" he gasps between chuckles. "I fucking *knew* something was up with you two."

"Language," Teagan snaps automatically, though Jamie isn't anywhere around. "Married? Are you out of your minds?"

"A little," I admit. "We were drunk. Really, *really* drunk."

"But we're sober now," Rourke adds, squeezing my hand. "And we want to make it work."

Teagan stares at us like we've lost it. "How can you possibly think this will work?"

I pull out the big guns. "The same way you and Connor made it work," I say, finding my backbone.

Teagan's eyes go wide. "That's different! Connor and I—"

"Met and fell in love in a matter of days, hon," Connor interrupts gently. "These two probably had more time together than we did."

Teagan's mouth snaps shut, her cheeks flushing.

"We know it's crazy," I continue. "But Teagan, I've never felt this way about anyone. He makes me want to stay in one place for the first time in my life."

"And she makes me want to be more than just a flirt...with incredible abs," Rourke adds with a grin.

Teagan looks between us, her expression softening slightly. "This is really happening? It's not just some Vegas hangover talking?"

"It's real," I say firmly. "Scary as hell, but real."

Connor comes over and claps Rourke on the shoulder. "Congratulations, man. Though I have to say, your timing could use work."

"What do you mean?" Rourke asks.

"Because the entire crew is gathered at the main lodge, wondering where you disappeared to. Brady's been fielding questions about whether Rourke finally got eaten by a bear."

I groan. "We have to tell everyone?"

"Unless you want them to think he was mauled to death," Teagan says dryly. "Though honestly, that might be less shocking than the truth."

Twenty minutes later, we're walking into the lodge hand-in-hand, facing a room full of curious faces. Graham and Sky look up from their coffee, Ewan and Hazel pause mid-story, and Brady and Imogen exchange glances.

"There he is!" Brady calls out. "We were about to send out a search party."

"Sorry," Rourke says, not looking sorry at all. "Got a bit...distracted."

Sky's eyes immediately zero in on our joined hands. "Oh my God, what's going on?"

"Actually," I take a deep breath. I'm just going to say it. "We're married."

The room goes dead silent.

Then everyone starts talking at once.

"Married?" Graham's coffee mug clatters against the table.

"When?" Sky squeals.

"How?" Hazel looks confused.

"Vegas," Rourke announces.

Ewan's booming laugh fills the room. "Well, I'll be damned! The Irish bachelor finally got himself caught!"

We all laugh.

"This calls for a celebration!" Ewan declares. "Let's break out the good whiskey!"

Hazel shakes her head. "Now we're in for it."

"It's three in the afternoon," Teagan protests.

"It's almost happy hour." Graham grins. "They're married! Live a little."

I decide to hold back on letting them know day drinking is part of what got Rourke and I into all this in the first place.

But as the chaos of congratulations and questions swirls around us, Teagan pulls me aside. "Can we talk? Privately?"

I follow her out onto the deck, my stomach churning with nerves.

"I'm sorry I didn't tell you right away," I start, but she holds up a hand.

"I'm not mad about that. Well, I am a little, but..." She sighs, fussing with her braid. "Tell me, as your sister, that this is what you really want?"

I smile just thinking about Rourke. I do. I really do. "It is. He's it."

Tears prick her dark eyes. "I'm so happy for you."

I pull her into a fierce hug. "Thank you."

We hold each other chuckling as our tears mingle, before finally pulling back.

"And your work?" she asks. "Your life in London?"

"I don't know yet," I admit. "We still have a lot to figure out."

She takes a deep breath and studies my face. "You know, we could use a *local* architect for the big projects we have planned."

My heart skips and I blink. "Are you serious?"

"Duh, as my sister you should know I'm serious about *everything*." She chuckles. "I mean…good salary, creative freedom, and you'd be close to family."

"And Rourke," I add quietly, as Connor joins us on the deck.

"Technically, he's already part of the family," she says with a small smile.

"It would be a partnership, actually, Opal," Connor says. "You'd have equity in the expansion projects, creative control, the works."

I stare at them, overwhelmed. "You'd do that for *me*?"

"We'd do that because you're amazing at what you do," Teagan says firmly. "*And* because you're family."

"Plus," Connor adds with a grin, "someone needs to keep Rourke in line."

Through the window, I can see Rourke inside, gesticulating wildly as he tells what I assume is an embellished version of our Vegas adventure to the crew. His laugh carries through the glass, warm and sexy.

"*This* Rourke Fogerty? I don't think anyone can do that."

They laugh.

"Worth a shot," Teagan says, patting Connor's shoulder.

I grin. "Looks like you're stuck with me, lil' sis."

She grabs my hand. "Best news I've heard all day. Well, second best."

I glance at both of them, confused.

Connor puts his hand on Teagan's belly.

"We just came from the doctor." She covers Connor's hand. "I'm pregnant again."

"Oh my god!" I jump up and pull her into another hug.

"That's why she hasn't been feeling so great lately," Connor says.

"This is wonderful! I'm so happy." I can't stop the tears from falling again. Another nephew or niece!

We head back inside, where the celebration is in full swing. Someone has indeed broken out the good whiskey, and Ewan is attempting to teach Jamie a Scottish folk song while Rourke plays guitar.

Connor gets everyone's attention and when he and Teagan break the news about the little one on the way, everyone is overjoyed. They all congratulate my sister and brother-in-law with hugs and shoulder pats and even some tears. Mostly from the big lumberjacks—the softies.

I slide up to Rourke, who immediately pulls me down onto his lap at the large dining table.

"*Mo ghrá*," he purrs, and I'll never tire of hearing his Gaelic sweet talk. "Everything okay with you and your sister?"

"Great, actually." I give him a grin. "How do you feel about having a wife who's permanently moving to Montana?"

His eyes widen. "What?"

"Teagan and Connor offered me a partnership."

"Feckin' brilliant!" He kisses me soundly, to the cheers of everyone around us.

"So you're really staying?" Sky asks, overhearing us and bouncing in her seat nearby.

"You bet," I confirm. "Hope you're all ready to shake things up around here."

"There goes the neighborhood," Graham snarks across from her.

Brady comes over and raises his glass. "To Rourke and Opal—may your love be as wild as your wedding story!"

"*Slàinte mhath*, to the happy couple!" Ewan cheers.

Sky pops up beside Rourke with a camera in hand. "This is gold for the camp's socials. #LumbersnackLoveStory!"

As everyone toasts and laughs around us, Rourke leans down to whisper in my ear.

"I love you, Opal."

If any *other* man had said that to me after only a few days, I'd be running for the hills.

But this is Rourke, my husband.

"I love you, too," I reply, easily, like it was always meant to be said...*eventually.*

He smiles and shifts me to the bench beside him to pick up his guitar again. "Sorry, love, I think it's time they hear my rendition of 'Love Me Tender'."

And as he begins playing the chords, I see a tiny speck of glitter in his beard...and grin.

EPILOGUE - ROURKE

SIX MONTHS LATER

The best sound in the world is Opal Fogerty cursing at inanimate objects.

Well, okay...*second* best to the sounds she makes when I'm ravaging her.

"You absolute bastard of a drafting pencil," she mutters, hunched over the dining table that's become her makeshift workspace. "Stop breaking your feckin' tip."

Six months of marriage and she's already picked up my Irish swearing.

Christ, I love this woman.

I move quietly behind her, coffee mug in hand, watching as she attacks a large blueprint with the determination of a warrior and the chaos of a tornado. Her copper hair is piled atop her head, secured with two bright colored pencils and possibly a chopstick from the Chinese dinner we had two nights ago at the Deepwood Mountain Inn. She's wearing my flannel shirt and not much else.

"Mornin', wife," I say, setting the coffee beside her and leaning down to kiss her neck.

She hums in appreciation. "Is that coffee or are you just happy to see me?"

"Both." I press myself against her back so she can feel exactly how happy I am to see her. "But the coffee's getting cold."

She spins in her chair, grabbing the mug with one hand and my ass with the other. "You're still my hero."

Our cabin looks like it's been ransacked by a wild animal, which is exactly what happened when Opal finally moved all her stuff from London last month.

Architectural drawings cover every surface, fabric swatches are pinned to the walls, and there's a mysterious box of door-knobs in the corner that she swears are "essential to the aesthetic integrity" of the new guest cabins.

It's perfect.

"How about some lumberjack pancakes for the wee terror-ist?" I ask.

"Only if you draw abs on mine," she replies, shooting me a grin. "Jamie coming over today?" She gulps down coffee like it's the elixir of life.

I start assembling ingredients on the stove. "Aye, Connor and Teagan have that doctor's appointment in Bozeman."

She nods, her eyes drifting back to her blueprints. "Good. I need his expert opinion on the playground design."

I chuckle. "He's three."

"Exactly. Target demographic." She taps her temple. "Market research."

I can't help but spin around and kiss her again, loving how her mind works.

"What time are we meeting the crew for lunch?" she asks, already reabsorbed in her work.

"Noon." I click on the gas. "Sky wants to go over the new demonstration platform before the spring rush."

"You mean she wants to make sure it's high enough for the ladies to properly appreciate Graham's ass during axe-throwing demonstrations."

I laugh, but she's not wrong. "Speaking of, I caught her and Graham going at it in the equipment shed yesterday."

Opal gasps in delight. "No! The same shed where we...?"

"Yes, ma'am. Apparently, it's a thing now."

"We should put a plaque on it," she suggests. "'Timber Run Love Shack: Where Lumberjacks Get Their Wood Handled.'"

I choke. "You're terrible."

"You married me."

"Best decision I never meant to make."

Her smile softens, and she reaches up to trace my beard with her fingertips. "Same, husband. Same."

My phone buzzes with a text from Ewan.

> Brady's panicking about the bachelor party again. Says we're planning something "inappropriate." As if.

I snort. Brady and Imogen's wedding is next month, and we are absolutely planning something inappropriate. Nothing too wild—we've all grown up a bit, mostly—but just inappropriate enough to make Brady squirm.

I text back.

> Tell him we canceled the strippers, but the llamas are non-refundable.

Ewan replies immediately.

> Evil. Love it.

∼

Later that evening, after we've returned Jamie to his parents (who report a clean bill of health for both Teagan and baby-to-be), Opal and I settle into our evening routine.

She's back at her drawings, I'm on the couch with my guitar, and somewhere between us is the comfortable silence of two people who don't need to fill every moment with words.

I strum softly, working out a melody for our summer wedding. Something old and Irish but with a modern twist, just like us.

"Play the one about the river," Opal says without looking up.

I smile and shift into "The Water is Wide," one of her favorites. She hums along absently, her pencil moving in rhythm with the music.

This is what happiness feels like.

Not the adrenaline rush of performing for a crowd or the temporary high of a wild night out. It's this—creating something together, even when we're focused on different things.

"Opal," I say, when the song ends.

She looks up, hair falling around her face, eyes bright with creativity and love. "Hmm?"

"I want a baby."

The words come out unplanned, surprising even me. But they're true, truer than anything I've ever said.

She doesn't look shocked. Instead, a slow smile spreads across her face. "Right now? Because I'm kind of in the middle of something."

I laugh, setting down my guitar. "Not this exact minute. But soon."

She rises from her chair and comes over to me, straddling my lap, her arms winding around my neck. "I think," she says, "that sounds like an excellent plan, *mo ghrá*."

"Only if you're ready," I reply.

She presses her lips to my cheek. "With you? I'm ready for anything."

∼

Want to read more from Deepwood Mountain?
Check out these series:

Deepwood Mountain Main Series
https://www.lexihayes.com/series/deepwood-mountain/

Husky Valley
https://www.lexihayes.com/series/husky-valley/

Frozen Heights
https://www.lexihayes.com/series/frozen-heights/

McCafferty Mechanics
https://www.lexihayes.com/series/mccafferty-mechanics/

Deepwood Mountain Collaborations
https://www.lexihayes.com/series/deepwood-mountain-collaborations/

Deepwood Mountain Holiday Specials
https://www.lexihayes.com/series/holiday-specials/

You can sign up for my newsletter and get a FREE book via my website:
www.lexihayes.com
It's the best way to hear about new and upcoming releases, plus get access to subscriber exclusives and bonus content.

And as always, if you liked this story, please post a review on any of your preferred platforms. Reviews are the lifeblood of independent authors like me, and I welcome your opinions and feedback.

Thanks for reading!

ABOUT THE AUTHOR

Lexi writes short, steamy, over-the-top romance with a heaping dose of humor. She's a long-time superhero lover, book sniffer, and Mr. Darcy fanatic. Raised in the same SoCal city as Will Ferrell, she now resides in sweltering Las Vegas with her husband and the ghosts of two spoiled cats. She dreams of lush green foliage, ocean waves, and Henry Cavill. Or Alan Ritchson. It's a toss-up really. ;)

Join Lexi's mailing list for new and upcoming releases (and FREE book!) here: www.lexihayes.com

instagram.com/lexihayesauthor
facebook.com/lexihayesauthor